The Duchess and the Dreamer

Praise for Jenny Frame

Wooing the Farmer

"This book, like all of Jenny Frame's, is just one major swoon." —*Les Rêveur*

"The chemistry between the two MCs had us hooked right away. We also absolutely loved the seemingly ditzy femme with an ambition of steel but really a vulnerable girl. The sex scenes are great. Definitely recommended."—*Reviewer@large*

"This is the book we Axedale fanatics have been waiting for…Jenny Frame writes the most amazing characters and this whole series is a masterpiece. But where she excels is in writing butch lesbians. Every time I read a Jenny Frame book I think it's the best ever, but time and again she surprises me. She has surpassed herself with *Wooing the Farmer*."—*Kitty Kat's Book Review Blog*

Royal Court

"The author creates two very relatable characters…Quincy's quietude and mental torture are offset by Holly's openness and lust for life. Holly's determination and tenacity in trying to reach Quincy are total wish-fulfilment of a person like that. The chemistry and attraction is excellently built."—*Best Lesbian Erotica*

"[A] butch/femme romance that packs a punch."—*Les Rêveur*

Royal Court "was a fun, light-hearted book with a very endearing romance."—*Leanne Chew, Librarian, Parnell Library (Auckland, NZ)*

"There were unbelievably hot sex scenes as I have come to expect and look forward to in Jenny Frame's books. Passions slowly rise until you feel the characters may burst!…Royal Court is wonderful and I highly recommend it."—*Kitty Kat's Book Review Blog*

Hunger for You

"I loved this book. Paranormal stuff like vampires and werewolves are my go-to sins. This book had literally everything I needed:

chemistry between the leads, hot love scenes (phew), drama, angst, romance (oh my, the romance) and strong supporting characters." —*The Reading Doc*

Byron and Amelia "are guaranteed to get the reader all hot and bothered. Jenny Frame writes brilliant love scenes in all of her books and makes me believe the characters crave each other." —*Kitty Kat's Book Review Blog*

Charming the Vicar

"Chances are, you've never read or become captivated by a romance like *Charming the Vicar*. While books featuring people of the cloth aren't unusual, Bridget is no ordinary vicar—a lesbian with a history of kink…Surrounded by mostly supportive villagers, Bridget and Finn balance love and faith in a story that affirms both can exist for anyone, regardless of sexual identity."—*RT Book Reviews*

"The sex scenes were some of the sexiest, most intimate and quite frankly, sensual I have read in a while. Jenny Frame had me hooked and I reread a few scenes because I felt like I needed to experience the intense intimacy between Finn and Bridget again. The devotion they showed to one another during these sex scenes but also in the intimate moments was gripping and for lack of a better word, carnal."—*Les Rêveur*

"The sexual chemistry between [Finn and Bridge] is unbelievably hot. It is sexy, lustful and with more than a hint of kink. The scenes between them are highly erotic—and not just the sex scenes. The tension is ramped up so well that I felt the characters would explode if they did not get relief!…An excellent book set in the most wonderful village—a place I hope to return to very soon!"—*Kitty Kat's Book Reviews*

"This is Frame's best character work to date. They are layered and flawed and yet relatable. Frame really pushed herself with *Charming The Vicar* and it totally paid off…I also appreciate that even though she regularly writes butch/femme characters, no two pairings are the same."—*The Lesbian Review*

Unexpected

Jenny Frame "has this beautiful way of writing a phenomenally hot scene while incorporating the love and tenderness between the couple."—*Les Rêveur*

"If you enjoy contemporary romances, *Unexpected* is a great choice. The character work is excellent, the plotting and pacing are well done, and it's a just a sweet, warm read…Definitely pick this book up when you're looking for your next comfort read, because it's sure to put a smile on your face by the time you get to that happy ending."—*Curve*

"*Unexpected* by Jenny Frame is a charming butch/femme romance that is perfect for anyone who wants to feel the magic of overcoming adversity and finding true love. I love the way Jenny Frame writes. I have yet to discover an author who writes like her. Her voice is strong and unique and gives a freshness to the lesbian fiction sector."—*The Lesbian Review*

Royal Rebel

"Frame's stories are easy to follow and really engaging. She stands head and shoulders above a number of the romance authors and it's easy to see why she is quickly making a name for herself in lesfic romance."—*The Lesbian Review*

Courting the Countess

"I love Frame's romances. They are well paced, filled with beautiful character moments and a wonderful set of side characters who ultimately end up winning your heart…I love Jenny Frame's butch/femme dynamic; she gets it so right for a romance." —*The Lesbian Review*

"I loved, loved, loved this book. I didn't expect to get so involved in the story but I couldn't help but fall in love with Annie and Harry… The love scenes were beautifully written and very sexy. I found the whole book romantic and ultimately joyful and I had a lump in my throat on more than one occasion. A wonderful book that certainly stirred my emotions."—*Kitty Kat's Book Reviews*

"*Courting The Countess* has an historical feel in a present day world, a thought provoking tale filled with raw emotions throughout. [Frame] has a magical way of pulling you in, making you feel every emotion her characters experience."—*Lunar Rainbow Reviewz*

"I didn't want to put the book down and I didn't. Harry and Annie are two amazingly written characters that bring life to the pages as they find love and adventures in Harry's home. This is a great read, and you will enjoy it immensely if you give it a try!" —*Fantastic Book Reviews*

A Royal Romance

"*A Royal Romance* was a guilty pleasure read for me. It was just fun to see the relationship develop between George and Bea, to see George's life as queen and Bea's as a commoner. It was also refreshing to see that both of their families were encouraging, even when Bea doubted that things could work between them because of their class differences…*A Royal Romance* left me wanting a sequel, and romances don't usually do that to me." —*Leeanna.ME Mostly a Book Blog*

Blood of the Pack

"[A] solid entry into the expanding Lesfic urban fantasy/ paranormal romance genre. I look forward to seeing more from the Wolfgang County series."—*Colleen Corgel, Librarian, Queens Public Library*

Soul of the Pack

"I enjoy the way Jenny Frame writes. Her characters are perfectly suited to one another, never the same, and the stories are always fun and unique…there is something special about her urban fantasy worlds. She maximises the butch/femme dynamic and creates pack dynamics which work so well with those."—*The Lesbian Review*

Heart of the Pack

"A really well written love story that incidentally involves changers as well as humans."—*Inked Rainbow Reads*

By the Author

A Royal Romance

Courting the Countess

Dapper

Royal Rebel

Unexpected

Hunger For You

Charming the Vicar

Royal Court

Wooing the Farmer

Someone to Love

The Duchess and the Dreamer

Wolfgang County Series

Heart of the Pack

Soul of the Pack

Blood of the Pack

The Duchess and the Dreamer

by

Jenny Frame

2020

THE DUCHESS AND THE DREAMER

ISBN 13: 978-1-63555-601-8

This Trade Paperback Original Is Published By
Bold Strokes Books, Inc.
P.O. Box 249
Valley Falls, NY 12185

First Edition: May 2020

Credits
Editor: Ruth Sternglantz
Production Design: Stacia Seaman
Cover Design by Tammy Seidick

Acknowledgments

Thank you to Rad, Sandy, and all the BSB staff for their tireless hard work. A huge thank you to Ruth for her guidance, patience, and advice. I'm deeply grateful to have you help me make my books the best that they can be.

Thanks to my family for their support and encouragement.

All my love and thanks to Lou and Barney, you are my whole world, and I couldn't feel luckier than to have you both.

To Lou
You make me laugh, you make me dream,
you make me happier than I ever thought I could be.
xx

Chapter One

The harsh noise of an alarm blared its way into Clementine Fitzroy's subconscious, making her jump out of sleep. She grabbed the phone beside her and blindly stabbed her finger at the screen to stop the wretched air raid siren noise, her vision and mind still blurry from sleep. She managed to stop the noise, but her heart pounded at the fright it had given her.

Clementine scrubbed her face with her hands and felt a twinge of pain in her neck. The neck pain meant she had fallen asleep at her desk again. Now that her mind was clearing from sleep, everything came back into sharp focus. She had been up all night trying to meet a deadline and set the alarm in case she fell asleep, which she did.

She moved her mouse to wake up her screen, to check how far she had gotten before falling asleep and sighed. "It's not even half done."

Being a freelance architect meant she had the flexibility to be there for her ill mother but also meant she lost a lot of work time doing so. Her mother was severely affected by Alzheimer's, and had until three months ago been cared for by Clementine, here at her home, the gatehouse to the Rosebrook estate.

Clementine looked around the drab front room. It was dated, neglected, much like her life. Her desk sat in the space under the stairs, directly across from the living room fireplace and the armchair where her mother used to sit while she worked.

Guilt crept up on her, although it was never far away. Her mother hadn't had an easy life, and Clementine had promised her that she would always take care of her. She meant that promise with every fibre of her being, but with worsening dementia affecting her mother's mind, she was persuaded by the doctors and her friend that a nursing home was the only place her mum would be safe.

The memory of the last time her mother had gotten out of the house played in her mind. She'd come downstairs and found her mother's armchair empty. She had gotten out of the house before, but now that the new locks were in place, she didn't think her mother could get out.

It had been Clementine's own fault. She had been careless, and after bringing some shopping in from the car, she had forgotten to take the key out of the door, and her mother had disappeared. It had taken her and the other villagers who turned out an hour to find her, and that had been the final straw. The move was for her mother's safety, but she'd broken her promise.

The ping of her email brought Clementine back to the present. She opened it and sighed again. It was the project manager for the job she was working on, asking if they could expect her work in the next few hours.

It wasn't possible. She'd need another day at least. Clementine leaned on the desk and covered her face with her hands, feeling tears come to her eyes. She was lucky to be given work by two companies run by university friends of hers, who understood her situation, but she couldn't stretch that goodwill too far, and she had lost so much time this week as her deadline loomed.

Despite being relieved of the twenty-four seven care of her mother, she visited every day and was always on call when her mother was distressed, and it had been a particularly bad week. Nothing calmed her mother but her own presence, and she received phone calls from the nursing staff to come almost every day.

"Okay, you can do this. Coffee, and get this finished," Clementine said.

She got up and hurried to the small kitchen to switch on the kettle. At the moment she did, the house phone rang, and Clementine's stomach twisted with tension.

She picked up the phone and held her breath. "Hello?"

"Your Grace, sorry to interrupt your morning."

Her heart sank when she heard the voice of Sister Fellows, the senior nurse in charge of her mother's care. She hated when she was reminded of her title, but she couldn't convince the care staff to drop it.

"Is my mother all right?" Clementine said.

"I'm afraid the dowager duchess has tried to get out of the building again and injured her ankle."

Clementine pinched the bridge of her nose, and her whole body tensed. "How did that happen?"

"One of the newer members of staff opened the window in her room to let some fresh air in. Her Grace sprained her ankle badly climbing out. I'm terribly sorry, ma'am, but she won't settle and keeps asking for you."

"I'll be there as soon as I can."

Clementine hung up the phone and felt panic fill her. She would need to ask for another extension. She was never going to finish her design project today. Clementine went back to her computer and quickly sent off the email. She wouldn't be surprised if the company took the job from her, and she couldn't blame them.

She grabbed her handbag and car keys and quickly made her way out to her car. Panic turned to despair when she saw a flat front tyre. Clementine's anger spilled over and she kicked her old car.

"Bloody hell. Of course I've got a flat tyre—just perfect, bloody perfect." She held her head in her hands. She didn't have time for this, so might as well just get on with it.

She couldn't afford breakdown cover, and her car didn't have a spare wheel, so she took the puncture repair kit and pump from the boot. It would at least get her to the care home. She had to get to her mother no matter what. Clementine put the puncture kit down by the flat tyre and looked up at the black wrought iron gates that marked the entrance to the grand—but severely neglected—Rosebrook House. On the gates a battered and weathered *For Sale* sign clung to the railings.

The feelings of anger, sadness, and failure hung around the building like a dark cloud. Clementine looked down at her hands, stained with dirt and oil, and gave a hollow laugh.

"Look at me, Duchess of Rosebrook, Countess of Thistleburn, Baroness Portford, kneeling in the dirt, trying to mend the tyre on an ancient car. Who would believe it?"

❖

"And they all lived happily ever after."

The children grouped around Evan Fox clapped and one little boy said, "Read us another one, Fox."

The other children joined in, "Yeah!"

There was nothing Evan enjoyed more than playing with children, but she had to get back upstairs to her office. The childcare centre located on the bottom floor of Fox Toys and Games was a regular hideout for Evan, when she wanted to get away from business pressures and the countless people who wanted just a few moments of her time.

"Sorry, kids, the boss will have my guts for garters if I'm any longer." Evan patted the Labrador service dog beside her and said, "I'm sure Rocco, here, would like to hear some stories from you guys."

The childcare manager, Evan's friend Jessica, joined them. "Okay, kids, say thank you to Fox for coming to see us."

"Thanks, Fox," they replied in chorus.

"No problemo. I'll be back soon. Have fun." Fox got up, then ruffled Rocco's ears and gave him a dog treat from her tweed suit jacket pocket. "You be good, big guy."

Jess walked her over to the door of the childcare centre, where she checked her appearance in the glass doors.

"You're not meant to feed the service dogs, Fox," Jess said.

Evan straightened her chequered tie and took her comb out of her top pocket and made sure her short dark brown hair was sitting perfectly.

"It's just one or two, or three. Rocco deserves a pat on the back for his good work with the kids."

Jess folded her arms and chuckled. "Only you would just happen to have dog treats in your pocket."

Evan turned around and brushed down her trousers. "You have to be prepared—you never know when you're going to meet an animal friend."

Jess stepped towards her and straightened the fox head on her lapel. "You know, if you were born in the eighteenth century, you'd be called a dandy."

"I'll take that as a compliment. I like to express myself through my clothes," Fox said.

Jess rolled her eyes. "Oh, I know."

Fox had met Jess at university while studying business. Jess already had a childcare degree, but had gone on to study business with the hope of opening her own business. When Fox Toys wanted to extend and revamp their own childcare facility, it was natural to bring Jessica on board to run it. It was a safe, fun environment where the staff could leave their children, and a great perk of working for Fox Toys.

Fox winked at Jess and said, "You look beautiful today, you know."

"Please, I've been crawling around with the toddlers next door. I'm a mess."

The nursery next door took care of babies and toddlers and had its own dedicated staff that Jess managed.

Fox kissed her on the cheek and said, "You've never looked lovelier."

"You're good for my ego, Fox," Jess said.

"Every woman should be appreciated for the wonderful person that they are."

Jess laughed softly. "Why you aren't snapped up and married with five kids, I'll never know."

Evan put her hands in her pockets and let out a breath. "You sound like my mother. I'm waiting for my grand love story—you know that."

Evan modelled her idea of a perfect relationship on her mum and dad. Her dad had told her the romantic story of how they'd met ever since she could remember, and Evan was a romantic soul at heart.

She wanted her own story.

In the meantime, while she'd had pleasant dates with women, none had felt right.

Her dad, Donald Fox—or Donny, as he was known to family or friends—had always told her that when she met the right one, it would feel like she'd gotten smacked across the head with a banjo. Her father was a very descriptive, passionate man, and Evan believed him absolutely.

Evan rarely got past the second date, but she loved women and enjoyed taking them out and making them feel special. One day, she was certain, her love story would come along, and a beautiful woman would knock her socks off.

"Grand love stories don't come around very often," Jess cautioned.

"All the more worth waiting on."

"Well, I can tell you one thing," Jess said. "Mrs. Fox, whoever she is, will be a lucky woman."

Evan felt a heat come to her cheeks. "How's things going with that woman you were seeing—the TV producer?"

Jess sighed. "I've called time on her. Let's just say, she didn't believe in an exclusive relationship."

"I'm sorry, Jess." Like Evan, Jess had never had much luck in love.

"Don't worry about me. I can deal with toads. There seem to be a lot out there."

Evan looked over the busy open-plan room full of kids. It was sectioned into age groups, each with its own staff, and Jess overseeing it all. "So how is everything going on down here? Any problems?"

"Nothing since our last meeting. The service dogs are such a great help, especially with our special needs children," Jess said.

The company supported many charities, but given Evan's love of animals, the service dog trust they had founded was close to her heart. She watched two other dogs sitting with other groups of kids, but one little boy, sitting by himself with a brown standard poodle, caught her eye.

"How is Jamie?"

"Doing great—now that he has Barney, they go everywhere together," Jess said.

Right on cue Jamie stood up, followed by Barney the poodle, and they walked together over to get another toy, Jamie with his hand on Barney's back.

"Animals are awesome, aren't they?"

Just then Evan's watch beeped with a text message. "It's the boss, reminding me I have a phone call to take. I better go."

Jess laughed. "You know Violet doesn't like you calling her that."

"Well, it's true. If it wasn't for her keeping me on track, I'd be playing in here all day with the kids. I better go. See you later."

"Bye, Fox," Jessica said.

Evan went out the door into the large entrance hall of Fox Toys and Games. The building was in the centre of London's business sector but was so different from the buildings around them.

Fox Toys had moved to this newly designed building when Evan's father had retired. Evan oversaw the plans personally. She wanted the indoors to feel like the outdoors, and she didn't want a stuffy old building. The entrance and reception were full of natural light from the glass construction of the building. There were trees and plants everywhere, and you could hear the gush and gurgle of the large fountain in the reception area. Plus, on the roof there was a garden, where employees could take their breaks.

Evan had commissioned a study that found staff employment satisfaction rose with the changes she'd made, and general well-being had improved. And as a company dedicated to ecology, the natural setting fit their corporate mission.

Evan arrived at the lifts and pressed for the doors to open. Three women from accounts walked out and gave her big smiles.

"Ladies, you're looking wonderful this morning," Evan said enthusiastically.

"Thanks, Fox."

She stepped into the lift and heard the giggles of the women as they walked away. She chuckled to herself. Wasn't life wonderful when you spread positivity?

Her mum and dad had brought her up to believe in positivity and always to spread that positivity, especially to women who—her mother, who was heavily involved in the women's rights movement and various feminist groups, reminded her—were bombarded with negative body images. It was no hardship. Evan thought women were wonderful, every kind of woman. Although her enthusiasm did get her into trouble sometimes, when a couple of women took her positive words for a romantic interest.

The door opened on Evan's executive floor and she immediately saw Violet on her feet tapping her watch.

"You're late."

Violet headed a team of four, three women and one man, who looked after her diary and administration.

Evan held her hands up in surrender, then sat on the edge of her desk. "I was caught up with an important security issue at reception."

Violet sighed and shook her head. "I may have to report your truthfulness to your mother, Evan. You were in the nursery."

Evan clasped her chest dramatically and said, "Please, anything but that."

Alissa, Ericka, and Rupert—Violet's team—laughed.

"You're all looking good today, team. Rupert, you look particularly handsome." Evan winked at him.

A blush came to the young man's cheeks. "If only you were a guy," Rupert said.

Evan moved close to Violet. "If I was a man, I'd be head over heels for Violet. Sorry, Rupert."

She gave Violet a kiss on the cheek.

"You are impossible." Violet pointed to her office door. "Conference call—now."

Evan saluted. "Yes, ma'am. See you later, guys."

As Evan walked to her office, Violet called after her, "Oh, Steff Archer is looking for you."

"Tell her to come up when she's free."

Evan entered her office and felt calm. There were plants, mini trees in pots, and other nods to her love of the environment. Everything Fox Toys did since she took over from her father was driven by environmental conservation. To the extent possible, all the supplies the company used in the head office were recycled. And Evan's greatest achievement since taking over was to bring an end to plastic packaging, the only toy company in the world to do so.

Evan took off her jacket and hung it over the back of her chair. Her office was also her fun bolthole away from the boring corporate world. She had a massive TV screen on one wall where she played all her games consoles, and train tracks that followed the shape of the room until they reached the station on her desk. On another wall was the motto that she lived by, in huge letters: *Dream Big and Never Give Up.*

Evan took a handful of sweets from the huge bowls on her desk. There were jelly sweets, Skittles, and Love Hearts—all vegan, as was her diet. She selected a Love Heart and read the words printed on the front: Marry me.

Her phone buzzed and Violet's voice said, "Putting your call through in one minute, Fox."

Evan picked up a plush stuffed fox toy that was sitting on the coffee table and walked over to the windows of her high-rise office. Mr. Fox, with his top hat, tails, and cane, was the emblem of Fox Toys, and she'd had this particular one since she was born. She'd named him Foxy and told him all of her secrets and worries as a child, and sometimes she still needed to. Evan held him and looked out over the city.

"I know Mrs. Fox is out there, Foxy. I'll find her."

"Fox?" A male voice from her speakerphone interrupted her thoughts. "It's Bill from marketing. We have a problem with our new movie licensing agreement."

"There are no problems, Bill, only opportunities. Tell me, and I'll run it through the old brain box."

Chapter Two

Clementine parked her car outside the care home and got out quickly. Panic, guilt, and pressure gripped her. She had to get to her mother. It had taken her too long to get here because of her stupid car.

She hurried up to the door and pressed the security intercom. A tinny voice greeted, "Hello, how can I help?"

"It's Clementine."

"Please come in, Your Grace."

She sighed at the use of her title, but in a traditional, private facility like this, it was useless to fight against.

She was met at the reception by Sister Fellows, who looked quite flustered.

"Your Grace, I'm sorry about this. We can't calm her down to attend to her ankle."

"Take me to her. I'll talk to her," Clementine said.

Sister Fellows escorted her to her mother's room, and she could hear her before she saw her.

"No, I want to go home!" her mother shouted.

Clementine ran the last few steps and burst into the room. Three nurses were trying to stop her mother from thrashing and further hurting herself. The tears running down her mother's face broke her heart.

"Leave her—I'll calm her down."

The nurses stepped back and said, "Yes, Your Grace."

Clementine knelt by the side of the bed and took her mother's hands. "Mummy? It's me. It's Clemy."

Her mother looked at her and said, "Clemy? It's really you?"

Clementine could see her mother trying her hardest to look through the prism of her clouded mind.

"It's me, Mummy."

"Have you just finished school?"

Her mother's mind seemed to be always stuck in Clementine's school years. "I'm here. I need you to calm down, so the nurses can look at your injured ankle."

Her mother grasped her hair, and with sheer despair in her voice said, "They're keeping me prisoner here. I want to go back to Rosebrook. I want to go home, Clemy."

Clementine closed her eyes briefly. Her mother always wanted to go home. In her mind and heart, they still lived at Rosebrook House. She silently cursed her grandmother, who'd selfishly lost their entire fortune and land. This was the evidence of that selfishness, and she hoped Isadora could see, wherever she was, what effect her actions had.

"Mummy, listen, listen to my words. Concentrate on them."

Clementine stroked her mother's brow and recited the Bible verses that usually calmed her. Her mother had always had a strong belief in God, and even when her mind was at its most cloudy, she remembered the words of her faith.

"*The Lord is my shepherd; I shall not want*—say it with me, Mummy."

As Clementine started the verse again, Marianne began to relax and mumble the words with her.

"*The Lord is my shepherd; I shall not want. He maketh me to lie down in green pastures: he leadeth me beside the still waters. He restoreth my soul: he leadeth me in the paths of righteousness for his name's sake. Yea, though I walk through the valley of the shadow of death, I will fear no evil: for thou art with me; thy rod and thy staff they comfort me.*"

Her mother was now calm, and while Clementine continued reciting the psalm, she nodded to the nursing staff to take care of her mum's ankle.

❖

A few hours later, Clementine wandered aimlessly around the supermarket near her mother's care home. After she'd calmed her, the nursing staff attended to her injury and gave her something to help her sleep. Clementine hated to leave her but she had to—her work project was essential, and they desperately needed the money.

She needed something to eat for dinner, but there was nothing in the house, and it needed to be something fast to eat at her desk. Clementine picked up a pizza, crisps, and a new jar of coffee—that would see her through. She passed the wine and spirits area, and thought how nice it would be to have a bottle of wine to keep her company while she worked. But did she have enough money?

Clementine wasn't brave enough to hope she had enough on her credit card to pay for these items. Her card was too near the limit, and she'd been embarrassed at the checkout before. She got out her purse and saw she had twenty pounds, maybe enough for the cheapest bottle of wine. Clementine was waiting on a few payments coming through from her clients any day now, but that would go straight to her credit card bill, as usual.

She picked up a bottle of cheap wine and made her way to the checkout. Her phone beeped with a text. She took her phone from her bag—a text from her friend in the village, Kay Dayton.

If you're near a shop can you get the twins a few things? Agatha just phoned me, they're out of bread, milk, and teabags.

Clementine sighed and walked back to the drinks aisle to put her wine back. The twins were two old ladies who lived in the village, and she and Kay always made sure they were looked after, especially since the local shop closed years ago.

She looked in her basket and realized she'd probably have to put the crisps and pizza back too. She might not have her ancestral land or home any more, but as duchess she still felt the responsibility to look after those people still left in the village.

Not that she had the means, but she did all she could. The elderly twins had looked after her all through her childhood, especially when her mother was suffering with depression. The illness had dogged her her whole life, but got worse after they lost their home.

Clementine texted Kay back, then gathered up all the twins needed and kept only the pizza and coffee for herself. As she walked out to her car, the stress and tension started to spill over. She got into the car and wiped the tears that had just started to flow. She was interrupted by a beep, alerting her to an email—a response to her email earlier today asking for more time on her project. Her heart sank. They couldn't wait any longer and had given the project to someone else.

"No, please."

Clementine covered her face with her hands as anger and frustration overtook her.

Nobody who passed the car and saw her visibly upset and in a ramshackle car with a temporary wheel would have a clue that she was Duchess of Rosebrook, the third highest dukedom in Britain. Her title was meaningless now. She couldn't do anything to take care of the village and the few people who were left.

Clementine wiped her eyes and thought, as she had many times before: *If only I could abdicate the dukedom.* But unfortunately the only way to get rid of the stupid title was to commit a felony or die—there was no abdicating being a duke or duchess—so here she was, trapped in a role with no meaning and no land or money to take care of her people.

Clementine looked up at the sky and spat, "I hope you're happy, Isadora."

❖

Evan was bouncing on the trampoline that she kept in the office while throwing a mini basketball through a hoop on the wall, while her latest audiobook played in the background. She loved reading but didn't always have the time, so audiobooks were ideal. Her phone beeped and Violet's voice said, "Steff Archer here to see you, Fox."

"Send her in." She then said to her iPhone, "Pause."

There was a knock and Steff Archer walked in. Archie, as she was known to her friends, was Fox Toys' environmental consultant, a post Evan created when she took over the business. After finishing her business degree, Evan went on to study environmental conservation at night school. Archie was a guest lecturer, and they struck up a close friendship, both being lesbians who were driven by the same purpose, to help save the planet.

"I've been looking all over for you, Fox," Archie said.

"Well, here I am." Evan threw the basketball to her and she caught it with one hand, since she was carrying an iPad in the other.

"Good catch." Evan bounced off the trampoline and landed on the floor. She adjusted her tie and smoothed her hand over her hair.

Archie wasn't quite the full-on dapper dandy that Evan was—designer jeans, tweed waistcoat, and shirtsleeves rolled up to her elbows was her style. Her shoulder-length hair was undercut and pulled into a tight topknot. Archie was five years older than her and the more sensible, but together they dreamed big and made some huge changes in the company, the main one being the game changer of using no plastic packaging. Generally, Evan dreamed big and Archie, who had a seat on the Fox Toys board, worked to make those dreams practical, and to make them happen.

Now, Evan sat on the edge of her desk and Archie put her iPad down.

"You were in the childcare centre, weren't you?" Archie said, as she threw the ball back to Evan.

Evan caught it and grinned. "Where else?"

"I think you'd rather be playing with the kids than be in the boardroom."

Evan spun the basketball on her finger. "That's what this company is about, encouraging the joy and imagination of children. So what's up?"

A big smile crept up on Archie's face. "Prepare to have your mind blown."

"What?"

"I've found the perfect location for your dream."

Evan's biggest dream was to find enough land to build a sustainable, ecological, diverse village, with affordable housing, where groups of like-minded people could live in a safe, supportive environment. The dream was inspired by her great hero, the social reformer Isadora Fitzroy.

Her heart started to beat fast. They had been looking for a long time for enough land, and the right kind of land, but nothing suitable had come up.

"Where?"

"Are you ready for this?" Archie grinned.

"Oh, come on. Tell me."

"Rosebrook," Archie said.

Evan couldn't quite believe it, and she struggled to form words in reply. "Rosebrook? Isadora's Fitzroy's village? You're winding me up."

Archie handed over the iPad. "See for yourself. Do I lie?"

Evan gazed at the webpage displaying the land details. "Is it just the land or—"

"No, the house as well."

Evan felt lost for words for probably the first time in her life, and her heart raced with excitement. She found herself walking around her desk to her chair, needing to catch her breath. "How is this possible? We've enquired before and the owner refused to sell at any price."

Archie took a seat across the desk and crossed her legs. "Apparently the country hotel and rural retreat they had in mind was all a little too much for them, considering all the work that needs doing to the house and land."

Evan gave a derisory snort. "Isadora would turn in her grave if her home and village were turned into some tacky leisure park."

"Why do you adore Isadora Fitzroy so much?"

"Because she's me, back in the past. A gay person, a woman ploughing her path, having dreams to make the world a better place—ever since I first learned about her at school, I felt this connection to her."

"She failed with her dream," Archie reminded her, "and lost her entire fortune."

Evan got up and started to pace. She always got animated when she felt passionate about something. "She didn't have the support systems I have, and she was swindled of her money along the way. Call the seller and make them an offer they can't refuse."

"Already have." Archie stood up. "It's yours if you want it."

Evan clasped her hands to her cheeks with surprise and joy. "I can't believe this is happening, at last."

Archie pulled a bunch of keys from her jeans pocket and dangled them in the air. "Do you want to go and see what you're buying?"

Evan grinned like a little child. "Archie, I think I love you. It's hug time."

She threw her arms around an uncomfortable Archie. "God, I hope you don't love me, because you're *so* not my type, and why always with the hugging? A firm handshake would have done."

Evan slapped her on the upper arm. "You are seriously repressed, mate. You need to learn to open up. No wonder you're continually single."

"Pot calling kettle black there, Fox."

Evan grabbed the keys. "That's because I'm looking for Mrs. Fox. Come on."

"You do realize how risky this project, this dream is?" Archie cautioned.

Evan walked backward towards the door and said, "The future belongs to those who dream."

"Eleanor Roosevelt?" Archie asked.

"Nope, saw it on a T-shirt." She waggled her eyebrows. "Let's go, I've got dreams to create."

Archie followed her to the door, shaking her head and smiling.

CHAPTER THREE

Evan and Archie left for Rosebrook straight away in Evan's trademark green vintage Beetle, which had been converted to electric. As they left the motorway and the landscape started to turn to fields and trees, Evan put down her window and breathed deeply.

"The English countryside, there's nothing like it."

Archie snorted. "All I can smell is manure."

"What about the sea air?" Evan said. Rosebrook's position on the Dorset coast made it even more attractive.

"It makes me twitchy to be so far away from the city," Archie said.

Evan laughed and shook her head. "You're so weird. An environmental activist who doesn't like the country. Most of your colleagues in the industry want to go back to nature, have a plot of land, and live on it, in tune with nature."

"Good God, no. I want to save the environment, the countryside, the animals that live there, the hedgerows, the unspoiled natural beauty, and teach people how we can live in harmony with nature, but I don't want to live in it. I'm a city person through and through. I panic if there's not a Starbucks within a five minute walk. Why you would want to live there, I have no idea. You've lived your whole life in London."

"Ah, but I spent all our family holidays, every weekend, visiting the country. Sometimes walking and visiting villages or stately homes, and sometimes litter picking with countryside clean-up groups. My mum gave me my passion for saving the planet. I was on an anti-nuclear march by the time I was three years old."

"What about your dad?"

"He generally went along with whatever she wanted to do. *She* is his passion, and whatever Cassia Fox wants, Dad wants."

"And that's why you are constantly talking about Mrs. Fox? You want someone to be your passion?"

"I want to *share* passion with someone who believes in dreams and in leaving the world in a better place than they found it," Evan said.

Archie shook her head. "Listen, I'm older than you, and maybe no wiser, but relationships like that rarely happen. Better to enjoy your passion for women in short doses."

Evan glanced to the side before returning her gaze to the road. "You are a congenital misery guts, Archie."

"No, just realistic."

"Realistic? Oh, that word gives me shivers. I hate that word—people say that when they've forgotten to dare to dream. Cheer yourself up a bit—look at the lovely cows in the field."

"I can smell them. Isn't that enough?" Archie said.

Evan laughed and brought her attention back to the road.

They passed a sign indicating three miles to Rosebrook. The road went up a steep incline, and when they reached the brow of the hill, Evan pulled in and got out of the car. Archie followed her and they both looked out over the scene.

Evan sighed. "How perfect and unique is this place? In one direction"—Evan pointed ahead of them—"rolling hills and farmland." Then she turned forty-five degrees and opened her arms up wide and inhaled deeply. "And in the other, the sea and the Jurassic Coast. Heaven."

"If you say so," Archie said. "Did you visit here when you were a kid?"

Evan nodded enthusiastically. "Oh yes, I think I was about ten when I learned about Isadora Fitzroy at school, and I had to know everything about her. I was obsessed with her story and persuaded my parents to take me here."

Evan pointed down the hill to the crossroads at the beginning of the village. "Through the trees on the right, there's a path that leads down to the beach. I spent hours playing on that beach with my dad, and there's a little wooden pier where you can hire small boats for sea fishing. I used to sit on that pier and fish for crabs, then search for fossils in the stones on the beach. It is the Jurassic Coast, after all. It was the best fun." Evan had such a feeling of excitement that it was practically boiling over. "This is an untapped oasis of possibilities. Come on, let's go see my village."

❖

"Oh, my dear. Thank you," Agatha Tucker said.

Clementine dropped by to give the twins the shopping they'd asked for. Agatha was the fitter of the two, and Adelaide, who wasn't the best on her legs, sat in a chair by the fire. While Agatha put the shopping away, Clementine walked over to Adelaide and sat down. "Ada, are you behaving?"

Ada laughed. "I hope not. How's your mum, dear?"

"Just the same really. She was quite upset, but I managed to calm her down."

"Good. We miss her—she was such a good personality around the village."

"Yes, she was," Clementine said.

Agatha came back from the kitchen and said, "Would you like a cup of tea and a cake, dear?"

"I won't, if you don't mind. I've quite a lot to do, but thank you."

Clementine gave them each a kiss on the cheek and said her goodbyes. After leaving she went to the place in Rosebrook that gave her the most peace. The beach. Clementine sat on the sand and closed her eyes. She concentrated on the sound of the waves, the smell of the sea air, and the feel of the sand between her toes.

All through her life, in times of stress, Clementine always found her way down to the beach. It was so peaceful, so quiet. This was a little-known cove, and only people who came to fish regularly and the odd tourist came down here. It was her sanctuary.

Clementine listened to the seagulls circling overhead and exhaled, hoping to rid herself of the stress she was feeling—it didn't work.

She opened her eyes and saw the little fishing boat belonging to Mr. O'Rourke meandering back in the distance. James O'Rourke owned the bait shop half a mile down the beach. He took out groups of fishermen, caught crabs and langoustine, sold fishing equipment and fossils picked up from the beach—whatever he could turn his hand to. The boat was the only sign of life on this beach.

It hadn't always been like this. Her mother had shown her pictures from the Victorian period onward, of this little beach packed with tourists. Behind her, up at the wall of cliffs, a row of beach bathing huts had been rented out in the summer, and ice cream sellers used to ply their trade up and down the shore.

But all that started to decline as the village began to die a slow death from her grandmother's mismanagement, and then the death knell came. She looked around and saw the evidence. Farther up and to the right were ugly cement block structures, half sunk into the sand. Towards the end of the Second World War, the Ministry of Defence sequestered land, buildings, and this beach for the war effort. The nearly private beach was perfect for training troops for the D-Day landings, and for anti-aircraft guns. After the war, the land the Fitzroys still owned reverted back to the family, later to be all sold up.

Just like this beach had lost its life and hope, Clementine had lost hers. Losing a job, still waiting on payments from her last two, and no sign of the next commission made keeping hope alive a losing battle. She had been offered permanent jobs with companies over the years, but had always stayed clinging to the edge, as a freelancer, so she could look after her mother.

It was looking more and more like a nine-to-five job was her only option, but not being available night and day for her mother broke her heart. She wiped away the tears that rolled down her cheeks, and as she looked around the big empty beach she felt truly alone.

CHAPTER FOUR

Evan parked the car at the church at the edge of the village and got out. She took off her sunglasses and popped them in her top pocket.

"Wow! What a fabulous building," Evan said, gazing at the medieval architecture.

Archie joined her and read off her iPad. "It was built in 1394 and added to over the years but deconsecrated in the seventies."

The graveyard in front was overgrown with weeds with the tops of the graves only just peeking out. She saw bees buzzing around the flowers.

"It seems a shame to tidy these weeds and flowers up. We have to set aside some plots of land for the bees, to make up for it. Note that down, will you?" Evan said.

"Got it. Bee world habitat," Archie said while noting down Evan's instructions.

Evan was heavily involved with bee conservation groups and thought it hugely important for agriculture to help bee populations thrive.

Evan walked up the steps to the church and placed her hand on the old oak door. "Can we look inside?"

Archie pulled out her bunch of keys and unlocked the door. "The agent did say it was a hard-hat area inside, but I suppose that's not going to stop you."

Evan grinned. "You know me too well. You've got to take the odd risk." She walked through the front door, past a wooden set of stairs, and into the main body of the church. "Wow, what a great space."

"Only you could say that. There's damp, plaster hanging off the walls, and it looks like some people have been using it as a drinking den."

Evan turned around in the space, taking in all that was beautiful about this old place. There was an upstairs balcony with seating, and downstairs the space was illuminated by the sun streaming through the beautiful stained-glass windows, although quite a few were broken in places.

She put her hand on the solid wooden pew next to her and said, "This would be a great community space, just like when it was a church."

Evan started to pace around and gesticulated with her hands energetically. "This can be a hub for the whole community, a gathering place to plan, to celebrate, to support the residents. Take this note. I want this space renovated first. If I'm going to sell my vision to the residents, then this would be the place to gather and meet. How many residents are left in the village?"

Archie quickly checked the agent's details. "Uh…eleven people in total. Four leaseholders and three owners. One the gatehouse to Rosebrook House, one house and plot that the owners run as a small holding, and one bigger house owned by its single occupant. The residents mostly live on the western side of the village. At its peak the village had one hundred and thirty-five residents, plus numerous land leases in the surrounding county."

"That's how the Fitzroys got rich."

"And lost it, remember," Archie said.

Evan winked. "Don't worry—I know what I'm doing. So, we need repairs to the stained glass and restoration of the building. Walk with me and tell me what other buildings are included with the land."

Evan set off at a fast pace out of the church doors and jumped down the steps. She had never felt so excited, so full of energy and ideas. She took in the small abandoned workers' cottages she passed as she walked down the main road through the village and was saddened at what had happened to the place Isadora loved, while invigorated by the chance to revive it.

Archie caught up with her and read from her iPad, "As well as the cottages and housing, there's the disused army barracks on the edge of the village, to the west, a hangover from when the army sequestered the village during the war."

"Yes, and there's some concrete structures used for anti-aircraft positions down on the beach. I'm not sure what to do with them yet—they are a piece of social history. I'll let it run through the brain box," Evan said.

Archie continued, "Other than that you have an empty factory that used to manufacture agricultural equipment, and there's the old beer factory—"

"The company that brought the downfall of the Fitzroy fortunes, and finally"—Evan slowed as they got near a boarded-up old building—"the pub."

"That looks like an old building," Archie said.

Evan smiled as she gazed at the whitewashed building. It was broken down and dirty, and the signage badly damaged, but you could still make out the lettering on the timber.

"The King's Arms, established 1660." Evan turned to Archie and said, "A pub is the heart of the community. It has to be top priority for refurb."

"That's got to be at least a Grade Two listed building. Any refurb would have to be done carefully," Archie said.

"We'll do everything by the book. I want this place to be perfect. Any info on the current duchess? I know her name is Clementine Fitzroy, but she's a bit of a recluse, and there's no info on the net about her. I don't know her age—I don't even know if she still lives in the vicinity."

Archie looked down at her information. "The agent says she lives in the gatehouse to Rosebrook house. She could be some old dear breathing down your neck as you make changes."

Evan slapped her on the shoulder. "I'm sure she'll be delightful. Positivity rules, remember?" She snapped her fingers. "And while I remember, I want electric car points set up throughout the village, to encourage using electric cars, and a community bike station where residents or tourists can borrow bikes."

"Got it. Where next?"

Evan rubbed her hands together excitedly. "Rosebrook House."

❖

Clementine walked from the beach path onto the main road through the village.

"Clem?" She heard a voice calling behind her.

She stopped and turned around. It was Kaydence Dayton and her son Toby. Kay was as close to a good friend as Clementine had in the world. She and her husband Casper, along with their children, Toby and

Dexter, moved to the village a couple of years ago. It was the first time the village had new blood in years.

"Hi, Kay—hi, Toby."

The Daytons were an unusual family. Both Kay and Casper had given up big jobs and big salaries in London's financial sector to start a new life of self-sufficiency in the country. She was sceptical when they first arrived, but they proved Clementine wrong and had turned the run-down cottage and land into a thriving enterprise, with animals, vegetables, and the like being sold at the local farmers' market.

Kay caught up with her. "Did you manage to get something for the girls?"

"I did and dropped it off with them. How's everyone at home?"

"Oh, great. I thought I'd bring Toby out for a stroll in his pram. Can I walk you home?"

Clementine smiled. "That would be lovely."

❖

"This is gorgeous." Evan stood in the huge wood-panelled circular entrance hall and gazed in wonder at the 1920s architecture. The veneered wooden panels depicted ancient Greek and Roman gods, the Parthenon, and other classical buildings.

"Had you never visited here when you were younger?" Archie asked.

"No, it was never open to the public. But I've seen pictures over the years. Nothing beats seeing it in person. I mean, look at the dome."

They both gazed up at the white plastered ceiling, punctuated by a dome made up of tiny little dots of glass, some missing, that let the light stream in.

"It's unlike any stately home I've ever seen. I mean, from the outside it looks like a normal large country pile," Archie said.

"Exactly," Evan said, "that's why it's so special. Architects say it's the best example of art deco style in Britain. It's amazing to think Rosebrook Castle used to be here. It was beyond repair, so the duke of that time, Isadora's uncle, knocked it down and started again."

She walked back over to the front door and indicated to the two hugely tall Grecian figures holding spears, guarding the doorway.

"Look at this—a century ago, people thought it was perhaps a bit garish. It is over the top, but that's what makes it wonderful. I mean, there's a picture I've seen of a bathroom upstairs, tiled in gold, with Grecian statues and marble, so over the top, but so wonderful. I hope it's still intact, but we'll refurb it anyway."

"What are you going to do with it, Fox? Open it to the public?"

Evan thrust her hands into her pockets and wandered back over to Archie. "Some of the house, but I want it to be my new home."

Archie looked taken aback. "You want to live here? In the country?"

"Don't look so shocked. It's always been my dream to live here," Evan said.

"But it's the middle of nowhere. I know you want to see this village and land turned into an example, a vision of how life could be, living an ecological life, and eventually a safe place for LGBTQ people, but how could you run the business?"

"I'm going to run the day-to-day business from here. The only part of Rosebrook that is part of the original castle is the medieval banqueting hall in the gardens. I plan to refit that for business and have a few members of staff working with me. Then I can shoot back to London whenever I'm needed. It's not that far."

Archie shook her head. "You know what, Fox? You're either a genius or bonkers."

Evan laughed and slapped Archie on the shoulder. "I don't know about being a genius, but I'm completely happy to be bonkers. Some of the best people are." She winked and made off for the stairs. "Come on. I want to see if those gold tiles are still there."

Chapter Five

Four months later

Clementine had become used to the noise of construction vehicles and lorries coming and going to Rosebrook House. Used to it, but not happy about it. In the last few weeks, the noise, the banging from the house, had gotten more frenetic, and she had lost count of the times her car had been blocked in by the many trucks and vans sitting at the entrance to the property. She was having a running battle with the drivers and had given them a piece of her mind on more than one occasion, her annoyance steadily building.

The house had been sold and resold many times since Clementine and her mother had left, but this time it felt different.

None of the other buyers had ever made her annoyed or nervous before. In the past, the *Sold* sign had gone up, and then nothing happened for months or years, as the purchaser realized how much money it would take to make the house liveable again. Then it would be sold on, and the cycle would start again.

This time was different. After the new *Sold* sign went up, the very next day there were workers arriving, setting up scaffolding around the house and putting in temporary amenities for the workers—not to mention a very quick refurbishment of the old church. It was the first time someone appeared to be serious about Rosebrook, and the very thought made anxiety squirm in her stomach.

Clementine poured herself a coffee and walked through to her desk. She had managed to get some commissions over the last couple of months, enough to keep her head above water. The current job she was working on was for a block of business units, boring and dull, but it was work.

When she left university, she imagined herself working on exciting, modern buildings and homes, bringing some colour to cities and towns. The reality of course was very different.

Clementine sighed and put her coffee down on her desk. "Oh, well, it's a job."

As she sat and prepared to begin work, she heard the loud beeps of a large vehicle reversing, and some loud shouts. She walked over to the window and looked out. She saw two extremely large moving company lorries, each being carefully waved through the gates to the estate.

Clementine felt tears fill her eyes and her heart hurt. *It's gone. I've finally lost Rosebrook.*

She turned and looked at the family picture on the mantelpiece, with her father as a young boy beside his mother—Isadora—and his stepmother. Rosebrook was gone, the final nail in the coffin, a long time since Isadora put her dreams before her family.

Clementine wiped her tears and was about to walk back to her desk when she heard a knock at the door.

"Knock, knock. It's me."

It was Kaydence. "Come in."

Kay, who was normally a cheery, positive person, appeared even more so than usual. "Did you see the moving vans? Looks like our new Rosebrook resident has arrived."

"Yes, I saw. Rosebrook has finally gone," Clementine said sadly.

Kay seemed to realize that this was a pain filled moment. "I'm sorry. I should have been more sensitive. I know a new resident in the house will be hard for you, but it looks like there's some hope for Rosebrook and the village."

"How so?" Clementine asked.

Kay held up an envelope. "Didn't you get the letter?"

"What letter?"

"Everyone get a letter from the new owner. It was hand posted through the doors last night. Didn't you check your post?"

Clementine was never eager to check her post as it usually contained outstanding bills. "No, let me take a look."

She went to her front door and checked the wire basket that caught the post and pulled out a few envelopes. She tossed a couple of brown ones aside and opened up the hand delivered letter. Clementine started to read and walked back to the living room.

Kay couldn't contain her excitement. "Can you believe it? After all these years, someone wants to rebuild the village."

Clementine looked up from the letter. "The owner of Fox Toys wants to rebuild the village?"

"Yes." Kay grinned happily. "Fox Toys are very popular in my house. Did you read the part where she said she has big dreams for Rosebrook and wants all us villagers on board to be part of it? She's having a reception at the church tonight. We're all invited. Evan Fox wants to present her plans to us."

Annoyance was building in Clementine. "Another dreamer who'll run out of money or get bored of the mundane running of a village."

Kay sighed. "I don't think the owner of Fox Toys could run out of money—they're a multinational company."

Clementine stared down at the letter. "The Fitzroys had a lot of money. My family is a testament to the fact that you can lose everything here."

"Clem, I know this is difficult for you, seeing someone barge in on your family's home and land, but would you rather see it dying like it is, or being rebuilt?"

Clementine said nothing, but inside she was struggling with anger, resentment, and hurt. This was it—she was losing her family's legacy.

"Clem, will you at least come tonight and listen to what Evan Fox has to say?" Kay asked.

Clem scrunched up the paper and said, "I've got no time to listen to dreamers. I'm working."

❖

Evan was nervous. It had been four months since she bought Rosebrook and its land, but even after all the intense work had been put in to restore the house and the former church, now was where the hard work started. Selling her dream to the residents of the village.

She paced around the church, now dubbed *The Meeting Place*, checking everything was in order to open the doors at seven o'clock. The church had been sympathetically restored to keep all of its original historical features.

Evan checked the list of residents on her phone for probably the thousandth time, trying to get the names into her head. She wanted the villagers to feel like they were part of this project, and in order to do that, she had to gain trust.

She was saddened by the fact that there was only one family with young children in the village, something she hoped to change. Evan looked up to the pews on the balcony and tried to imagine a scene, five years from now, where those seats were filled with happy villagers, meeting to discuss community projects. It was a dream and she would make it happen.

Archie pulled her away from her thoughts. "Fox? There's just a couple of minutes to go."

"Okay, is everything set?"

"Yes, the drinks table is set up, and the waiters are at the door ready to serve drinks and canapés."

"Good." Evan looked around to see the small area she had set up for the kids. She'd hired a balloon artist to entertain the couple of kids attending. She wanted them to have a good impression of her and the project too, and not bore them with a stuffy meeting.

Again, she checked her phone and this time reread the information she had found on how to address a duchess. She was one of the most important people to get onside. Evan assumed that the duchess still had some sway with the villagers and could colour their judgement, and besides, she wanted to make a good impression anyway—this was Isadora Fitzroy's granddaughter.

She mumbled the instructions she read on her phone. "Social inferiors first greet the duchess as Your Grace." Evan felt the nerves build inside her. "I'm definitely a social inferior. Then, madam or ma'am."

She heard the doors being opened and the chatter of voices. This was it. Evan put on her best smile and walked towards the group of people coming in.

First of all she was greeted by the young family in the village, plus two older ladies. One was in a wheelchair.

"Hello, thank you for coming. I'm Evan."

A smiling woman said, "I'm Kay, this is my husband Casper, and our two boys, Toby and Dexter, and these are Agatha and Adelaide Tucker."

Evan shook hands with Casper, and then politely kissed the hands of Kay and the two older ladies.

"Oh, isn't she so gentlemanly," the lady called Agatha said.

"I'm delighted to meet you, ladies, and you, Casper and Kay." She then crouched down to the children. "Hey, buddies. How are you doing?"

The boy—Dexter, his mum had called him—said, "Do you make Fox Toys?"

"I sure do, and I've got a couple of stuffed animals for you." She pointed to the balloon modeler. "If you go and see the balloon guy over there, he'll give them to you and make some balloons for you."

The two boys squealed and ran over.

"I think you've won my boys over to your cause," Casper said.

"Please go and get some drinks, some food, and make yourselves comfortable."

After them she was introduced to a delightful, well-dressed older gentleman with a white beard and warm manner. His name was Mr. Fergus, but he insisted on being called, simply, Fergus.

Then she met a lovely, smiling young woman named Ashling and her father, James O'Rourke, who was not as smiley. And neither were the two farmers, Mr. Mason and Mr. Murdoch, and his wife.

"Pleased to meet you all. Go through and get a drink."

The man named Mr. Murdoch muttered as he walked, "This better be good."

Archie whispered, "Tough crowd."

Evan wasn't going to let that deter her. She waited by the door but no one else arrived. She looked at her watch and wondered if she should give the duchess longer, but her guests were already getting nervous. She walked up to the pulpit and had her PowerPoint slides ready to go.

"Good evening, ladies, gentlemen, and children. Thank you for coming out tonight. I want to give you this presentation to give you an idea of who I am and what I plan on doing with the village and land. First, let me tell you a bit about me. I've been a lifelong admirer of the late Duchess Isadora Fitzroy and what she planned to do here. Like the duchess, I believe in building communities, with low cost housing and village amenities that allow residents to grow and become the best they can be."

Kay and her husband, Mr. Fergus, and the elderly ladies were listening intently, but the farmers were muttering among themselves.

"So I want to regenerate this village, rebuild the derelict cottages, refurbish those cottages that are leased, and bring a shop, a pub, and all the usual things a thriving village needs."

Evan moved the presentation on to the most exciting slides, the ones about conservation.

"Now the other thing about me is that I'm passionate about the environment, and so I want to build on Isadora's ideas by making this village an example to the nation."

She was getting more animated by the second, her gestures getting bigger and bigger.

"My dream is to turn this rural place into an eco-village, where we live by giving back to nature, not taking, and where our main focus is making the world a better place, by saving power, reducing our carbon footprint, and taking care to conserve the environment and the animals we live alongside."

Evan saw Archie smiling from the front seats as she got more enthusiastic by the second.

"But over and above that, I want to make this village a safe place for people who have been marginalized by society, a place where LGBTQ people and those of all different minorities find a home and supportive place to live. Ladies and gentleman, we can make Rosebrook a shining example to the nation, and I hope you will come along with me to make it happen. Thank you."

She got a round of applause and then asked, "Any questions?"

Mr. Murdoch stood up with a look of anger on his face. "Are you one of those carrot-crunching vegans?"

Obviously *vegan* was a dirty word to these Rosebrook farmers, but she had to be honest. "Yes, I am a vegan."

Mr. Murdoch looked to his friend Mr. Mason and said, "Told you so." Then he turned his attention back to Evan. "I tell you this, you will not stop us farming because of your environmental tosh. We have existing leases."

"No I don't want to—" Evan was about to put their minds at rest, but they stood up and marched out, along with Mr. O'Rourke.

His daughter Ashling was trying to reason with him. "Dad, stay and see what she has to say." But he didn't, and Evan was left with only the few who were happy to listen.

Archie stood and said again, "Tough crowd."

Chapter Six

The next morning, Clementine heard a knock at the door. She hoped it wasn't one of the villagers to tell her what a wonderful future the village had now that Evan Fox had arrived. Going by Mr Fergus's visit this morning, and Kay's exuberant phone call, Evan Fox had managed to hook most of them into her unrealistic dream last night at the church meeting.

As Clementine walked to the door, she said to herself, "I mean what kind of woman's name is Evan Fox, anyway?"

She opened the door and felt what her mother had once described as collywobbles—the feeling you got when you were instantly and unexpectedly attracted to someone. Her mother had told her that she felt these so-called collywobbles when she first met her father, but Clementine had never quite believed in them. Attraction was lust and felt in a completely different area.

Nonetheless, the aforementioned collywobbles did indeed instantly gather in her stomach at the sight of this unknown dapper butch standing with a bunch of flowers in her hand, and for some reason a stuffed toy fox in the other.

This someone was dressed in a tweed suit and waistcoat, with a colourful tie and pocket square. She had never seen a dapper butch before in real life, only online, on social media, where she liked to follow the styles and butch looks that attracted her, but the run-down Rosebrook village was certainly not the usual habitat for a butch lesbian, dapper or not.

The dapper butch smiled, and Clementine felt her chest tighten.

"Good morning, Your Majesty…Your Lady—no, Your Grace, ma'am."

Clementine had to stop herself from smiling at the adorable way the dapper butch stumbled over her title.

"It's Clementine, and you are?"

Her eyes were drawn to the tie and lapel pins in the shape of a fox's head, along with the stuffed animal she was holding, and her stomach dropped. It was her. The one who had finally brought her family's association with Rosebrook to an end.

"I'm Evan Fox, ma'am, Clementine, ma'am." Evan Fox then thrust the bunch of hand-tied flowers and the toy fox at her. "A small token, ma'am. I wonder if I might have a few moments of your time?"

Clementine was taken aback in many ways. She recognized this was a bunch of wildflowers—unusual—and that the giver was highly unusual as well. Evan Fox was not only dapper, she was a dandy, going by her precisely styled hair as well as her immaculate dress. She was really good-looking but must be a good bit younger than herself.

Clementine sighed. "Thank you, but I fail to see the relevance of the stuffed animal."

Evan seemed surprised. "Why?"

"They're for children," Clementine said flatly.

"Surely not, I have loads of soft toys, and this little chap is the mascot of Fox Toys."

Looking at Evan's appearance, with her now visible red braces peeking out from underneath her tweed jacket, Clementine didn't doubt she had children's toys. "I'll give it to my friend's children. Come in."

As Evan followed her in she said, "Oh, you mean the Dayton family? Toby and Dexter? I met them last night. Great kids, they have one each already, so keep Mr. Fox for yourself, please."

"Sit down," Clementine said.

Evan felt a distinct frostiness coming from the duchess, and she hadn't been expecting that. She also hadn't been expecting such a young, normal-looking but naturally beautiful woman, dressed simply in a jumper and jeans.

She had expected an older lady—that's how she pictured a duchess—but Clementine had opened the door, looked her in the eye, and then she had been whacked in the head with a banjo, or so it felt. Hence why she got the titles so embarrassingly wrong at the door.

Her dad had described the feeling of meeting her mum as being hit in the head with a banjo, and Evan, being a romantic, had set that as her benchmark for love and had been waiting a long time to feel it.

And I called her Your Majesty. Evan felt the embarrassment still but shook it off and decided to charge on with positivity.

"You look wonderful today, by the way," Evan said with enthusiasm.

Clementine gazed at her with suspicion from the chair across the room. "Excuse me? I don't need flattery, Ms. Fox."

There was that cold breeze again. But Evan was undeterred. She was an expert at bringing people around through good humour and her infectious personality. That's why she was so good in business negotiations.

"I don't flatter, ma'am. I spread positivity." Evan grinned.

Clementine snorted. "Well, don't waste your positivity on me. Especially since I'm wearing jeans, a jumper, and no make-up."

Wow. Again, tough crowd here in Rosebrook. *Just keep charging on*. "I was disappointed not to see you last night at The Meeting Place."

"The Meeting Place?" Clementine repeated.

"Sorry, the church. We've renamed it The Meeting Place because I want it to be the centre of the community I hope to build here."

"I read your letter, Ms. Fox—"

Evan interrupted, "Evan or Fox, please, ma'am."

"Only if you stop calling me ma'am, Evan."

"Got it. Please, carry on."

Clementine sat back in her chair and started to talk. Evan lost track of her words as her eyes followed Clementine's fingers as she placed an errant piece of hair behind her ear. She had elegant features and the cutest nose, but the thing that captivated Evan's attention most was the fire in those green eyes of hers, even though the fire appeared to be directed at her.

Evan's heart thudded with excitement. She'd never expected the Duchess of Rosebrook to make her head turn to mush and her heart melt into goo.

Oh my God, she's the future Mrs. Fox. When you met your wife, first you felt like you've been hit with a banjo, then your brain turned to mush and your heart melted.

She shivered and realized she had no idea what Clementine had said.

"Are you listening?" Clementine said sharply.

"Um...sorry, could you repeat that?" Evan said.

Clementine sighed. "Your letter implied you wanted to build some kind of new community in this village, and I have no interest in that. I just wish to be left alone."

Evan was surprised. She cleared her throat. "Ma'am—sorry, Clementine. If you could just hear me out. First of all, it's such an honour to meet Isadora's granddaughter. You must be so proud of her."

"You must be joking. If she had taken care of her family and her duties as duchess, my mother and I would be sitting in Rosebrook house, not you, Evan."

Evan was taken aback by her attitude to Isadora. Isadora was generally thought of as a heroine and pioneer with good ideas. She'd had setbacks, certainly, but the ideas were good.

She decided to be as nonconfrontational as possible, "I'm sorry to hear that. I wrote the final essay of my business degree on Isadora. She is my hero, but leaving that to one side, I wish you had been at the village presentation last night. I would value your knowledge of the people, village, and the land."

The fire in Clementine's eyes got fiercer. "Do you know how many people have owned the house and land since my family left? Many. And of those people the furthest they got was putting up scaffolding around the house before they realized how much money it would take to make this village live again, and they ran, leaving the few of us with a village in its death throes. I don't trust people with plans and dreams, Evan."

Evan looked up at the mantelpiece and saw a picture of Isadora with her partner, and she assumed Clementine's father as a boy. She stood up and picked up the photo. From her research, when Isadora first inherited Rosebrook estate, she was full of life and enthusiastic about the future. Isadora would be unhappy about the current state of Rosebrook and her granddaughter's opinion of her. Maybe it was Evan's mission to change both those states of affairs.

Evan put the picture down and turned to Clementine. "Just listen to me for five minutes, and then you can kick me out on my backside."

Clementine nodded, so Evan began. "My life's ambition is to fulfil Isadora's dream of a cooperative community, with houses for fair rents, and jobs that pay a decent wage. A place where the people have good healthcare, education, childcare, recreational spaces, but adding some of my own dreams onto Isadora's vision."

Evan started to pace backwards and forwards in front of Clementine as her passionate speech gathered momentum. "I want to build a green village that aims to increase health and happiness, and reduce the effects of peak oil, climate destruction, and economic instability. Also a place that is a welcoming and a safe community for all from the LGBTQ community—"

"A gay village?" Clementine interrupted.

"No, a village of safety and acceptance for all."

Clementine rolled her eyes, but Evan charged on using big hand gestures that matched her excitement.

"A place where the community will have a say on how it's run. Every member a stakeholder. I'll rebuild the cottages to make them as ecologically sound as I can, and build more housing to attract young families, a truly safe and supportive place for sections of our community. I want it to be a shining example to the rest of the country as to what we can achieve when we set out to try to leave the world a better place than we found it."

Clementine closed her eyes and shook her head. "I live in reality, not dreams. I may not own the land any more, but I still feel the responsibility to my people here. You are going to put these people through disruption and get their hopes up for the future, and then once you are fed up with your new toy, you'll leave them high and dry. You're a toy manufacturer, not a landowner. You have no qualifications to take care of this village," Clementine said.

Evan was normally extremely good natured and hard to anger, but Clementine was making it difficult simply by her obstinate attitude.

"What kind of qualifications would I need? I took environmental studies at university, and I have my very own environmental consultant who works for me."

Clementine gave a hollow laugh. "University course? How about five hundred years of experience, passed down from one Fitzroy to the other. It's in my blood—I was born to take care of the land and the village. I was trained for it, but thanks to my grandmother and you, I can't do it."

My God, thought Evan, *this woman has one almighty chip on her shoulder.*

Again Evan tried to be conciliatory. "That's why I was so disappointed you didn't come last night. I would value your advice immensely."

The noise of a lorry reversing interrupted their conversation. She saw Clementine look past her shoulder and out of the window.

"Bloody dirty things." Clementine stood up quickly. "You want my advice? Follow me."

What had she gotten a bee in her bonnet about now? Evan never imagined this conversation would be this hard. She got up and followed Clementine out the front door.

When Evan met her, Clementine pointed to an old car parked in front of the gatehouse, which was now boxed in by the lorry.

"You see?" Clementine said angrily. "Four months this has been happening, and no matter how much I complain to your foreman, it keeps happening. My mother is very ill, and I need to be ready to get to her at a moment's notice, if her nurses call. One morning I waited an hour before someone moved one of your vehicles, and I was late getting to my mother."

Evan felt immediately sorry. Clementine was obviously dealing with a lot of difficult responsibilities, while she, some new city businesswoman, came and pitched up in her ancestral home.

She put her hand on her heart and said, "I'm truly sorry this has caused you problems. I promise after I talk to them, it will never happen again, on my word of honour. Plus, I'm living here now, so if you have any complaints or problems, come straight to me."

Evan saw confusion and emotion in Clementine's eyes. She had obviously been looking for a fight and not gotten one.

"And what about that?" Clementine pointed to Rosebrook House's roof.

"What about what?" Evan replied.

"Those ugly solar panels on the roof," Clementine said.

"It's the first step in making the house and the village ecologically sound. The second stage is to get a wind turbine in the grounds, which will feed a Powerwall battery and make the house run virtually off-grid."

"Wind turbine?" Clementine said angrily.

"Hey, it may not be the prettiest, but if we don't make these small sacrifices, we may not have a world to live in."

Clementine walked up close to her. So close that she could smell Clementine's perfume. Her heart started to race.

"Just remember, this village is not your latest toy. You're dealing with real lives, real historic, living, breathing buildings."

Instead of replying with annoyance or anger, Evan smiled, leaned in close to Clementine's ear and said, "You're so pretty when you're angry, Clem."

Evan was sure she saw Clementine shiver slightly. Then she turned on her heel and walked back into her house and slammed the door.

"Well, that was eventful."

Even though Clementine was back in her house, Evan could still feel her. She closed her eyes and smelled her perfume and felt unquenchable excitement after being in Clementine's company, even though the duchess was angry with her—maybe especially because she was angry.

If a frown made Evan feel like this, she could only imagine what a smile would do to her. One thing was for sure. Evan wanted to experience more of the Duchess of Rosebrook. She was beautiful, sad, and carrying the weight of the world on her shoulders, but still she held herself with a natural nobility.

Evan put her hands in her pockets and looked up to the sky. "Isadora? Not only am I going to bring your vision into reality, but I'm going to rebuild your granddaughter's belief in dreams again." If she really was Mrs. Fox, Evan was going to have fun finding out.

CHAPTER SEVEN

"What do you think, Mum?" Evan said while bouncing on a trampoline.

"I think you're making me dizzy. Sit down, Evan," her mother said.

Evan slowed her bouncing and sat on the edge of her large trampoline. One of the many modernizing elements she'd brought to Rosebrook was to have the disused basement rooms turned into a large gym and a games room, and this one housed her large trampoline.

She had always promised herself that if she ever moved from her London flat, she'd have a large trampoline like she'd had when she was growing up, and here she had it in this historic house. An image of Clementine flashed across her mind. If the grumpy but gorgeous duchess saw this in her former home, she'd probably want to kill her, but that would be good too.

An angry Clementine was still a Clementine, and she had thought about her constantly since she met her.

"So, do you like the place?" Evan said to her mum.

She had video-called her mum and taken her on a short tour, ending in the trampoline room.

"It's a beautiful house, sweetheart, but it's a big place to rattle around in by yourself," her mum said.

That was one thing that bothered Evan. It was very quiet. She was a people person, and being on her own troubled Evan. She really needed to get the pub back open as soon as possible, to get the community socializing again.

The other thing was furniture. She'd had no idea how to furnish this place. Sure, she had her trampoline room, games room, toy room, and her bedroom set up with essentials, but she'd had to let an interior designer fill the house with appropriate furniture, and it didn't quite feel like it suited her personality.

"I'll be okay, Mum. I bet Dad would love my trampoline. Where is he, anyway?" Evan asked.

Her mother was in Geneva at a climate change conference with one of the Fox Toys environmental charities. Her father always went along with her, wherever she travelled, now that he was retired.

"You're right. He'd never get off the bloody trampoline thing. Your father is at a collectors' fair he found out about. Honestly, whatever country we go to, he always finds an antique toy shop or fair. He's on the hunt for some train set or another."

"Cool," Evan said with a big smile. Both Evan and her father were not only passionate about toys, but they were passionate about their respective toy collections. Where her dad collected trains and clockwork toys of the forties and fifties, Evan had an impressive collection of action figures, in their original packaging, including Star Wars, Marvel, and DC action heroes. Now she finally had the room to display them. They were still packed away, but that was her next project. "When can you both come and see the place?"

"Not for another month at least. I have a few more commitments after this convention, but as soon as we can, we'll be there."

"I know. Thanks, Mum."

"So, what's the reception like from the locals to your big plans?"

Evan immediately thought of Clementine and sighed. "They've been great. It's a small community, but when I met them at the refurbed church, they were really interested, well mostly. The farmers were slightly distrustful."

Her mother smiled. "You could interest anyone in anything with your positive attitude. I'm sure you can get anyone onside."

Evan shrugged. "I don't know about that. The resident duchess is not on board and in fact can't stand the sight of me, it seems."

"You've met her?" Cassia asked.

"Yep, when she didn't turn up to the community meeting, I went to her door. I was so excited to meet Isadora's granddaughter, but she wasn't happy to see me."

"What is she like?"

Evan couldn't help the smile that crept up on her face. "She's beautiful, passionate, and she has these fiery green eyes—as I said, she can't stand the sight of me. But I don't think life is easy for her.

She doesn't seem to have much money and has an elderly mother in a nursing home."

"Hmm," her mother said, "think about it from her point of view. She's a duchess—not only that, but I've read that the dukedom of Rosebrook is the third highest ranking one in Britain—and she has no land. That's what the title is for, and it's useless if you don't have your land and people to go with the title. And to top it all off, you are now standing in her family home, which you've changed, and come at her with all these plans in that excited way you have. Like a child that's had too much sugar. I'm sure it does remind her of her grandmother Isadora."

"That's what I feel like my purpose is, to finish the job Isadora started," Evan said.

"You might remember Isadora Fitzroy as a pioneer, but I remember what your gran told me at the time. When they lost everything, the family was embarrassed beyond all recognition."

"What should I do?" Evan asked.

"Don't go storming in like some wild idealist throwing your money around. Show her and the village they are a part of what's happening. Let them see your plans, your costings, open up, give them a proper voice on the plans, and I'm sure you'll convince the duchess that way."

"You mean make the Rosebrook regeneration a trust instead of my own personal project? Invite the people onto the committee and to become part of the changes?"

"Exactly," her mother said. "As you know, the Fox family have many trusts, and your dad and I have always found that the best way to make change. Give the people working on the ground a sense of ownership."

Evan had a new burst of energy. She couldn't wait to get started, but then one thing popped into her head. "There's one teeny, tiny problem left, Mum."

"What? You always say there are no problems, only opportunities."

"This is a bit different, though. I think Clementine Fitzroy is my wife. She's turned up at last."

Her mother burst out laughing. "What? Why do you think that?"

"Within five minutes of meeting her, I experienced all three criteria that Dad told me to expect when I met my wife, what he felt when he met you. First you feel like you've been hit with a banjo, then your brain turns to mush and your heart melts."

"Oh, sweetheart, I know you're an incurable romantic like your father, but it's not an exact science. It's probably just attraction. You don't even know if you'll like her personality."

"I've been attracted plenty of times before, and this felt different, more overwhelming. I trust my feelings, Mum," Evan said.

"Evan, your father's perhaps over-romanticized our beginnings. Don't base your love life on us. Is she even gay?"

"I've no idea, but I'm going to find out. Stage one, make her smile."

Her mother smiled and said, "That's always a good place to start. Your dad always made me smile. Whatever happens, sweetheart, you're at the start of a grand adventure."

Maybe a romantic adventure, her own love story.

Evan gazed around her new office space with wonder. Her team had converted the medieval banqueting hall. It was beautiful. All the original stone work and big wooden beams on the ceiling echoed of an earlier time, but mixed with the new computers and TV monitors hanging on the walls, it was well and truly ready to become Evan's country office.

"You've done a fantastic job," she said to Archie.

"It wasn't easy getting a fast, reliable internet connection in here, but we got there in the end."

There were still some technicians floating around the room, fiddling with wires, and setting up computers for the staff that would be joining her here, but Evan's desk and computer were ready to go. She sat down and lifted her iPad to check the notes she had made.

"Okay, so I've set up the Rosebrook Trust with my lawyers. I just need to give them the names of the trustees."

Archie sat on the side of the desk. "Are you sure this is a good idea, Fox? Giving over some of the control to the villagers?"

"Yes, it's perfect. Isadora's original plans included a mini parliament, where residents would come to consensus and vote. I need these people working with me, not just me barging in and telling them what's what. My mum reminded me of that."

Archie sighed. "It's your business, your dream, but I'm not one for giving up control."

Evan laughed. "I bet, but just loosen up a little. Besides, I need to get our resident duchess involved."

"Why? Won't she just interfere?"

Evan tweaked the bow tie she was wearing. "Her interference might help us. You see, she has local knowledge and hundreds of years of experience passed down to her on how to run an estate and village. There will be things we'd miss. Besides, the others will follow her. Clementine Fitzroy is their natural leader, even if she doesn't know it herself yet."

Archie indicated to the empty desks. "So have you got staff lined up?"

"I've managed to persuade Violet to let me have Rupert. He and I have a good rapport, and he's keen to start a new life in the country. Violet's working with him to headhunt a few faces to come with him. He'll be down next week, if the staff cottages are ready."

As well as refurbishing the main house, Archie's team had been updating the former estate workers' cottages to modern standards.

"We'll have one good to go by next Monday, another two by the end of the month. I'm sure your new office staff can commute or share until they're ready."

"One cottage was meant to be for you," Evan said.

Archie looked up to the ceiling. "You know I don't want to live in the country. This is your dream, and I'll help achieve your project, but you'll be at the head office two days a week, and I'll travel up and down by car."

"Okay, okay, if you're that against it."

They were interrupted by one of the workmen walking in and saying, "Excuse me, Fox, there's a Mr. Fergus here. He'd like to see you."

Evan stood up. "Of course, send him in."

"I'll leave you to it." Archie left just as Mr Fergus was arriving.

"Fergus, come in and take a seat." Evan directed him to a seat.

She liked Fergus. He was happy, jolly, and shared her manner and dress sense. Today he was wearing an old-fashioned Harris tweed, similar to the pale blue tweed trousers and waistcoat she was wearing.

"Nice suit, youngster."

Evan grinned. "My tailor made me a whole wardrobe of country suits. I can't wait to try them all out."

Fergus smiled and rubbed his pure white beard. "Good show, good show. You left a message with my housekeeper that you wanted to see me."

"Yes, but you didn't need to come all the way up here. I would have come to you," Evan said.

"Not at all. I wanted the walk. Besides I have to admit to being curious as to what you've done with the place."

Evan held out her hands proudly. "What do you think?"

"It's wonderful. You know, I remember the last time I was here—Isadora was showing me her new plans. It was five years after the War when my partner and I moved to Rosebrook. She wanted to sell off some land and try to restart her big project, but she had already lost so much, and her wife and son were dead against it. It never came to anything."

"It's amazing that you knew her. Can I offer you tea, coffee, water?" Evan pointed to the other end of the room where there was a coffee machine, tea facilities, and a drinks fridge.

Fergus looked across, and then at his watch. "Well, the sun is definitely past the yardarm. You wouldn't happen to have a little snifter, would you?"

Evan laughed and walked up to the drinks area, and from a cupboard brought back a bottle of malt and two glasses.

"Here you are. I have a love of malt whisky."

"Another thing we have in common. Cheers. Now, what can I do for you, youngster?" Fergus said.

Evan rolled the whisky glass between her hands. "I need your help."

"My help? Of course, anything. What do you need?"

"Your advice, experience, and influence. I told you about my dream the other night, to make Isadora's new style of community come to life, and to help make the planet greener, but I've come to the realization that I'm doing this the wrong way. I need to bring the village together and address their issues before I charge on with my own ideas."

"You mean our resident farmers, Mr. O'Rourke, and the duchess?"

Evan nodded. "I need the duchess onside to bring the others along. Even though she doesn't own the land any more, the people do still seem to follow her."

Fergus nodded. "History and tradition run deep in this village. She is a symbol of what held this community together for so long."

"Why is she so hostile when I'm trying to rebuild her village?" Evan asked.

"She was brought up to fulfil a role, a role that has hundreds of years of expectation and history behind it. Clementine may have studied to become an architect, but being the duchess was always meant to be her life, her vocation, and now she can't do it."

"When did she leave Rosebrook?"

"She was sixteen, I think, but older than her years. Marianne, the dowager duchess, always had troubles—you know, mentally. So Clementine has had to be the responsible one since she was a young woman. Marianne declined after they were forced to leave the house."

Evan let out a breath and took a sip of her drink. "Now here I am, sitting in her house, and acting like a bull in a china shop?"

Fergus chuckled. "Something like that, but you can make her come around."

"I need your help to do it. This isn't my world, and I don't know how it works. I was so enthusiastic about my project that I forgot about some aspects that I haven't a clue about. I've moved from a flat and I'm living in a stately home, with no staff, and no idea what staff I would need."

"Forgive me for being vulgar and talking about money, but your family is wealthy—didn't you go to boarding school and mix with people who had big country piles like this?"

Evan shook her head and smiled. "Nope, my mum and dad are lifelong passionate Labour supporters and don't believe in the private school system. I went to my local school. Their views on social reform rubbed off on me."

"What would you like me to do?" Fergus asked.

Evan stood up and walked around her desk. "I want to have another meeting, come about this from a different angle, and I need Clementine there. I thought maybe neutral territory?"

"My house? No problem at all. Good idea. I'll help you in any way I can, youngster."

Evan smiled and held up her glass. "Cheers."

❖

The summer sun was hot in the July sky, Clementine had completed another two projects for the firm who had contracted her, and her mum had been settled for the last week. As she lay back on her sun lounger on the beach, life seemed calmer and manageable. She opened her eyes when she heard the sound of Toby's and Dexter's laughter in the water.

Beside her Kay removed the sunhat from her face and shouted, "Don't go in too deep, boys."

Kay had persuaded her to have a lunchtime picnic with her and the boys at the beach, since she had no more work on. So they came down to the bay and got the sun loungers Mr. O'Rourke kept at his fishing hut and enjoyed some sandwiches. Initially apprehensive, Clementine was happy she had come. It was relaxing.

"Another drink, Clem?" Kay opened the cool box beside her and pulled out two bottles of sparkling apple juice.

"That would be perfect. Thanks." Clementine took the bottle and quickly took a drink. The cool liquid felt wonderful as it ran down her throat.

"Isn't this just heavenly?" Kay said. "My family and friends often ask why we moved the family out to this isolated village." She spread out her arms. "This is why. A just-about-private beach, where the kids can play safely, and back home our own little mini-farm, living off the land as nature intended. Not bad, eh?"

Clementine smiled. "No, not too bad at all."

That was the first time she could take a breath and enjoy a day without being overly stressed. She looked out to sea and saw Mr. O'Rourke's fishing boat sitting out on the water. He had one of his fishing parties out enjoying the day.

"Lovely day for fishing."

"Yes, when I was at the boat shop, Mr. O'Rourke said he had two bookings today. Unusual, but I suppose when the village is rebuilt, he'll be more than busy."

"Hmm," Clementine said noncommittedly.

"Oh, come on, you can't still be annoyed at her. She's lovely. I've seen her driving through the village a few times in that cute little green Beetle of hers."

"Kay, she wants to turn the village into some kind of environmental experiment, meanwhile building some kind of utopian dream for the LGBTQ community. It's all pie in the sky. We're just a rich woman's plaything."

"I don't think so. She has trustworthy eyes," Kay said.

Clementine sat up straighter in her lounger. "Trustworthy eyes? Really?"

"Yes, and she's sweet. Every time I see her, she has a smile and a nice compliment for me."

"Flattery," Clementine said, "pure flattery. I wouldn't believe a word of it."

Kay snorted. "It's not flattery, it's kindness. Besides even if it was, I'd take it. I'm a harassed mother of two kids. I don't get too many compliments." Clementine said nothing and a few silent moments went by before Kay suddenly said, "Is she your type?"

Clementine just about spat out her apple juice. "My type? What on earth are you talking about?"

"Your type of woman." Kay grinned.

"I don't think I've ever told you that I'm gay, have I?"

"You're not denying it then. I thought so. I'm good at reading people, although I don't know why you kept it a secret. I'm your friend."

Clementine sighed. She wasn't going to deny it. "It wasn't a secret, but it just never seemed important. I've never seen anyone I like or had a relationship since I came home to look after Mother."

"Fair enough, so is she your type?" Kay asked.

Clementine thought back to the way her body reacted when she opened the door to Evan and felt a shiver at the memory. Collywobbles.

"No, not my type."

"I don't know why," Kay said. "I'm straight and she's just about my type. So well-dressed, so gentlemanly, so…what's the word?"

"Dapper," Clementine finished for her.

Kay snapped her fingers. "Dapper, that's it."

Clementine shook her head. "She's too dapper. She's a dandy, more like, and I'm sure she loves everything about herself."

Kay shouted to her sons, "Toby, that's too far out. Come back in a bit."

Hoping the conversation about Evan was over, Clementine shut her eyes and tried to dispel the memory of those weird feelings she had when she thought of Evan.

Just as she was settling, Kay said loudly, "Who is that?"

Clementine sighed and opened her eyes. "Who's what?"

Kay pointed to the other end of the beach where a figure was descending the stairs to the bay. "You don't see many people coming down there, especially that way," Kay said.

The stairs down the cliff, at the other end of the bay, had been built a long time ago, and were steeper and much more difficult to descend than the other routes to the beach. The top of the stairs was quite overgrown now, and only the locals really knew about it.

The figure made it down and ran along the beach. Whoever it was, they were fit. As they got closer, Kay whispered, "It's her."

"What? Her, who?"

"Look closer. It's our dapper dandy," Kay said.

Finally, she was close enough to make her out. It was Evan, and she shivered even though the heat was scorching. As she got closer, Clementine's gaze was glued to Evan's running form and the play of her muscles in her legs as she ran. To make matters worse, Evan's shorts weren't long, and she wore a sleeveless T-shirt, so Clementine got to see so much of Evan's well-toned body.

Then, all of a sudden, Evan was there. She stopped by them and caught her breath. Evan's normally perfect styled hair was loose, her fringe hanging sexily over her face. Evan pushed back her floppy hair and tipped her imaginary hat to them.

"Ladies, so nice to see you," Evan said.

"You too, Evan." Kay giggled like a schoolgirl and replied for them.

Clementine couldn't reply. She was too transfixed by the hot, sexy mess in front of her. Those collywobbles were going haywire, running all through her body, over her skin, and out through her fingertips.

"Would you like a cold drink, Evan?" Kay asked.

"I'd love it."

Kay handed her a bottle, and Evan began to down it in one, her head held up to the sky and eyes closed. Clementine couldn't take her eyes off the beads of sweat running down Evan's neck as she gulped down the cold drink. She also noticed that her own fingernails were tracing down her throat, and making her shiver all the more.

Stop it, Clementine chastised herself. *Look at her. No one is that good-looking and not full of themselves. Don't give in to her game.*

When Evan finished the drink she gave a loud, "Woo!" and said, "What a day, isn't it amazing to be alive? And may I say how beautiful you both look today."

Kay giggled like a schoolgirl again. What was wrong with her? Clementine thought. "Thank you, Evan. You're good for morale."

Evan put her fist on her heart. "I only speak the truth, and how are you, Your Grace—sorry, Clem?"

"It's Clementine, and I'm perfectly well."

"Good, good. What a day, eh?" Evan turned towards the sea and waved to Toby and Dexter. "A bit of a day out, is it?"

The kids waved back enthusiastically.

"Yes," Kay replied. "I managed to persuade my reclusive friend here to get some sun."

Clementine rolled her eyes. She was going to kill Kay.

"Good, good, when you live in a beautiful place like this, Clem, you should get out and enjoy it."

Clementine looked up at her and said, "Only my friends call me Clem."

She expected that cutting barb to silence Evan and make her scuttle away, but instead she clutched her heart, feigning she had been shot.

"Oh, good shot, Your Majesty, Your Duchess-ship." Then with a smiling face she added, "I'm going to be your friend, Clem, so I'm just starting early. You'll catch up."

Clementine felt a ball of…was it rage?…some overwhelming emotion erupt from somewhere deep inside, and began to say, "Now, see here—"

Kay butted in before Clementine finished her admonishment and said, "Excuse me for asking, Evan, but how did you know about that staircase down to the bay? It's overgrown and a bit dangerous. Only the locals really know about it."

"I spent many a day trip to Rosebrook when I was young, spent so much time on this beach that I know it off by heart."

This admission made Clementine's ears prick up. "You came here, when you were a child? It's not exactly a tourist destination."

"Yes, my parents brought me here and we had picnics on the beach, went litter picking"—Evan pointed down to the mesh drawstring bag hanging on her hip, filled with chocolate and crisp wrappers—"something I still carry on to this day."

Kay grinned at Clementine. "Imagine that. A Rosebrook regular."

There were more layers to Evan Fox revealed every time she met her. Could there be substance to her?

Evan held her arms out. "If you get weather like this, Rosebrook can rival anywhere."

Toby and Dexter called out to Evan and asked her to come and play with them. She surprised Clementine and Kay by shouting, "Woo! Yes, great idea. A dip in the sea will cool me off."

Evan pulled off her T-shirt, revealing a crop top style sports bra. Clementine didn't know where to look.

"Kay, could you look after my litter bag for me?" Evan said.

"Sure, but don't feel obliged to play with my boys if you're busy," Kay said.

"I'm never too busy to play with children." Evan winked and set off her collywobbles.

Evan walked a few steps towards the shore but then turned around and snapped her fingers. "Oh, I almost forgot. Fergus is hosting a planning evening at his house tomorrow night. I wonder if I could persuade you to come along, Clem?"

"I thought you already pronounced your plans at the church?" Clementine said.

"Yes, they were my plans, but I've had a rethink, and I want the villagers to have more control over the new work."

Clementine shook her head. "I told you I'm not—"

Evan dropped to her knees and clasped her hands together. "Please? If not for me, then for your village?"

Clementine was getting hotter, and not just from the sun that was baking her, especially with so much of Evan's toned body on show, and that normally perfectly styled hair flopping over her face. She was finding it really difficult to say no to those deep blue eyes of Evan's.

She opened her mouth to force a no, when Kay interrupted her. "I'll talk her into it, Evan."

Before Clementine could say any more, Evan said, "Thank you, beautiful lady." Then she rushed down to the shore and into the waves.

"What just happened?" Clementine asked.

"Oh, she's bloody dishy, isn't she?"

As Clementine watched Evan dive into the waves, with her hair now wet and ever so sexy, then lift Dexter onto her shoulders and making the kids giggle with laughter, Clementine had to admit that, yes, Evan Fox was dishy, but dangerous.

CHAPTER EIGHT

The next day, Evan was in the grand entrance hall to her house, zipping around the highly polished floor on her Segway. It was a great big area to use it on. While she sped about, she spoke aloud into the memo app on her phone, taking some voice notes for the next board meeting.

She nearly fell off her board when Archie walked in the front door and said, "Busy, I see?"

Evan sped over to Archie and stopped just before smashing into her. "I'm working through lunch break. I'm taking notes for the board meeting, and I think better when I play with some sort of toy. Anyway, how can I help you, this fine lunchtime?"

Archie handed her the iPad she was holding and said, "We've found a good plot of land for the recycling centre, and I've contacted the environmental cattle feed company that you asked me to. They'll get back to me with a name of someone who can talk to your farmers."

She looked down at the iPad and smiled. "Good, good."

"Do you think they'll even listen to you?" Archie asked.

Despite being a vegan herself, for environmental reasons, Evan didn't want to bulldoze her way through this traditional farming community and expect them to change their ways overnight. She had always found that it was more productive to work with people to reduce their impact on the environment. She supported many areas of research into more environmental ways of farming, like changing the cattle feed to one that caused less methane production in the animals.

"I think they'll listen when they find out that I'll subsidize their purchases. Everyone's a winner."

"Hmm," Archie said, "I'm not as confident as you. Some of these old-school farmers can be very set in their ways."

"Then we try to convince them in another way. We will get there, Archie. Have some faith. What about the pub? How's work going with it?" Evan said.

Archie folded her arms. "We have some plans for you to sign off on, and then we can get to work. We'll need to headhunt a manager from somewhere, along with restarting the beer factory."

Evan spun in a circle while reading Archie's notes. "Those two things are crucial. The beer factory will bring employment to our new residents, and the pub is the heart of the community, but I need people I can trust and the community can trust. I had thought of Griffin, but I can't get hold of her."

Griffin was an old friend who had very successfully dabbled in microbrewing.

"I'll keep working on it," Archie said. "Oh, I passed our resident grumpy duchess on my way here."

"She's not grumpy, just had a difficult time in life," Evan said.

The more she saw Clementine, the more she was convinced she had found the woman who was meant to be her wife. She had been waiting a long time for life to send the woman to knock her socks off, just as her mum had done to her dad, but she was here, Evan was sure. Unfortunately, Clementine didn't seem to get the same memo.

Yesterday at the beach she could hardly take her eyes off Clementine. Every time Evan said something that ruffled Clementine's feathers, her heart thundered in her chest and made her a little giddy.

Clementine was beautiful, and she could sense that she was lonely, and Evan didn't want to think of her with no one else in the world. She would use everything in her power to make Clementine feel happy again, even if she didn't want to feel it at first. Besides, with Evan's long obsession with Isadora Fitzroy, it seemed like her fate was to fall for her granddaughter.

"Ever the optimist," Archie replied.

"What was she doing?"

"There was something wrong with her car. She had her head under the bonnet. I tried to offer my help, but she wasn't having any of it."

Evan stepped off her board and handed the iPad back to Archie. "I need to run. Can you hold the fort at the office?"

She grabbed her suit jacket hanging by the front door and quickly combed her hair, glancing in the mirror next to the coat stand.

"Where are you rushing off to?" Archie said.

Evan turned around and grinned. "To help my damsel in distress."

❖

Evan parked her car just outside the gates of Rosebrook and caught her breath when she turned and saw the duchess bent over, under her car bonnet, in a short skirt and heels, and her mouth watered.

"Good God, you are gorgeous, Mrs. Fox." She thought of her favourite historical romance novels and added, "Faint heart never won fair lady."

Then she looked down at her collection of small toy figures stuck to her dashboard, including her favourite SpongeBob figure. "What do you think, SpongeBob? Have I got any chance with a duchess?" Evan nodded in response to their imaginary conversation. "You're right. Positivity rules. I'll spread the love."

She checked in the mirror that her tie was straight and got out of the car. As she walked over, Evan could not take her eyes off Clementine's shapely behind. She didn't want to give Clementine a fright, so she cleared her throat, hoping that would attract her attention. She did look up, and Evan saw Clementine's beautifully manicured hands were covered in oil.

"Can I help you?" Clementine said. The frustration in her voice was clear.

"I wondered if I might be of any assistance?" Evan said.

"Unless you are a mechanic, no," Clementine said flatly.

Evan leaned on the car and didn't let her smile falter. "No, I must admit I'm not good with cars, unless I'm building model ones, but I can offer you a lift to anywhere you want to go."

"Why would you want to do that?" Clementine sounded suspicious. "You want to butter me up, to go along with some plan of yours?"

Evan refused to let the negativity affect her. "No other motivation than helping you out."

Clementine looked down at her watch, then at her hands covered in oil. "I need to be in Bournemouth within the hour. Do you know the way?"

Yes, she was coming! "No, but satnav does. Why don't you take five minutes to go and wash your hands, and I'll meet you at the little green Bug over there."

Clementine looked at her strangely. "Why are you doing this?"

"What? Being helpful? It's the way I was brought up. Manners and helpfulness are my middle name. Now, go—you're running out of time."

At last Clementine turned and hurried back into the house.

"Yes, I did it." Evan punched the air.

❖

Evan checked her appearance in the car door mirror, then heard the clattering of heels coming her way. The very sound made a ripple of pleasure run through her body. She loved femme women, and heels were part of that.

She hurried around to the passenger side and held open the door. "My wheels are your wheels."

Clementine said a quiet, "Thank you," and slipped in the car.

Evan shut the door, hurried around to the driver's side, and slid in quickly. She was so excited. She had Clementine all to herself for at least an hour or so, the woman who made her feel like she'd been smashed in the head with a banjo. Now was the time to build bridges between them.

"Okey-dokey." Evan rubbed her hands together. "Do you have a postcode for our destination?"

Clementine took a letter out of her bag and handed it to Evan. "It's on the top."

"Got it."

Clementine had not anticipated being in this situation today. If it wasn't for the blasted car, she wouldn't be. This meeting was important. The client was rebuilding a large home overlooking the Bournemouth seafront, and the job carried a large fee. Large enough that she was ready to ditch her principles and take Evan's offer of help.

She looked over at Evan typing in the postcode to the satnav and puzzled at this strange newcomer to her life. Evan was eccentric, from her fox accessories to the children's figures sitting across the dashboard to her car, to the car itself, a green Bug, as Evan had called it.

Clementine had tried to paint the image of Evan in her mind as a conceited ladies' woman. It was easier to think of the woman who had taken over her family home in that way, not as this helpful, strangely goofy character.

"Okay, directions all plugged in. Wagons roll, eh?" Evan said.

Evan put her iPhone in the holder on the dashboard and pressed the ignition button. As soon as she did, a sultry voice started to play through the Bluetooth speaker.

"Her fingers trailed down from her lover's neck to her chest. She squeezed Julia's breast—"

"Bugger," Evan said as she reached for her phone in panic and started manically pressing all the buttons on the screen. Unfortunately, she seemed to hit the volume button and instead of the sound pausing, it got louder and louder.

"You're soaking wet, do you want me to fuck you?"

"Oh my God, stop, stop!" Evan said desperately.

Clementine couldn't help but laugh at Evan's predicament.

Evan finally managed to find the pause button, and the car went from sex to silence, with only the sound of Evan's laboured breaths filling the air.

"I'm so sorry, Clem. I know what it must have sounded like, but I'm not driving about listening to porn. It's a romance novel—look." Evan showed her the audiobook screen, and Clementine saw that it was indeed a lesbian romance novel from one of the big publishers.

"You read romance novels?" Clementine couldn't quite believe it. The thought of Evan reading romances killed the idea that she was a player.

"Uh, yes. I'm a romantic. Just like my dad. Let's get you on your way."

Evan's cheeks were bright red. It was sweet how embarrassed she was.

Who are you, Evan Fox? Clementine thought. She decided to let her off the hook and not ask any more questions—for the moment.

Finally Clementine said, "Thank you for doing this. I'll pay for the petrol, of course."

"No, you won't," Evan said quickly.

Clementine hackles were raised once again. "Excuse me but—"

"It's electric. No fuel needed," Evan said, smiling.

Clementine's wanted to find something to snap back at Evan for, but she couldn't. She turned her gaze back to the windscreen and said nothing.

"Let's get on the road then," Evan said.

Finally they were on their way. An awkward tension lay between them, and Clementine wondered if Evan felt it too. They bumped along the potholed village road until they got out onto open country roads. Evan drove steadily, carefully manoeuvring around tight bends.

"What a beautiful day. I think there's nothing like a sunny day in the countryside, don't you?"

Clementine was silent for a moment then said, "When I was younger, but now everything I want in my life is in the city."

Evan looked around quickly before returning her eyes to the road. "You'd leave your ancestral home? Rosebrook?"

"It's not mine any more—it's yours," Clementine said sharply.

There were a few moments of silence before Evan replied, "I can't take away your place in this community, Clem. You'll always be Duchess of Rosebrook."

Clementine sighed. "That doesn't mean anything any more. Once my mother passes, well, I'll leave and start a new life."

Evan tightened her grip on the steering wheel. "That would be a sad loss for Rosebrook. So, you're an architect? Just like your grandmother Isadora?"

"How did you know that?" Clementine asked.

"Your friend Kay. Lovely woman, by the way, and such great kids and husband."

"He's a nice man. Gentle, caring—wait, have you been checking up on me behind my back?"

"No, you just came up in conversation. Shall we have some music?" Evan asked.

Clementine shrugged. "If you want."

Just as Evan was about to turn on the music, a call came through. "Excuse me a moment."

She answered the call with such enthusiasm. "Peyton! Hi, how's sunny Cal?"

"Beautiful, you need to move to LA, or that pasty skin of yours will never have any colour."

Clementine watched with fascination as Evan conversed with Peyton, whoever she was. Evan was loud, over the top, and unnaturally bright. She'd never met someone as positive as Evan before, but was it all bluster?

After a bit of banter, the caller said, "The publisher's willing to deal, and would like a meet, but it'll cost you a hundred thousand on top of your original offer."

"Well, what's another hundred thousand? Call Violet and set up the meet…"

Clementine's mouth hung open. What's another hundred thousand pounds? How could she be so glib about money? Evan's business operated in a world where money was no object to dreams. Presumably that was why she felt so confident about regenerating Rosebrook. But there had been a time when money had been no object the to Fitzroys, and look what happened.

When Evan hung up on her call she said, "That was my lawyer in the US. She's negotiating a toy deal with the children's author Gabriel Harrington. It's going to be huge with a capital large."

Clementine had heard of the famous children's author, of course, but what she was wondering was why Evan had the time to be driving her to an appointment, when she was involved in such big business decisions every day.

Evan couldn't seem to contain her excitement. "You know Fox Toys is the first toy manufacturer to ban plastic packaging?"

"Really? That's quite an achievement," Clementine said.

"My advisors thought I was crazy. It would cost a fortune and give us such big logistical challenges, but I stuck to my guns, and it's paying off. We were one of many toy manufacturers hoping to get this deal, and Gabriel Harrington chose us because he is a passionate environmentalist. You put good out there, you get good back."

Clementine didn't agree but wasn't going to ruin Evan's excitement. "Can I ask you something, Evan?"

"Of course, I'm an open book to you, Your Graceship."

"Why do you have time to drive me to an appointment? Or stay in Rosebrook?"

"Sorry? What do you mean?" Evan asked.

"You're obviously an extremely busy businesswoman, and yet you're spending your time trying to rebuild Rosebrook and driving me to an insignificant appointment."

Evan furrowed her eyebrows. "It's not an insignificant appointment."

"It is to you. Answer the question."

"I've got everything I need at Rosebrook. I've set up an office there, in the banqueting hall, I have a full staff, and I still go to London two days a week."

Clementine felt panic when Evan mentioned the banqueting hall. "What have you done to the banqueting hall? It's the oldest building in Rosebrook, you know, the oldest in the county."

"Calm down. I haven't done anything to it. My team have just run in the electrical equipment for the computers, but everything's been done tastefully. Why don't you come up and see it, see the house too? I'd like you to see it and feel safe that you can trust it in my hands."

"No, thank you." It might have seemed a harsh response, but she didn't think she could bear to see her ancestral home changed and mucked about with. It would be too painful.

"Clem, have you thought about the meeting at Fergus's house? Will you come?"

"No, I told you that I didn't want to be involved in pipe dreams."

A silence fell over the car.

Evan parked outside the building where Clementine's appointment was being held, despite Clementine telling her she'd get public transport home. Evan wouldn't hear of it, of course, and sat listening to her audiobook while she waited, but her mind wasn't on the story—she couldn't stop thinking about Clementine. She didn't take her refusals to see the house or come to the meeting personally. Evan could clearly see Clementine carried the scars of all she had lost and a troubled life.

Kay had told her that Clementine's mother was not in a good way at all, and that Clementine had been her carer for many years before the decision was taken to move the dowager duchess into a nursing home. It must be a heavy duty to carry all that on your shoulders without any partner to help or confide in.

Evan felt a need to help Clementine and be her shoulder to cry on. Not just because she found her so attractive, or because she was her hero's granddaughter, but because she saw such a deep sadness and weariness in Clementine's eyes. That first hit across the head with a banjo when Clementine first opened the door to her had awakened an unquenchable need to help and be near her.

But first things first, she had to show Clementine that she had a place, a future in Rosebrook village, and she had every confidence in herself that she could do it.

Evan heard the sound of heels on concrete and quickly turned off her audiobook. Clementine opened the car door, slipped in, slammed the door shut, and sighed.

"How did it go?" Evan asked, although she could sense it hadn't gone well.

"They already had an architect on staff, but they wanted me to quote-unquote *work together*"—Clementine put air quotes around the phrase—"with him on the new residential building, so they could use my name. Designed by the Duchess of Rosebrook, granddaughter of the famous Isadora Fitzroy."

"I'm sorry." Evan felt so bad for her. It was another kick in the teeth.

"I can't even make a name for myself, for my own skills. I mean, who cares about titles any more? The world has moved on, and yet this dukedom is hanging around my neck, strangling me."

Evan had to choose her words wisely and didn't want to turn Clementine off from her even more. Perhaps a change of subject, change of scenery.

"Why don't we go and have an ice cream on the beach? It's just a few minutes away."

Clementine looked at her like she was insane. "An ice cream?"

"Yes, it's a gorgeous summer's day. Come on?"

"I'd just like to go home," Clementine said firmly.

Evan tutted and shook her head, pretending to be annoyed. "Well, I think you owe me one for driving you here."

Clementine gave her an annoyed look. "I thought you just wanted to help—that's what you told me."

"I changed my mind. Come on, it'll be fun." Evan covered Clementine's hand with hers briefly, before starting the car and setting off to find a car parking space near the beach.

Evan found a space and got out of the car. She went to the boot of the car and got out the drawstring bag she used for litter. Clementine arrived at her side and looked quizzically at the two bigger bags in the boot.

"One's for plastic and one for bottles and cans," Evan said.

"You had that bag on the beach—do you take it everywhere?" Clementine asked.

"I try to. My mum has had me doing this since I was a little kid. It's just ingrained in me now." Evan took off her jacket and rolled up her shirtsleeves. "It's a scorcher today. Sometimes it's hard to maintain my dapper look in hot weather."

She checked her hair in the car mirror and heard Clementine say in a sarcastic voice, "I'm sure."

As usual Evan didn't respond to that negativity. She straightened her bow tie and then offered her arm to Clementine. "Shall we, Your Graceship?"

Clementine looked surprised, unsure at the offer, and wonderfully for Evan, she took her arm. Yes! If Clementine was Mrs. Fox, then she would look back on this as the first time Clementine trusted her.

"Let's get some ice cream."

They walked down to the large wooden pier at Bournemouth beach, getting looks from passers-by. Evan knew she was the one drawing the looks, for despite how much society had changed, a woman in a traditional male suit and tie—or bow tie—was still unusual.

She leaned over to Clementine and said, "I don't think they've ever seen a woman in such a jaunty fox bow tie."

Clementine actually smiled. It was a small blink-and-you'd-miss-it smile, but a smile all the same. Evan, buoyed by that, walked up to the ice-cream booth. She asked the seller, "Do you sell vegan ice-cream?"

The girl behind the counter looked at her like she had horns.

"No," she said flatly.

"Oh, well, one large 99, with sauce, and one um…" Evan studied the menu. "An orange Calippo."

When the server went to get their items, Evan said, "Do you ever wonder why an ice cream with a Flake is called a 99?"

"I've never thought about it too deeply. What is a Calippo?"

Evan feigned shock. "You've never had a Calippo? You've never lived, Your Majesty. It's a large orange ice pole kind of thing. Delish."

Once they had their items, they walked along the beach wall, Evan picking up some stray litter as they went. The beach was busy with people, since it was a hot summer's day.

"You're a vegan? Is that for environmental reasons?" Clementine asked.

"Yes, I was brought up vegan. I think that worried a few of your farmers," Evan said.

"I can imagine."

Evan pointed down at the wall and said, "Will we take a seat?"

"I'm wearing a skirt," Clementine said.

"Oh, come on, it won't fly off. Sit with me. Here, I'll hold your ice cream."

Clementine sighed as she sat down carefully and took her ice cream from Evan. "Why am I sitting on a beach wall eating ice cream?"

Evan plonked down beside her. "Because you owe me one."

The idea of owing a debt to anyone, especially the woman who had taken over her ancestral home, was abhorrent to her.

"If I'd known there was a debt involved, I would never have taken your offer of a lift," Clementine said.

"I've hardly demanded your firstborn, have I? I just wanted to cheer you up after your interview."

Clementine said nothing and they both looked out to sea. There were sailboats in the distance and a ferry crossing the water. She had to admit that she was starting to let go of some of her annoyance and anger.

Out of nowhere, Evan said, "It's nothing like Rosebrook beach, is it?"

It wasn't. Nowhere gave Clementine the calm contented feeling of sitting on the beach there. She turned to look at Evan, who was eating her large orange ice pole, and kicking her feet against the beach wall. She couldn't have looked less like a CEO of a large company.

"Do you enjoy what you do, Evan?" Clementine asked. "I mean the toy business."

A big grin erupted over her face. "Absolutely, it's my life. Why do you ask?"

"You don't seem like the typical CEO, that's all," Clementine said.

"I hope not. Toys are in my blood. My dad and grandpa gave me that love, but it's not really about toys. Toys are just lumps of plastic or stuffed pieces of material, but they fuel the imaginations and dreams of children. That's the part that I love most."

Clementine was quite taken aback at Evan's answer and how animated she looked. Her eyes matched her beautiful smile and almost danced with excitement. Clementine felt her heart speed up and her skin bristle with excitement. Collywobbles again.

Clementine cleared her throat. "You sound passionate about it. Are you as passionate about the environment, or is that just a hobby?"

Clementine wanted to gauge how seriously Evan took this village project.

"You can have more than one passion in your life, but yes. My dad gave me my passion for toys, and my mum gave me my passion for the environment. She belongs to environmental and feminist activist groups. That's how she met my dad, actually."

"Really, how?" Clementine licked her ice cream, becoming drawn in to Evan's conversation. It was hard to keep up that distance she was trying to, when Evan was so engaging.

"Well, her activist group staged a sit-in at Fox Toys headquarters, and my grandpa, who was still running the company then, sent my dad down to negotiate with them."

"What were they protesting about?" Clementine asked.

"It was a new toy playset we'd brought out in blue for boys, and pink for girls, and the figures were totally gender stereotyped. My dad says when he saw my mum, it was like he had been hit about the head with a banjo." Evan looked at her softly, then finished, "He knew there and then that she was meant to be his wife."

Clementine had become a bit lost in Evan's eyes as she told that story and snapped out of it when she felt the cold of the ice cream hit her hand.

"Oh no, it's melting." Clementine rummaged in her bag and found a handkerchief to wipe her hand. "So what happened about the sexist toy?"

Evan grinned. "Discontinued. My mum re-educated my dad and the company on gender and environmental issues."

"Did she stop protesting?" Clementine asked.

"No way, she was arrested only last year for boarding an oil drilling vessel," Evan said proudly.

"Gosh, what happened?"

"She got community service, ironically litter picking. Something she had been doing and teaching me to do."

Clementine laughed and then caught herself. She had actually laughed and forgot about her disastrous interview and her troubles at home. That hadn't happened before. Clementine felt she had been born stressed. It's all she could remember from her childhood. But now her money troubles, work troubles, and her mother were forgotten all by sitting on a beach wall, eating ice cream, and talking to Evan.

Evan continued, "My mum is my hero, and my dad adores her."

"She sounds wonderful."

"She is. Mum taught me to respect women, and to reinforce how wonderful they were, any time I could, but then that's no hardship, since I love women. Women are wonderful."

Was that why the compliments flew easily from Evan's mouth? Maybe she wasn't this conceited lady's woman she had thought her to be?

Evan then said suddenly, "Will you come to the meeting at Fergus's house tomorrow?"

Clementine was totally taken off guard. "What? Is that what this is all about?"

Evan recoiled and frowned. "Do you really think I would do that? I wanted to help you, but I would take it as a great personal favour if you would come."

"Why are you so intent on me hearing your plans? It's your village." Just saying that made Clementine sad.

"But it's not. The hearts and minds of the village still look to you. As I said, your farmers, Mr. and Mrs. Murdoch and Mr. Mason, didn't take to my plans quite as enthusiastically as the others. I admit my first meeting with the village, and you, I was in bull in a china shop mode, but I want to change my focus, think about things from the village point of view."

Clementine's resolve not to get involved was weakening.

"Just one meeting," Evan said, "and I'll not mention it again."

She sighed. "Okay, one meeting."

"Yes!" Evan said. "You won't regret this."

They finished their treats and started to walk back to the car. While they did, Evan said, "You know about my passions, my dreams now. Is being an architect your dream?"

"I don't have any dreams," Clementine said flatly.

That's what she told herself and anyone who asked, but that wasn't quite true, if she was honest with herself. Her dream was to be the mistress of Rosebrook House, and to make the village live again, but that was never going to happen, so why dream?

Chapter Nine

The next day was a busy one for Clementine. Kay's husband Casper came to look at her car but told her it needed to go into the mechanic's, so he lent her the family's second car, until Clementine could work out what to do.

She drove to visit her mother after lunchtime and read to her for a while. The room was calm for a change, and quiet, apart from Clementine's voice. As she read, Clementine stroked her mother's brow. She thought about how many times her mother had done this for her, and now the tables were turned.

She finished reading the psalm and kissed Marianne's head. Her thoughts drifted to Evan. Evan hadn't been far from her thoughts last night, either. How yesterday had surprised her. Either Evan was putting on an Oscar-winning performance, or she was genuine.

Not only genuine but like no one she had ever met. Her youthful exuberance was obviously infectious because Clementine couldn't remember the last time her problems were not at the forefront of her mind, but yesterday, sitting on the beach wall with an ice cream, her problems were a million miles away.

When Clementine got home she took to the internet to find out everything she could about Evan. She was surprised to find out that she was twenty-eight. She would have guessed much younger—still, at thirty-six, way too young for her.

Huh?

She shook herself of the thought and saw her mother looking up at her. Her eyes were clearer, less troubled.

"What's happening in the village?" her mother asked.

Her mother did have periods of lucidity sometimes, and Clementine treasured those. She kept stroking her mother tenderly and said, "We have a newcomer to the village, Evan Fox. She took me to Bournemouth beach yesterday."

"We need newcomers to the village. Where is she staying?" Marianne asked.

Clementine couldn't tell her she had bought Rosebrook, because in her mother's mind they still lived there.

"One of the cottages." Clementine told a white lie.

"Is she nice?"

Clementine smiled. "Yes, she bought me an ice cream."

"You should bring her home to play one day."

There it was—her mother's mind stuck firmly in her childhood. "I'm seeing her tonight, actually." The thought gave Clementine a buzz of excitement. That was new, since she had met Evan.

"Bring her up to the house. I'd like to meet her."

"I will, Mummy."

❖

Later that evening Clementine was standing at the mirror in the hallway, fixing her make-up. Tonight she had picked a floaty summer dress to wear instead of jeans.

She looked at herself in the mirror and said, "Why are you doing this? You don't need to impress Evan. She's too young, she has your house and land, and you have too much going on in your life for complications." And Evan would be a big complication.

And yet, despite all this, Clementine had that excited feeling and it was growing. She heard the door knocker and quickly put away her make-up. Her heart was racing and she chastised herself for it.

"Just be a minute," Clementine shouted towards the door.

She hurriedly put her things away, then opened the door, ready to apologize for keeping Evan waiting, but Evan jumped in first.

"Wow, you look absolutely wonderful, Clem. What a lucky woman I am to have your company."

Clementine didn't really hear what Evan was saying. She was too fixated on Evan's clothes. "What on God's green earth are you wearing?"

Evan smiled and looked down at her outfit. "You like it? My tailor made a selection of suits fit for the country. What do you think?"

Evan was wearing a tweed shooting jacket and hunting breeks, with heavy woollen socks up to her knees, each adorned with a huge red tassel. Brown leather shoes, checked shirt, wool tie, and flat cap. All that was missing was a shotgun in the crook of her arm.

Clementine hadn't seen anyone wearing an outfit like that, here at Rosebrook, since her grandmother's day.

"You're not saying anything, Clem." Evan brushed some fluff from her jacket. "It is authentic, isn't it?"

Clementine could hardly contain her smile and laughter. "No, it's very authentic…" She muffled a laugh. "It looks like you've just come off the set of a period drama."

"I can see you want to laugh," Evan said, giving her a playful look.

Clementine covered her mouth to stop the laughter. "No, no, you look…unique."

Evan appeared to take that in good spirits. She held out her arms. "I live to be unique and cut a dandy, dapper dash. Anyway, it's fun for a pleb like me to play at being the classic English gent. Shall we?"

Clementine shook her head, still smiling, and locked the door. No one had made her laugh so much in years. Evan offered her arm and Clementine took it.

"You're not a pleb. You're an extremely successful business-woman."

"Money doesn't buy you class—you were born with it."

"Oh, please," Clementine said, as they walked along the road to Fergus's house. "What's my second name, Evan?"

"Fitzroy," Evan replied.

"Do you know what that means?"

"The *fitz* means something—it's on the tip of my tongue. Tell me," Evan said as she gazed down their entwined arms. This was so nice. Clem wasn't scowling. She had actually made her laugh, and she loved doing it.

"*Fitz* means born out of wedlock, so Fitzroy is a bastard child of a king. King Charles II, in fact."

"Who was?" Evan asked.

"The first Duke of Rosebrook. His mother was mistress to King Charles II for many years, and the King was his father. Like all of King Charles II's out of wedlock children, he got a title, a lofty title. So we didn't have high-class beginnings."

"Amazing! What was his mother like?" Evan asked.

Clementine furrowed her eyebrows. "You really want to know?"

"Yeah, it's so interesting. I focused on Isadora when I wrote an essay about her and Rosebrook, but I didn't go that far back in your family's history."

"Well, she was a formidable woman. Maria Warwick. She was born of poor farming stock, went to London, and became a dancer and entertainer. She caught the King's eye at a performance and became his mistress, a position she guarded jealously. The King had many mistresses, but Maria lasted the longest."

Evan nodded her head. "From poor farmer's daughter to King's mistress and the founder of a dynasty in a generation."

"Yes, that fear of being poor drove her, I think. I wouldn't be duchess if it wasn't for her too. My second cousin would have gotten it."

"How so?" Evan asked.

"After the first duke died as a young boy, there was no male heir—she'd had three daughters by the King after that. Knowing her position was dependent on having a child with a rich estate, she persuaded the King to change the writ to allow females to inherit. There are very few titles in England that go through the female line, mostly the older ones."

Evan was astounded by Clementine's knowledge and loved the way her whole being came to life while talking about it. That was Clementine's passion, no matter how much she tried to hide it. Rosebrook was everything to her—Evan was sure of it.

"That is so interesting."

They walked along in silence for a minute or so, the only sounds of the early evening the birds chattering in the trees. It was idyllic, and Evan felt so much more relaxed here than in London.

Then a thought occurred to her. "So who inherits after you?"

Clementine took her arm from Evan and clasped her hands. She seemed nervous, Evan thought.

"If I don't marry a man and have a child—my cousin and then his children."

Clementine left that phrase hanging there between them. *If she didn't marry a man.*

Evan had assumed from the start that Clementine was gay, her intuition told her so, and surely whoever was in charge of these things didn't banjo her across the head for a straight woman. No, no, no. It couldn't be. Evan's stomach dropped.

"Have you anyone in—" Evan tried to ask casually.

"No, I've never wanted to marry a man."

Evan nearly jumped and clicked her heels together. *Yes, my future wife is gay. Praise be!* She managed to remain cool and said, "Oh. Your cousin inherits, then?"

Clementine sighed. "Yes, not the nicest man, but he's in his sixties, so hopefully I'll outlive him and it'll pass directly to his daughter, Lucille. I'm her godmother. Still, it's a useless title without the house and land."

Perfect. Mrs. Fox was still a possibility, if Evan could convince her that it was the best idea ever.

Evan held open the gate to Fergus's large cottage. It was the biggest in Rosebrook. Fergus had told her that it used to be the estate manager's house.

"Nice house," Evan said.

"Yes. Fergus is the only one with money enough to keep his house well-maintained. Apart from you, obviously." Clementine smiled.

Evan sighed with contentment at that beautiful smile. If only Clem did it more often.

"What's the sigh for?"

"Oh, nothing." Evan quickly chapped the door.

Fergus opened the door with a huge smile of his own. "Good evening, Your Grace, and to you, youngster."

Clementine couldn't get the older gentleman to drop the title when he first greeted her, just like the nurses at her mother's nursing home. He was from a different age when things like these seemed so important.

"Good evening, Fergus."

"You're looking very snazzy, young Fox," Fergus said with a grin.

"Thanks, got to look the part," Evan replied.

Fergus waved them through vigorously. "Go through to the dining room—you know the way, Clementine. Everyone's here."

Clementine opened the dining room door, and everyone around the table stood—Mr. and Mrs. Murdoch, Mr. Mason, James and Ashling O'Rourke, and Kay.

"Please sit down, everyone," Clementine said, a bit embarrassed at the attention.

Evan followed her in, and Clementine saw the looks of astonishment at Evan's outfit and watched Mr. Mason and Mr. Murdoch mumble between them. All except Ashling and Kay, who smiled. A strange thing happened to Clementine then. She felt annoyed and protective of Evan, something that surprised her greatly.

Evan was right—she did have the hearts and minds of these people, and she had to at least encourage them to hear Evan out. She took Evan's arm and ushered her in.

"Good evening, everyone. I'm glad you could all come to hear what Evan has to say. I'm eager to hear it myself."

Everyone around the table looked at one another, probably astonished that she was even prepared to listen to any of these new dreams and ideas.

"Drinks for everyone." Fergus went to his drinks table and began taking orders and pouring out the drinks.

"Thank you," Evan whispered as they sat down.

"What for?"

Evan gave her a serious look. "You know what for. Thank you."

Everyone chattered incessantly while the drinks were organized. Evan was taken up with talking to Kay, while Ashling O'Rourke walked around the table to sit beside Clementine. She always had time for Ash. She was exceptionally bright and kind-hearted, but at twenty-five had seen little of the world and had put her life on hold to be a support for her father.

It reminded Clementine of her own situation. Ash had lost her mother to breast cancer aged seventeen, and her father James O'Rourke had fallen into a deep depression, and so Ash hadn't gone to university like she had always dreamed of. She'd stayed here in Rosebrook, unable to leave her dad on his own.

"How are things, Ash?" Clementine asked.

"Oh, you know, same as usual. I'm really excited about the changes Ms. Fox is going to make to the village. Of course, Dad thinks it's a loopy idea. I told him, the more people who are attracted to come here, the busier the fishing business will be."

This was exactly what she had been frightened of—the villagers getting their hopes up for a brighter future and it not working out, or Evan getting bored of her new plaything.

"What does he think about that?"

Ash pursed her lips and shook her head. "He says it's all pie in the sky, but he lost his ability to dream a long time ago."

Clementine was in the same boat as James O'Rourke. Dreaming

was dangerous, but Evan was starting to shake that belief. She gazed at Evan as she got prepared to speak and heard Ash whisper, "So gorgeous, isn't she?"

Yes, Clementine's mind replied quickly.

❖

Evan had tried unsuccessfully to bring the meeting to order, but luckily Fergus hit a gong that sat next to the drinks cabinet.

"Let's listen to what Ms. Fox has to say."

The murmuring and talking subsided. "Thank you, Fergus, and thank you everyone for coming to meet with me today."

Evan turned to Clementine and saw her nod in encouragement. This was her chance to get everyone onside. She had seen how much respect they all had for Clementine. Whether she liked it or not, Clementine was their leader, and her support was crucial.

"I realize that the last time we spoke, I may have been a bit like a bull in a china shop with my ideas."

"You can say that again," Mr. Mason said. "You're a townie, and you come down here with all your New Age vegan propaganda nonsense and expect us just to roll over—well, that's not happening."

Vegan propaganda?

Then William Murdoch stepped into the conversation. "If you think you're going to stop us or our dairy farm, you've got another think coming."

His wife Barbara put a hand on his to try to calm him.

"Now, now. Let's listen," Fergus said.

Evan held her hands up. "I don't want to stop you from farming. The only thing I ever want to do is make things work in a more efficient way. I have some ideas I hope you might listen to, but of course it's your decision."

That appeared to quiet them down for the moment, and she did have a plan to encourage them to cooperate, so she forged ahead.

"As I say, I was a bit of a bull in a china shop, and I get like that when I'm excited about a project. But I've been made aware of some concerns, and I'd like to address them. Number one, before I forge ahead with my own plans, there are lots of things you as the residents need fixing before we even think about putting my environmental plan in place."

"What are you proposing, then?" James O'Rourke asked.

"I propose giving you, the residents, an official say in our work here. I propose a trust."

Clementine, who had been quiet up until now, piped up. "A trust?"

Evan smiled. "Yes, a trust. A charity organization with a board of trustees and budget. That would give you all a chance to list your priorities, things that need doing first and foremost, and then we can get to my plans for the future."

"Who would be on the trust board?" Kay asked.

"All of you and me. We tackle all of Rosebrook's problems together. How does that sound?"

Fergus raised his glass of whisky and said, "That sounds like a capital idea. Don't you think so?"

Everyone turned to look at Clementine to gauge her reaction. After a few seconds she said, "That sounds like a great idea."

Evan had to act quickly to get her plan into action. She winked at Fergus and said, "I propose the duchess as chairwoman."

Fergus quickly responded with, "Seconded. All those in favour, say *aye*."

"Aye!" came a chorus from around the table.

❖

"No, no, no. I told you." Clementine marched ahead of Evan.

"Clem—" Evan tried to say.

"You ambushed me, Evan. That wasn't fair. It was all a big set-up, from start to finish. I wondered why you were holding the meeting at Mr. Fergus's cottage. Now I know."

Evan ran a few steps to catch up with her. "It wasn't, well, not really. This role is perfect for you. You know the land inside out, and you're an architect. I'd like you to work with our architects on the project."

Clementine stopped and turned on Evan. "I don't have the time. Remember, I work, and I have to take care of my mother."

"But this is why it's perfect for you. I'll put you on salary, so you don't have to be self-employed, and you'll have more time to visit your mum, and not worry about those idiots yesterday not giving you a commission."

"Work for you? I don't need charity." Clementine was angry. One, because she had been manoeuvred into a situation, and two, because the thought of helping to make the village something special again felt like a terrible tease.

"You wouldn't be taking my money. It's the trust's money that pays the staff," Evan said.

"And who provides the budget for the trust?"

Evan sighed. "Technically Fox Toys, but that's just a small detail. My family has many trusts that work this way. The chairperson is always salaried. It's not a charity from me to you."

Clementine covered her face with her hands. She felt so torn between offence and excitement, but then she remembered her grandmother and where excitement had gotten her. She shook herself and said very calmly, "No. I told you from the start I wouldn't get involved in any of your outlandish dreams. I'm not my grandmother, no matter how much you idolize her."

Evan nodded and said, "So that's not a no then?"

Clementine snorted. "How did you get that from my answer?"

"Positivity." Evan grinned.

Clementine started to walk off on her own. Behind her she heard Evan say, "I'm going to be in London for the next couple of days at the office. It'll let you think about my proposal."

She reached her front door and unlocked it, then she turned to face Evan and said, "I gave you my answer."

Evan's smile faded slightly. "Listen, the truth is, I've bitten off more than I can chew. I'm rattling around up in that house with no idea how to run or staff it, apart for a cleaning company that comes twice a week. Then there's the garden and a million other things to think about. I could really do with your advice on it. You were born here and trained for it. If I had a chairwoman like you by my side, I know I could make a difference here. That's all I want to do—make a difference."

Evan's faltering positivity softened Clementine's resolve. Plus, she thought about the excited smiles on Ash's and Kay's faces. Could they make a difference?

"I'll think about it over the next few days. That's the best I can do."

Evan's infectious grin reappeared. She took Clementine's hand and kissed it. "Thank you, Your Graceship, ma'am."

Clementine felt goosebumps spread up her arm, which made her feel a little giddy. "Stop that. I'm not promising anything."

Evan nodded. "Hope is all I ask for. See you in a few days."

Oh God, Clementine thought as she watched Evan walk away. She was turning her life upside down in such a short time.

But what frightened her even more were the feelings Evan was invoking in her. Evan was sweet, funny, infectious in her positivity, and *so* her type, that she didn't know how she would cope with ongoing collywobbles. Even worse was not knowing what the feelings would turn into.

Chapter Ten

Evan loved this part of the toy making process. With the consent of their parents, some of the children from Fox Toys' nursery were brought to what they called The Playroom, to test new toys.

Jess was standing beside Evan, looking through the glass window at the children playing. Two of the nursery staff were in there with the children, making sure everyone was okay.

Evan loved to see children's imaginations overflowing with the help of toys. There were five new toys today. Evan was hopeful that some of these would make it past the testing stage and launch for the Christmas market.

"So," Jess said, "how fun was it playing at lord of the manor?"

Evan smiled. "Great fun. Rosebrook is just so beautiful. I go running every morning through idyllic English countryside and finish with running on the beach. There are not many places you could do that."

"And the people?"

"Lovely people. The salt of the earth," Evan replied. And they were, but it was hard work to get people used to a sleepy village in its death throes to match her energy and pace of ideas.

"But?" Jess said.

Evan turned to her friend. "How did you know there was a *but*?"

Jess laughed softly. "I know you. Tell me."

"Well—I'm a bit much for them, ideas wise, and the farmers aren't too keen on having a vegan owning the land."

"I can imagine. Your brain works too fast even for me. Has Archie moved down there yet?"

"No, she's not coming. She wants to commute. Says she's allergic to the countryside. A bit strange for an environmentalist."

"It doesn't surprise me in the least. She would panic if she wasn't within five minutes of a juice bar. So everything else is okay down there?"

"Apart from the gorgeous duchess who I think might be Mrs. Fox, and whose house I'm staying in?"

"Duchess?" Jess said excitedly. "Tell me more."

"Clementine Fitzroy. She lives in the gatehouse to Rosebrook. Her family had to sell up when she was younger, and she isn't too happy about all the changes I'm making."

"So she's gorgeous and you think she's Mrs. Fox, even though she isn't happy with you?" Jess said.

"Yeah, I went to meet her for the first time and…" Evan's voice trailed away as she remembered Clem opening the door for the first time.

She felt a nudge from Jess. "And what?"

Evan shook herself slightly. "I was banjoed right in the head."

Jess crossed her arms and wrinkled her eyebrows. "What on earth is banjoed?"

"Something my dad has always told me about meeting my mum. When he saw her for the first time, he described the feeling as being hit across the head with a banjo, and that's what I think I should feel when I meet *the one*."

"Wait a minute, so all this time you've been talking about meeting Mrs. Fox and going on first dates with a lot of women, you were waiting for this to happen?"

"Yup. It's the sign," Evan said.

"But what if you had passed on one of these lovely women who you didn't go on a second date with, and they were the one? Sometimes love is a slow burn, and just because your dad felt that way—"

"But it did happen. Clem opened the door and wham! My heart started to go crazy. She's so classy, too classy for me, probably, but I'd like to try to meet her expectations."

"So what happened after this wham with a banjo?" Jess asked.

"After a brief conversation, she asked me to leave, then gave me a bollocking about my refurb team blocking in her car."

"And you still think you have a chance with this woman?" Jess said.

Evan gave her a big smile. "Never give up! She just needs a bit of positivity brought back to her life, and besides"—Evan leaned in and said in a stage whisper—"she let me buy her an ice cream."

Jess burst out laughing. "You sound like you're still at high school."

Evan nodded her head and grinned. "You can mock, but telling me to get out, to having ice cream with me, is progress of a kind."

"I suppose. One thing's for sure, you never give up, so this duchess may have to like you if she wants to or not."

Evan prayed that Clementine had changed her mind about becoming the chair of the trust. As an architect herself, it would be too perfect to have her involved in the planning of the village. Clem would add her love and authenticity to the new Rosebrook, two things that were extremely important when building a new community. But there were some plans she had up her sleeve already, and one in particular that would show that she did care about the people of the village. She excused herself and took out her phone.

"Violet? I need you to arrange something for me."

Clementine hadn't seen Evan for two days, and yet she'd never been out of her thoughts. Even today as she sat at Kay's kitchen table nursing a cup of coffee, her mind was churning over the proposal Evan had made.

At the kitchen counter, Kay and Casper filled bags with food they had made for the Tucker twins, lovingly bickering as they went. Every week Clementine and Kay meal-prepped dinners and delivered them to the ladies, each taking a turn at cooking.

What will I do? Clementine thought.

Evan would probably be back for the weekend tomorrow, and relentlessly looking for an answer. Her initial answer of no to the chairwomanship had softened over the last few days. She tried not to think about the possibilities of becoming involved in Evan's dream, but it was extremely difficult.

In her heart, the job of chairing the trust and leading Evan's team of architects was exciting, an emotion she hadn't felt in a long, long time. Clementine could use her professional skills as well as her hereditary duties and life skills as duchess to mould the rebuilding of Rosebrook to what it was in its heyday.

Her mother and father would be proud of the rebuilding job, but only sorry that their daughter wasn't in Rosebrook House, but she was still torn.

She would be allowing herself to become involved in a project just like Isadora's. Clementine always promised herself she would never get involved in something like that, especially if it involved Rosebrook. Then there was the fact of working for Evan, because that was the reality of what the job would be, despite Evan's protestations to the contrary. She half suspected Evan had offered her this role because Evan knew she was struggling to get work contracts.

Clementine was independent and never wanted to be beholden to anyone, but part of her knew that Evan would never use that power over her. She appeared kind, and sincere, despite having her head in the clouds.

Then there was the little detail of feeling her stomach flip like a twelve-year-old girl's whenever she was in Evan's company, and this job would mean even more time in her company. But what would win out? Her heart or her head?

"Clem?"

Clementine was shaken from her deep thought by Kay. "Sorry? What did you say?"

"We're all ready. Casper is packing the car."

Clementine got up. "Sorry, I was miles away. Let's go, then." She followed Kay out to her car and Casper held the door open for her. "Thanks, Casper."

"See you later, ladies."

"Remember to pick up the boys, Casper."

"I will."

Kay turned on the engine and said, "Any news on the car yet?"

"No, it needs a bit of work done to it."

In fact the garage was giving her time to decide whether to do the repairs or scrap the car. It was going to cost a fortune.

"You know you can use our car anytime. Are you going to see your mum tonight?" Kay asked.

"Yes, thanks, Kay. I don't know what I'd do without you and Casper."

"You do plenty for everyone, Clem." Kay started to drive the short distance to the outer edge of the village where the Tuckers lived. "So have you decided yet?"

"What about?"

"You know, Evan's offer. Is that what you were thinking about so deeply in the kitchen?"

Clementine rested her elbow on the window and leaned her head against her hand. "Mmm. Yes, I've thought about little else. It's impossible but—"

"You know, Clem, I understand your reluctance and your difficulty trusting an outsider, a townie, with your village—"

"It's not my village, Kay. You know that."

"Maybe technically, but in your heart, and in the heart of every resident in Rosebrook, it's yours," Kay said.

"What's your take on it, then?" Clementine asked.

"I like Evan—you know that. She's trustworthy, I think, but we don't really know her. But the way I see it is this—it's going to happen whether you or we like it or not. This is Evan's land, and she seems determined to make her vision happen."

Clementine turned to look at Kay. "What are you saying?"

"Well, wouldn't you rather be on the inside, driving the agenda, influencing her and the rebuilding of this village, than outside watching it happen?"

Clementine hadn't thought if it that way. If she was the chairwoman of the trust, she would hold influence, and if she led the team of architects, even more. It made complete sense.

"If you can't beat them, join them, kind of thing?" Clementine said.

"Exactly, and the villagers would be happier knowing you are working on the project, plus you can't deny having a regular job would help with the dowager duchess's expenses."

That was very true. She was already behind in her monthly fees. Luckily the nursing home staff were very accommodating due to the title. It was good for something, at least.

They were just about to turn into the Tuckers' driveway, and Clementine said, "Yes, maybe I should swallow my pride and accept—" She stopped midsentence when she saw two work vans already in the driveway, and Evan and an associate standing by the vans.

"What are they doing?" Clementine said with annoyance. "They shouldn't be bothering the ladies." Clementine got out of the car quickly and marched over to where Evan was standing. "What the hell are you doing?"

Evan took off her sunglasses, smiled, and tipped her imaginary hat to Clementine. "Good morning, Your Graceship, m'lady. I don't think you've met my environmental consultant Archie before?"

"Pleased to meet you, Your Grace," Archie said.

"Hello," Clementine said quickly and turned her fire back to Evan. "Again, I'll ask you, what the hell are you doing?"

Archie looked uncomfortable and excused herself before walking off.

"There's no need to be excited, Clem," Evan said.

This infuriated Clementine all the more. "I'm not excited. I'm annoyed that you are bothering Agatha and Ada. These women are very important to us."

Evan put her hand on her chest. It was then that Clementine noticed Evan's latest tie and handkerchief combo had poodles on them. It looked so sweet, but then Clementine remembered she was mad at her.

"I would never bother them," Evan said. "I'm here to help. I'm donating two electric mobility scooters to them, so they can get out and about again."

Clementine wasn't expecting that answer. "Oh, did you ask if they wanted them?"

"Yes, we had a cup of tea and a good chat about it all, and they both were excited by the idea."

"So what are these two vans and workmen about?" Clementine asked.

"Well, to make things easier for them, the scooters are better outside, so we've had to erect a waterproof hut at the side of the cottage, and my electricians are putting in the necessary wiring and sockets for charging."

"Oh," was all Clementine could say.

"Have I allayed all your fears?" Evan said.

Clementine was confused. This was a really kind gesture, if it was what the twins wanted, but was Evan just trying to buy favour?

"Why did you want to do this?" Clementine asked.

"One, because it gives me pleasure to help others, and two, I'm doing what I pledged to do, start my rebuilding from the ground up, and I think getting two wonderful ladies back out and about their home village is a good start."

Damn. Why did she have to be so bloody kind?

"Is everything all right?" Clementine turned around sharply when she heard Kay's voice behind her.

Clementine sighed. "Yes, Evan has donated two mobility scooters to the twins."

"Oh, my goodness. That's so kind, Evan," Kay said.

Evan smiled and said, "They'll be zipping around the village in no time."

That thought made Clementine slightly worried. "Let's get the food inside, Kay."

Evan followed them over to Kay's car. "What is it you do for them?"

Kay answered for them. "We meal-prep dinners for the twins every week, and then all they have to do is put the meals in the microwave."

"That's really kind. Here, let me carry the bags in for you, ladies," Evan said.

Before Clementine could object, Evan had gathered the bags and set off with them.

"Scrummy, isn't she?" Kay said.

Clementine's body answered yes with a shiver, but she said nothing.

❖

"Excellent, Agatha," Evan said.

The Tucker twins were learning to use their new scooters with mixed success. Agatha took to it straight away, but Ada was having more difficultly.

"Evan," Ada said, "it keeps stopping and starting."

"Just try squeezing the accelerator gently, but not too hard."

Ada tried again and set off at a snail's pace. Kay walked along with her, leaving Evan with Clementine.

"You know this could end in disaster," Clementine said.

"Or it could give two lovely older ladies a chance to get out and about in the fresh air again. Think positive."

"It's not in my make-up. I thought you'd be in London all weekend."

"Watch out, Your Grace." Agatha zoomed past them.

Evan clapped for Agatha as she went past. "Go, Ms. Tucker. No, I want to spend my weekend down here. I love it, apart from the house being a bit quiet."

Clementine watched as Ada's scooter stuttered again. "Is Archie going to move down here too?"

"No, she's strictly a townie, so she insists. She's more of an exclusive restaurant and wine bar type than a relaxing country weekend type."

Archie and Evan seemed so different, but their friendship and working relationship appeared to work.

Out of the blue, Evan said, "Would you like to come to dinner tonight?"

Clementine's impulse was to say no, but she couldn't help remembering Evan describing the house as lonely. What did she have to do anyway?

"If you like," Clementine said.

"Really?" Evan said with surprise. She probably was expecting a no.

"Yes, why not?"

Evan was full of smiles. "That's fantastic. You remember I'm vegan? You don't mind eating vegan food?"

"Fine with me. I love my vegetables. I don't eat a great deal of meat anyway," Clementine replied.

"I hope you'll enjoy it."

"I'm sure I—" Clementine stopped midsentence as Agatha's scooter shot off at top speed into the wall.

They ran over to assess the damage. Agatha was fine, and very apologetic.

"I'm so sorry, I got the brake and the accelerator mixed up."

Evan whispered to Clementine. "Maybe you were right. I think they need some more lessons before hitting the road."

"Yes, I think that would be wise."

Chapter Eleven

Evan stood in her dressing room, putting the finishing touches to her hair. She loved having this wooden panelled room for dressing, something she didn't have at her flat in London. The agent who gave her the details on the house had listed this room as the duke's bedroom and dressing room.

Clearly in the past the duke and duchess preferred having separate rooms. She couldn't imagine sleeping separately from her wife. She was too demonstrative and tactile for that.

She combed her hair one time before declaring it perfect, then sprayed on some of her favourite cologne and popped on her suit jacket, today a grey tweed. To accessorize, she decided to go full-on Evan Fox, with her fox bow tie, pin, and handkerchief.

Evan held out her hands and grinned. "I'm rocking this country look." She checked her watch. "Six fifty-five, not long now."

Then she rubbed her hands nervously. She had been nervous all day. Worrying about what Clementine would think of the house refurb, worrying about saying something stupid and making a fool of herself, and of course worrying whether Clementine would like the vegan meal she had made.

Earlier this afternoon she had prepared her pulled barbecue mushroom dish that she was going to serve with tacos and toppings. Now all she had to do was to heat it and bring the dish together.

Evan wandered into the main bedroom and over to the bedroom window. Her stomach flipped when she saw Clementine enter the gates at the bottom of the driveway. "She's here." Clementine was wearing a light blue summer dress that blew in the early evening breeze. "You are so beautiful, Clem."

Evan didn't know if she'd ever have the chance to say that to her face, but just voicing it helped at the moment. Tonight could go one of two ways. Clementine could accept the job she offered, not be horrified by her house refurb, and become closer to her, or she could detest the house, refuse the job, walk out, and any possibility of becoming Mrs. Fox would be no more.

Evan straightened her bow tie. "No pressure, then."

She hurried out of the bedroom and down the stairs. She could have taken the lift, but it was too slow for her. Maybe she could install a fireman's pole? That would be efficient and fun.

Just as she reached the bottom, the doorbell rang, and her heart started to pound. "Shit."

Evan remembered she hadn't put on any music. She pulled her phone from her pocket and opened her music app. She chose her *Happy Mello* playlist, and the music was soon playing throughout the house on her Bluetooth speakers.

The doorbell rang again. "Shit." She put her hand on the doorknob and said, "Just be cool, okay?"

Evan took a breath and opened the door. Clem took her breath away. Clem had put her dark blond hair up into a loose chignon, and even this far away, Evan could smell her floral perfume. She inhaled it and a fire was lit in her body.

"Evan?"

Evan realized she hadn't greeted her guest but instead stared at her while her mind went all sorts of hot places.

"I'm sorry. Good evening. You look radiant, Clem."

"Thank you. Am I too early?"

"No, no, just right on time. I thought I'd show you what I've done to the medieval banqueting hall, before we look at the house. Is that okay?"

"Of course."

Clementine was glad in a way that they were delaying the tour of the house. It had been an uncomfortable experience walking up the driveway and ringing the bell to her own family home. She thought of the many times she had played out here in the driveway, on her bike or her toy car, and now she was a guest. It hurt somewhere deep inside her.

She fell into step beside Evan and inhaled her cologne. It was gorgeous and made her head swim.

Don't do this, Clementine warned herself. But how could she control the way her body felt around Evan? There was something about her, like a magnetic energy pulling her towards Evan. *Maybe it's just because she has your house?* Yes, that was it.

Happy with that explanation, Clementine turned to look at Evan, who had been unusually quiet.

"Have you done much to the banqueting hall, then?" Clementine asked.

"You mean have I messed it up? I hope you won't think that. I tried to keep things as original as possible, whilst making it a functioning office space."

They arrived at the building and Evan pulled open the door. She bowed extravagantly and said, "This way, m'lady."

Clementine couldn't stop herself from chuckling at Evan's silliness. What she found when she walked through the door surprised her, and it was a nice surprise.

The medieval stone walls were showing and simply restored and the beams on the ceiling were looking great as well. The only change was the floor, which had been covered over with a sympathetic new wooden flooring.

As for the office side of things, there were desks, some screens on the wall, but nothing outrageous.

"Well?" Evan said. "What do you think?"

"It's quite a surprise," Clementine said, taking in everything.

Evan sat on the edge of her desk and folded her arms. "Is that a bad surprise?"

"No," Clementine smiled, "quite the contrary. The refurb has been done really sympathetically."

The look of relief on Evan's face was palpable. She really did care about her opinion and doing the right thing.

"That's so good to hear. What were you imagining?" Evan asked.

"I don't quite know, but loud colours, and I didn't expect you to keep the original walls exposed."

"I'm not a philistine, you know," Evan joked. "I tried to keep it tasteful. My London office is a bit different."

"How so?" Clementine asked.

Evan stood up from her desk and rubbed the back of her head bashfully. "Eh, there might be a few train tracks around the walls, and a trampoline, amongst other things."

Clementine burst out laughing. "You've really reined yourself in here, then?"

"Yeah, I've made an effort." Evan stepped closer and her tone became more serious. "I didn't want to ruin the history of this place, ruin what your family have built."

Clementine looked into Evan's blue eyes and felt the unmistakable urge to caress her cheek, but she stopped herself at the last moment and walked away from her. "This was just used as a storage room in my time. I used to play in here as a child with my friends."

"There is one mystery about this place—maybe you can explain?" Evan said.

"What?"

When Evan walked to the corner of the room, Clementine knew what she was heading for. The new flooring Evan had put down hadn't covered a square of old oak floor with a handle on it.

"You didn't cover it over?"

Evan crouched down and lifted up the small, discreet trapdoor. "No, I thought it must be important. What is it?"

Clementine leaned over and looked down the claustrophobic space that disappeared into darkness.

"It's a priest's hole."

Evan looked up at her with confusion writ all over her face. "A *what* hole?"

"A priest's hole. Quite a few old country estates have them. During the sixteenth century, Catholics were persecuted under Queen Elizabeth I. Gangs of priest hunters were sent out to arrest, torture, and kill any priests they found. So wealthy Catholic families had these hiding places built, so they could hide the priest who tended their spiritual needs when the priest hunters came."

"Good God," Evan said, "you mean someone actually went down there?"

"Oh yes, it was either that or suffer horrendously if they were caught. The family that owned the medieval castle that stood here in the sixteenth century were Catholics. They lost their land eventually when they were found out to be still practising."

"Wow, you really are a fount of knowledge," Evan said as she stood up.

"Not really, I just know my family history. It's in my blood and was drummed into me as a child. In fact they say a priest was actually sealed in this hole as a punishment. His spirit is meant to walk the land, moaning and screaming."

Evan let the lid of the trapdoor fall in fright. "Really? Not the best place for an office."

Clementine laughed. "It's only a story. So you and your team work in here?"

"Yes, me, Archie, and four on my admin team. They don't start till Monday. This would be where your desk would be if you took me up on the offer to be chairperson."

Clementine tried to imagine herself here, with a desk across from Evan, and she felt pure excitement, both about the challenge of rebuilding the village and the idea of being around Evan all day. Her positivity was infectious, and Clementine had to admit that she hadn't smiled or laughed as much in years since Evan came along.

She didn't want to give too much away so she just said, "We can talk about it later."

"Okay then, let's go up to the house."

Clementine felt so strange as she stood in the Rosebrook entrance hall. The last time she was here was when a family member had promised her funds to buy the house back, but then it all fell through.

It had been on the market for an extended period when the agent showed her around that time. The plaster was falling off the ceiling, there were leaks, puddles of water, and dirt and grime everywhere. Now it looked like she had been transported back to a bygone era. Everything looked like new—from the scenes depicted on the highly polished wood panel, to the large round white couches sitting in the centre of the reception area.

"What's wrong, Clem?" Evan said. "Don't you like it?"

Clementine took a tissue from her bag and dabbed her eyes. "No, it's not that. It's just a strange experience seeing it all restored. Like nothing ever changed. How did you know about the white couches?"

"My interior designer researched everything," Evan said.

"I don't think it's been in such good condition since Isadora was a young woman."

"Thank you. That means the world to me, Clem. Listen, why don't we eat, and then I can let you see upstairs?"

"Yes, I think I need a glass of wine," Clementine joked.

Evan put her hand on the small of Clementine's back, and the touch made her shiver.

"Follow me."

Evan led her down to the kitchen. This had been one of the

challenging things to refurbish. The wiring and damp coming in had to be dealt with effectively, and it had taken some time. The original walls were painted stark white and there were spotlights in the ceiling.

The kitchen had an island with stools, which was where they were going to eat, and a large cooker range built into the wall a few yards away. Behind the island was a comfortable couch facing a TV on the wall. Evan spent a lot of time down here. It reminded her of her flat in London.

"Take a seat and I'll open the wine," Evan said.

Clementine sat on the stool and said, "Something smells good. Did you get in a caterer or something?"

"What?" Evan was a little offended at that comment. "No, I cook for myself. I would never serve you food someone else has made when I asked you to dinner."

"You're a good cook, then?" Clementine asked.

"No, not really, but my mum made me learn the basics. I can make a few things well, and I just rotate. I really hope you don't mind eating vegan food."

"Of course not. I'm looking forward to a new experience."

Evan smiled and uncorked the wine. She poured it into the glass and said, "You enjoy this wine then, and I'll pull the meal all together."

"What have you made?"

"Pulled mushroom tacos," Evan replied. She turned on the heat under the frying pan to warm up the mushrooms.

"Is that like pulled pork?"

Evan turned around and said with a wink, "Yeah, vegan style. It's my favourite meal. I learned how to make it during my gap year at uni. When I went travelling, I had this in a vegan restaurant. I begged the chef for the recipe, and here I am all these years later, still making it."

Clementine enjoyed watching Evan hop around the kitchen making the food. She had a tea towel over her shoulder and was tasting and checking each pot. She sang along with the music playing in the background. Evan appeared to do everything with enthusiasm and found joy in everything she did. It was refreshing to be around someone with so much vigour for life.

Evan dished up the food into small bowls and placed them on the kitchen island.

"How long have you been a vegan, Evan?" Clementine asked.

Evan placed a plate of warm tacos in front of her. "All my life. My mum and dad are both vegans—well, my dad became one when he met Mum." Evan smiled.

"Your mum sounds like quite a woman," Clementine said.

Evan laughed. "Quite a force of nature certainly. She gets things done and doesn't let anything or anyone stand in her way. She wants to save the world."

"Just like you? In fact she sounds a lot like you," Clementine said.

Evan put a plate with rice at both their place settings, then sat down and rubbed her hands together. "So we have tacos, spicy rice, pulled barbecue mushrooms, and lots of toppings." She pointed to each of the smaller bowls. "So for toppings we have salsa, guacamole, chillies, and roasted peppers."

"Here's to my first vegan taco," Clementine said. She added some toppings and took a bite from her food. The sweet smoky flavour from the mushrooms was a big surprise. They were delicious. "Wow."

Evan looked nervous. "Do you like them?"

"They are delicious. I never expected so much flavour. You really don't miss the meat."

"That's great. It's nerve-racking when you cook for a meat eater. You want them to have a good impression of what a meal without meat would be like," Evan said.

Clementine dabbed her mouth. "I don't really eat a lot of meat. I love my vegetables. I used to grow them in the garden, but—Well, I don't have time now, but this is great."

Evan cleared her throat. "How's your mum doing? I hope you don't mind me asking."

Clementine felt a stab of guilt that she was enjoying a nice meal and good company while her mum was alone and confused. She put down her cutlery and dabbed her mouth with her napkin.

"She's much the same really. The only difference is whether she has a calm day or a bad day. On those days she only calms when I'm by her bedside."

Clementine was surprised when Evan reached across and squeezed her hand. "I'm sorry. That must be so hard for you both."

Clementine took a sip of wine. "It is. I just wish I had more hours in the day to be with her. I go every day, but it never seems to be long enough. It breaks my heart to leave her. Like this afternoon."

"Did you get your car fixed, then?" Evan asked.

Clementine hesitated. She hated to admit that it still wasn't fixed. People would guess it was because of money.

"No, not yet, but Kay is letting me borrow her car."

"You know I could help—"

"No, thank you, Evan. I can work this out for myself." Clementine had to nip in the bud whatever Evan was thinking. She wasn't going to be the charity case who lived in the gatehouse.

Most people would have taken offence at her slightly harsh reply, but not Evan Fox.

"Okay," Evan said, "but if there's anything I can ever do, please let me know, and I'll be only too happy to help."

Clementine nodded. She didn't know why, but it felt so easy to talk to Evan, and she felt compelled to add something after her slightly frosty reply.

"Mama is stuck in the past, and I can't shift her from it."

"What do you mean?"

"Her mind is stuck years back, when I was a girl, and we were living here. She thinks she's being kept from taking care of me and forced to stay at the nursing home. She gets so frustrated just sitting or lying in her room."

"How long has she been there?" Evan asked.

"Two years. I fought with the doctors about putting her in. But no matter how careful I was, she kept getting out of the gatehouse and hurting herself."

"I can't imagine having to make that decision, Clem. You're very brave."

"I'm not brave, anyway this food is delicious, Evan." Clementine hoped that would bring the conversation about her mother to an end.

Evan didn't disappoint. "I'm glad you like it. Eat up, there's nice cream for dessert."

Clementine looked up from her food sharply. "Did you say *nice* cream?"

Evan grinned. "Yeah. I know there's a lot of vegan ice cream on the market, but this is so much more healthy. You blend up different fruits with frozen bananas, and it comes out like soft-serve ice cream."

"Another new experience. I can't wait."

❖

Evan was so happy about how the evening had gone so far. Clementine had been open and had enjoyed a new kind of food. They had chatted comfortably while they ate, and Evan actually made the duchess laugh a few brief times, which was a feat in itself.

She finished putting the dishes in the dishwasher and went over to the couch with the bottle of wine. Clementine sat waiting for her.

"Dessert was delicious, Evan," Clementine said.

"Thanks." She sat down and topped up Clementine's glass. "It's nice to have some company for a change."

"When we met on the beach, you said your parents used to bring you here when you were younger."

"Yeah, I loved the beach, and the village. There was so much to do—play in the water, play at soldiers in the World War II gun placements, look through the gates to this house."

"How old are you?" Clementine asked.

"Twenty-eight."

"I'm thirty-six. It's funny—we probably were on the beach at the same time all those years ago."

It was a strange thought. She smiled thinking how much her younger self would have loved showing off for the older Clementine.

"We probably were. We usually came here most bank holidays, and for a week in the school holidays. We stayed in a country hotel in the next village."

Clementine tapped the wine glass with her fingernail, and for some reason Evan found that extremely sexy, and she couldn't stop looking.

"That's not how I imagined a rich business owning family would spend their holiday time. I thought it would be Barbados, the Seychelles, Disneyland."

Evan laughed and leaned her arm on the back of the couch, getting closer to Clementine. "Oh no. The Foxes don't do those sorts of holiday. We spent our free time on things we cared about. We went to Africa and helped build houses, install clean freshwater supplies, go litter picking, anything that could make the world a better place."

Clementine laughed softly. "You are an unusual rich family."

"Mum and Dad always taught me that money was a means we could use to make the world a better place through our trusts and charities."

At the mention of the trust, Clementine took a drink of wine and looked away awkwardly.

"Have you thought any more about working for the trust?" Evan asked.

"I've thought a lot about it, but I need just a little more time. Why don't you show me upstairs?"

As they walked back upstairs to the reception hall, Evan plucked up the courage to ask the question that had been burning in her head. "Can I ask you, was Isadora still alive when you were younger?"

"Yes." Clementine sighed. "But by the time I was old enough to know who she was, she was a sad, bitter figure, sitting in her bedroom. My dad made allowances for her all the time, and my mama tried to look after her the best she could, but Mama said that she had lost the very last sliver of hope when her partner died."

"Oh yeah, I read that she really adored Louisa." Evan pointed to the lift. "Shall we go upstairs in style?"

"I used to play in this lift when I was little. Then it broke and never got fixed, like most things around here."

They got into the lift and were upstairs in a few seconds. They got out and Evan said, "I've decorated all of the rooms upstairs, but there's nothing really interesting in them. I'll show you the two rooms that might annoy you most, then the duke's bedroom."

Clementine narrowed her eyes. "Why would they annoy me?"

Evan gave her a sheepish smile and said, "You'll see."

Clementine followed behind Evan with trepidation. They stopped in front of what the Fitzroys called the blue room. It was more like a large suite and used for important guests who came to stay in the past.

"Here we are. I didn't have room to display my collection in my London flat, but the rooms here are perfect."

"What kind of collection? Nothing like chains or whips, I hope?" Clementine joked.

"Of course not, not those kind of toys. I have the mind of a seven-year-old. Take a look."

Evan opened the door and she saw the room was filled with lit display cabinets. She walked in and as she got closer she saw there were children's action figures and toys behind the glass.

Clementine looked back at Evan, who appeared nervous, and said, "You collect toys?"

"Yeah, just like my dad, except he collects toys from the twenties, thirties, and fifties. Mine are all seventies on. What do you think? Would your ancestors be enraged at having a display of toys in their house?"

"Some might, some not, but all the dukes and duchesses before me had their own eccentricities."

"Yeah?" Evan was smiling again. She had no doubt Evan thought that she would be enraged at the very idea, but the more she saw, the more she realized Evan really cared about Rosebrook House.

Clementine walked along looking at the toys, and Evan said, "Every toy you see on display, I have the same one, still in its packaging and kept over in the wooden cabinet over there."

She looked over, and the cabinet was huge. "My goodness. I wouldn't feel too bad about your collection. The sixth duke had a zoo out on the land at the back. He had a lion, an elephant, and all sorts of monkeys."

"Really? I would have loved to see that. While you're still in a good mood, can I show the other room that I've made big changes in?"

"Lead on."

Evan led them to the next room and put her hand on the handle. "This is where I unwind."

Clementine gasped as she saw the huge trampoline filling the room. "A trampoline? Seriously? Who has a trampoline that size indoors?"

"Me." Evan grinned. "Come and see." Evan took her hand and pulled her into the room.

Evan kicked off her shoes and climbed up onto the trampoline. She got her iPhone out and chose a more upbeat playlist.

"Watch."

Clementine couldn't help the smile as Evan somersaulted, jumped, and mainly showed off. Evan's showing off didn't feel as annoying as other people's. Evan had this childlike outlook on the world, and Clementine was beginning to find it endearing.

Evan stopped and knelt down on the edge of the trampoline. She held out her hand. "Come up and try, Your Majesty. You'll love it."

"Oh no," Clementine said quickly.

"Please, you'll feel so relaxed afterwards. Live a little."

"I don't want to," Clementine said more firmly.

"Just two bounces and we can leave. Come on," Evan said.

"I'm not exactly dressed for it."

Evan leaped off the trampoline. "Kick off your shoes and I'll help you up. Please?"

Clementine was afraid of making a fool of herself, but it appeared important to her host, so with a sigh she gave in. "Okay, but just for a minute," Clementine said.

"Yes, you'll love it."

Evan helped her up and joined her on the trampoline. Clementine wobbled on her feet when Evan came up, but Evan grasped her hands. "It's okay, I've got you."

Evan took her hands and they started a small bounce.

"I feel stupid," Clementine said.

"Then we're being stupid together. Relax and bounce with me."

Evan was surprised she'd managed to get Clementine up here, but now that she had, Evan was determined that Clementine enjoy herself.

They started to bounce higher, and Evan sang along with the music, making Clementine laugh.

"Isn't this fun?" Evan asked.

Clementine laughed. "It's definitely silly."

"There's a lot to be said for silliness, from time to time," Evan said.

Evan bounced them higher and higher. "Evan, I think we're high enough."

"Come on, you'll be fine."

Then suddenly, they were falling. Clementine squealed and hit the surface of the trampoline, and Evan fell on top of her. Clementine couldn't help but laugh at being in such a silly position.

"Are you okay?" Evan said through her laughter.

"I'm fine, absolutely fine."

Evan put her hands on either side of Clementine's head and raised herself up. "I told you it would be fun."

Clementine looked into Evan's eyes, and the mood changed. There was no laughter. Her heart started to beat out of her chest, her mouth went dry, and she had the unmistakable need to pull Evan into a kiss.

Evan must have felt it too because she started to caress her cheek with the backs of her fingers. Clementine had never felt such an urge to kiss someone before, but it was almost overwhelming. Almost. She closed her eyes and got control just as Evan was about to lower her lips to hers.

Clementine put her hand on Evan's chest. "I think we should get off now."

"Yeah, sure." Evan nodded.

The moment of need was gone, now replaced with a slight sense of awkwardness. Clementine's attraction to Evan was making everything all the more complicated. Evan helped her down, and Clementine felt the need to fill the awkward silence.

"That was fun. Thank you, Evan."

"You're welcome. Why don't I show you the duke's room now?"

"Yes, okay."

❖

This was the room Clementine wasn't looking forward to. Her mother and father's room. She walked in and found it tastefully decorated, not over the top at all. In her mind's eye she could see herself running in here as a little girl and jumping on her parents' bed.

"What are you thinking?" Evan said as she leaned against the post on the bed.

"About when I was a young girl, running in here from my bed early every morning."

"Did you like living here when you were young, Clem?" Evan asked.

Clementine considered her answer and whether she should be truthful. She felt she could. Evan had been nothing but respectful to her ancestral home.

"By the time my father inherited Rosebrook, it was a big country pile with no money to fix it. There were leaks everywhere, the heating didn't work properly, and I always felt this dark cloud of stress hung over the house. My father felt impotent, not able to make things right, and the more stress my parents felt, the more I began to resent my grandmother. She was one of the wealthiest people in Britain when she inherited, and it was gone in a lifetime. The family paintings and special pieces of furniture were being sold just to make ends meet…"

"I feel a *but* coming," Evan said and walked over to Clementine.

"You're right. It was still an amazing place to grow up. An adventure playground all to myself, and I always felt connected by my ancestry, by my very DNA. That's why it hurt so much to leave."

Evan took a huge chance and reached out for Clementine's hand. She didn't rebuff her, and that meant the world to her.

"I might not be your ideal caretaker for your ancestral home, but I promise you I will take care of it." Evan found herself taking a step towards Clementine. She could smell her scent and it was intoxicating. "Clem, I'd like to fill Rosebrook with sunshine again and wake the village up to be a vibrant, safe, ecological haven, and an inspiration to the country. Imagine a village where people like us can live together in safety, families who know they won't be judged. I have a vision, a dream, and I want you to believe in it too."

Clementine was looking at her intently, her lips slightly parted, and Evan shivered when Clem wet her lips with her tongue.

I want to kiss you so badly, Evan thought.

"What do you mean, people like us?" Clementine said.

"Gay, lesbian, the whole LGBTQ community."

Clementine raised an eyebrow. "You're making assumptions."

"No, you told me you wouldn't marry a man to pass on your title, so I think you're like me, Your Majesty, Your Graceship," Evan said smiling.

Clementine squeezed her hand. "Maybe."

The air between them was thick with sexual tension again, just like on the trampoline. How Evan wanted this woman. If Clementine hadn't put a hand on her chest, Evan would have kissed her atop the trampoline.

It felt like fate to Evan that she should fall for Isadora's granddaughter and bring the last Fitzroy back to be the mistress of Rosebrook. But if she moved too quickly, she might scare Clem off. The way she felt right now, it was either kiss her or ask her the big question again.

She made her choice. "Come and work for me, Clem—I mean, the trust, work for the trust."

Clementine gulped and then thought silently for a minute.

"I will give *you* an answer if you'll give me an answer to this question. How does it feel living here? Before you left for London you said you'd bitten off more than you could chew. What did you mean?"

"Ah, that question."

She had to open herself up to Clementine or she wouldn't trust her. "To be super honest, it's not quite what I imagined."

"In what way?"

Evan let go of her hand and straightened her tie. "Sometimes I get carried away with my dreams and don't think of the practicalities. It's been my dream to buy Rosebrook for years, and don't get me wrong—I'm in love with the village and the house…"

"But?" Clementine said.

Evan stuffed her hands in her pockets and put her head down.

"You don't want to tell me?"

Evan sighed. "No, I just hate to admit to negativity. I live my life by having a positive attitude and making the best of bad situations."

Clementine reached for Evan's tiepin. The simple intimate touch made Evan forget to breathe.

"Evan Fox, the happy-go-lucky jumping bean, who wants to save the world, but who is she when the lights go out?"

Evan felt like this was her one chance to make an emotional connection to Clementine. She had to take it.

"I'm lonely. When I pictured living here, I never thought about having dinner on my own, going to bed alone in the huge echoey house. I came from a two bedroom flat, so it's hard. I don't even have a staff yet. I don't know what I need. I mean, I have a cleaning firm come in twice a week, but I don't know how to staff a house like this."

Clementine pursed her lips and nodded. "Sounds like you need some help, Evan. What time do I start on Monday morning? Half past eight?"

Evan felt such elation. Being honest about negative emotions had gotten her past some of Clementine's walls.

"Thank you so much! We're going to be an unbeatable team. It's hug time." Evan picked Clementine up and spun her around.

"Evan, put me down this instant."

Evan eased Clementine down and said, "Sorry, I get carried away. We are going to do amazing things."

"And I'll be there to rein in your more outlandish dreams and bring you back to reality," Clementine said, smiling.

"That's what great teams are, yin and yang." Evan remembered the university essay that she'd dug out. "Oh, I almost forgot." She walked over to the bed and picked up a folder, then brought it back to Clementine. "I wondered if you would take a look at this."

"What is it?" Clementine asked.

"My university essay on Isadora. I thought maybe you'd like to see her from an outsider's point of view, and maybe correct me on any of the family history I got wrong."

Clementine held the folder and said after a few seconds, "If you really want me to."

"Thank you. I'd appreciate it, and I'll give you the files on our plans for you to look at over the weekend. Then on Monday, when you come to work, you can set us all right."

Clementine gave her a cheeky grin at that point. "I do like setting people right."

Chapter Twelve

"A bit more to me, Archie."

Archie put down her end of the desk with a thump. "Fox, it's seven thirty on a Monday morning, I've just fought through the most almighty traffic jam to get here on time, and we've been moving this desk around for half an hour."

Evan eased her end of the desk down. "If you moved out here, then you wouldn't have to sit in traffic jams on a long commute."

Archie rolled her eyes. "Believe me, I would rather sit in a jam than live in the country."

"Where did this phobia come from, Archie? Maybe you need to talk to a professional," Evan said jokingly.

"Oh, shut up. Can we finish moving this bloody thing?"

"Okay, okay just a little more to me." Evan picked up her side and they manoeuvred it into position. She looked to her desk, now only a few feet away, and was happy. "Perfect."

"Can I point something out?" Archie said. She pointed to the four desks used by the admin team. "You realize we started over there, and we've ended up a few feet from your desk?"

"And?" Evan folded her arms.

"And you seem to want her grumpy duchess-ship close to you," Archie said.

"She's not grumpy—she just has a lot to deal with in her life." Evan had a rare defensive tone in her voice. "I don't want to hear anyone refer to her like that. Do you realize how hard it must be for the duchess to come and work here? To work for a company controlling her birthright? She's had to swallow a lot of pride, and I think she is an amazing woman."

"Uh-oh," Archie said. "You're the most positive, happy person I've ever known. You only get close to frustration and anger when a woman is involved. You don't want to go down that road."

"I'm not going down any road, but even if I was, why wouldn't I want to?"

"I'm sorry to say these things, but sometimes you're so positive you don't see the pitfalls. Remember Miranda?" Archie said.

Evan relived the sense of foolishness she endured at that time, one year ago. "Miranda was an exception. I normally have really positive experiences with women I've been out with."

"You were besotted within a week, and within two she was wanting money off you. You came to your senses, but it took six months to stop her showing up everywhere you went."

"I wasn't besotted. I fell for her hard luck story and felt obliged to help her. I didn't know she wouldn't take no for an answer."

Miranda's stalking behaviour was an embarrassing episode. One she wouldn't want to repeat again.

"There's a huge difference between someone like Miranda and the duchess. She isn't affected by money—she works, and works hard. She may be a duchess, but she wasn't born with a silver spoon in her mouth. She's a classy woman, too classy for someone like me."

They were interrupted by the admin staff walking in. Archie said in a low voice, "She's a toff with a chip on her shoulder. You have her house and her land, and you could be her ticket back there. Just be careful."

Evan nodded quickly, then stood and extended her hands. "Good morning, happy team. You settle yourselves in, and I'll make the coffee."

A short time later Clementine arrived, and after short introductions, Evan had her sitting at her own desk and was showing her the ropes of their computer system.

"This is the shared drive, where you can find all the information on Rosebrook and the concepts and vision for the village. Now as head of the trust you'll have your own system in place. I asked my IT guys to design a trust website for you. I'll email you the details. You're the administrator of the site, and you can use it as you see fit."

"I will have your backing, won't I?" Clementine said.

"What do you mean?"

Clementine leaned further in to her. "The architects' team, for example. I need to know if I make a choice or suggestion that they're not just going to run to you."

Evan groaned internally. She was so close to Clementine that she just wanted to lean in, inhale her scent, and kiss her elegant neck.

"Evan?"

Evan realized she had been dreaming. "What was the question again?"

Clementine sighed. "Will I have your backing if your staff come running to complain to you about something I'm trying to do?"

"Of course you have my backing. If we don't agree on something, we'll discuss it. There's always a compromise. Now back to the computer—"

"Yes, yes, I've got all that," Clementine interrupted. She lifted her briefcase from the floor and pulled out some files. "I read over your plans over the weekend and I've got a few suggestions."

"Excellent." Evan rubbed her hands together.

Clementine handed her two plastic folders and a pen drive. "The first is a report on the village regeneration plans, and the second is on the house itself. You said you wanted advice on how to staff and run it?"

Evan leafed through a few pages of the extremely professional and comprehensive reports Clementine had prepared. Wow, she was efficient.

"This is, well, excellent," Evan said, trying to take some of the information in.

"It's all on this drive, but I thought you might like to leaf through it on paper. Now on the staff I've suggested. It's much more desirable to employ people who live in the village. That way everyone has a stake in making the house and the community work."

Evan was impressed but also patted herself on the back for persuading Clementine to help her. "You're right. I would never have thought of that. So what's your plan? Give a quick summary."

"My thoughts are these. You're going to rent the properties you refurbish and build—"

"At an affordable and reasonable price," Evan finished for her.

"Quite, so you should hire permanent staff from that group of people, and get temp agencies in until then," Clementine said.

Evan loved the sparkle in Clementine's eyes. Before, they were sad and weighed down by the world. Today was new—today Clementine was doing what she was trained to do since birth. "Excellent idea. Anyone would think you were trained to this."

Clementine stood up, gathered her things, and gave her a bright smile. A smile that banjoed her right across the face and in the heart. "I'd like to show you the advert my PR team has come up with for our new community. We'd like to release it to the major press this week."

"Email it to me. If you don't mind, I'd like to get to work. I need to review the files before the meeting with the architects."

With that Clementine walked with purpose across to her desk, her heels clattering on the wooden floor, and Evan couldn't stop her eyes wandering down Clementine's legs in the short skirt she was wearing.

What a woman, Evan silently muttered to herself.

Clementine had to admit, she was loving being in an office environment again, and even more, loving the fact that she was working on her village and trying to make it better. Kay was right, if you couldn't beat them, join them. But one thing she kept very clear in her mind—her main task was to rein in Evan's dreams, to make sure Rosebrook wasn't left bereft again.

She opened the drawer in her desk and looked at the picture frame she had brought from home. It was a photo taken of Grandma Isadora and Granny Louisa when they first inherited Rosebrook. A warning to Clementine that dreams can run away from you and become nightmares.

The other aspect to the job was the salary. She could finally get caught up with her mother's nursing home fees. She shut the drawer and turned her attention back to her computer and the noise that had been grating on her nerves for the past half hour—Evan walking up and down the office floor, talking loudly on her headset, while bouncing a rubber ball incessantly.

She gazed up at Evan and watched her nearly bounce along the floor herself, gesticulating with one hand, and throwing the ball with the other. She was a jumping bean and that bloody ball was giving her a headache, and if Evan was on the phone everyone knew about it. She didn't seem to possess an indoor voice.

"Ten percent, Roberto? You've got it. See you in Rome. Ciao," Evan shouted. She then turned to her PA Rupert and said loudly, "We're ready for liftoff with the Ferrari tie-up." She rubbed her hands together, and you could see her mind was already onto the next thought.

Clementine watched her start another call and bounce that bloody ball again.

She emailed Rupert the architects' report and walked over to him, trying to distract herself from the noise.

Rupert stood up nervously. "Can I help you, Your Grace?"

Clementine smiled. He was a nice boy, and the girls were pleasant too. Young and eager to be helpful. "You don't have to stand, and it's Clementine, remember?"

"Yeah, sorry. Do you need something?"

"Yes, I've emailed you a report. Could you print out twenty copies for the meeting?"

"No problem. We'll get that done in no time."

Clementine was just about to walk away when she asked, "Rupert? Does she always do that?"

"Oh, the ball? No, only since she came here. In her London office she has a mini trampoline."

Clementine raised both eyebrows in shock. "A trampoline?"

"Yeah, she has too much energy, you see. She can't sit still."

"I can see that," Clementine said. Then as she looked at Evan, she realized, she had the energy of a child, a child who was running a multinational toy company. She was quite sweet, really, but they had to do something about that bloody ball.

❖

Evan was enjoying taking a back seat on this meeting. The team of architects commissioned to work on the Rosebrook project had arrived thirty minutes ago and were extremely surprised to find the project now run by a trust, not just Evan, and under the clearly formidable Duchess of Rosebrook.

It was fun to watch Clementine come into her own and to imagine the kind of duchess she would have been if Isadora hadn't lost the family home and fortune. The three men and two women on the team of architects looked at each other in disbelief as Clementine critiqued their designs and plans point by point.

"The former army barracks should not be torn down—it's part of this village's history. Rosebrook played a part in winning the Second

World War. They may not be the most beautiful of buildings, but we can make them special, worthwhile, so that when the community uses them, they remember their link to the past."

What a brilliant idea, Evan thought. Her mind spun with a million community spaces the barracks could become. Clem was earning her money already.

One of the senior male architects interrupted Clementine, saying, "With the greatest respect, Your Grace."

"Questions can come at the end, Mr. Foskit." Clementine swiftly put him in his place.

Evan had to stop herself from laughing by putting her hand over her mouth. *Go you, m'lady.*

The frustrated Mr. Foskit sighed loudly and shot a look to Evan. She just smiled and shrugged.

Archie leaned over and whispered, "Are you all right with this? These plans have been in place for some time now."

"Oh yes, she's shaking things up and reminding us of our duty to the history of this place. That's what I want."

Archie added, "She's a bit of a boss, isn't she?"

That's what Evan was starting to love about Clem. "She's a duchess. She's being who she was born to be."

Clementine continued, "The last point, but the most important one, is the designs for the rebuild on the existing cottages and the new houses. We have to go back to the drawing board. These houses were built over centuries, employing different building techniques. They each have to have their own character, their own signature."

The more Evan listened to Clem, the more she could see Isadora in her. Clem just needed to recognize that.

"We already have our brief and plans costed—"

Clementine looked up at Evan. "I'm sure Ms. Fox wouldn't mind you relooking at your plans and bid."

"Absolutely no problem at all. I want to get this right, not rush into it."

Clementine smiled and was clearly buoyed by Evan's encouragement. "Okay, get to work on some new designs, maybe ten new ideas. Walk around the village, take notes, take pictures for inspiration, and then we'll meet up here in a week's time and compare designs. I'll make some designs myself."

The architects gathered their papers and grumbled among

themselves. Clementine stood quickly and said, "You'll have to excuse me. I have a phone call to make."

Evan's gaze was stuck to Clementine's curves in that short skirt of hers, as she strode with purpose from the room.

"What a woman," Evan said.

❖

"Thanks, Stan," Evan shouted to the car delivery driver.

Stan had just delivered an electric car to the gates of Rosebrook House, right next to Clementine's gatehouse. Fox Toys liked to promote electric cars and so leased them for employees. Some were discounted and some came as part of a salary package. Stan gave her a thumbs-up and jumped back into the cab of his truck.

As he drove off, Archie walked around the car and whistled at how nice it looked.

"This is some car. In fact, it's nicer than yours."

Evan walked around to Archie and patted the Mercedes SUV on the roof. "It's perfect for Clem, and anyway I like my little old Beetle. It's part of my personality."

"But a Mercedes?" Archie said.

"I wanted an SUV so she would have plenty of room for her mother's things—and a wheelchair, if she needed it. In the electric range the only SUV that suited was a Merc."

"You are into her, aren't you. It's the posh voice and the title, isn't it?"

"Do you really think me, of all people, brought up by *my* mother, the social campaigner, would be hooked with a title?"

"Maybe not, but you didn't deny the posh accent," Archie said.

Archie was right but she wasn't going to admit it. "Shut up. Right, I'll text her to come out, okay?"

"Are you sure you want me here for this?"

"I want you here to back me up. I know she's going to reject it first off—"

"Why would a woman reject a Mercedes SUV when she can't afford to get her own car fixed?" Archie asked.

"Pride. She might not have much, but she's proud. We had to fight over who was buying the ice creams at Bournemouth beach."

Archie raised an eyebrow. "When were you getting ice cream with her at the beach?"

"It doesn't matter. Just back me up."

"Okay, okay. I'll back you up."

Evan took out her phone to text Clementine but hesitated. Maybe she should send Archie in? She kept fiddling with her tie nervously.

"You *are* into her. Look how nervous you are," Archie said.

"Okay, I am into her. I think she's my Mrs. Fox. Are you satisfied now?" Evan said with frustration in her voice.

Archie rolled her eyes. "Oh God. Why are you so eager to give your freedom away? You're successful, rich—have fun."

"Archie, I'm not like you. All I've ever wanted is someone to love me and have a family. Go for Sunday drives to places like this"—Evan held her hands out wide—"play with my kids, drive them to their little clubs, football, karate, art club, whatever they like, um, cut the grass on a Saturday—"

Archie held her hand up. "Jesus, now you've gone too far. Cut grass? It makes me shiver."

"Why?" Evan asked.

"I hate the sound of lawnmowers. It's an image of a wife, two-point-four kids, and a ball and chain around my leg, but if that's what you really want, Fox, then good luck to you."

Evan decided texting Clementine was what she should do. She started to type in the message and said, "I'll remind you of this conversation when you're head over heels."

"Don't hold your breath," Archie said with a laugh.

❖

Clementine hadn't seen much of Evan that afternoon. At lunchtime Evan had gone out for a run, then when she returned, she'd been in the conference room taking part in a video conference.

She wanted to speak to Evan because she was starting to worry that maybe she had overstepped her remit. She was only chairwoman of the trust, after all. She was enjoying the work enormously, though. Having a say in her ancestral land was something she had dreamed about since she had left Rosebrook House.

Rupert and the other office staff began to drift away home. Archie had left as well about thirty minutes ago, so she had to wait till someone came back before she left.

She packed up her things, and a short time later a text popped up on her mobile.

Meet me at the gates, m'lady, your highness. Evan xx

Clementine could only smile. Evan always liked to make a joke of how she had first addressed her. She was sweet.

Wait. That was twice today that she had thought of Evan as sweet. She didn't want to fall into that trap, because Evan Fox was so good looking, and if she added sweet on top of that, there could be trouble.

She got up and started walking from the banqueting hall down to the gates. Why they had to meet there was strange. As she got closer, she noticed Evan and Archie standing by a car talking.

Evan turned around and noticed her. "Clem, come and join us."

She walked out of the gate and joined them at the car. Okay, this was weird. Was she getting the big heave-ho after one day?

"What's wrong?" Clementine asked.

"There's nothing wrong. I just wanted to give you your company car."

Clementine was sure her mouth was hanging open. "What? What do you mean?"

Evan opened the door to the car and indicted to her to get in. "This is your car."

She looked around the front of the car and saw it was a Mercedes. No, this was charity.

"I can't accept this," she said firmly.

"Why?"

"I'm not taking charity from you. You know my car is in the garage, and you want me to take this because you feel sorry for me."

Evan shook her head. "No, it's not like that. Fox Toys encourages employees to switch to electric cars. We lease them for our employees. Like Archie, you have one, don't you?"

"Yes, I have an electric car from the company," Archie said obediently.

Clementine was suspicious. "And is it a Mercedes?"

"Eh—" Archie stumbled over her reply, so Evan stepped in.

"No, not everyone gets a Merc, but I chose this one for you because it was the only SUV available, and I wanted that because I thought you might need the extra space for your mum's things, a wheelchair, something like that, if you had her out for the day."

"Oh." Clementine had the wind taken right out of her sails.

Archie clearly felt uncomfortable because she excused herself very quickly. "I'll leave you to it."

Once she left, Evan said, "Any more frowns I can iron out?"

"It's still an expensive thing. I'm supposed to be working for the trust, not you."

Evan took her hand and guided her to the driver's side. "Fox Toys funds the trusts we have. Who do you think provides the vans and cars for the service dogs that I told you about, and their handlers? We have a good contract with a vehicle leasing firm. Now will you get in and try it out?"

Clementine gave in and sat in the car. It was gorgeous. There were screens—for satnav and on-board computer, she assumed. The console was like she imagined a state of the art jet fighter or something.

Evan got in the other side and immediately started to talk. "This is totally electric. I've already had two car charging points put in outside the old village shop. I've got a few up at the house, but I'm having one installed here at the gates for you."

Clementine placed her fingers on her forehead and sighed. "This doesn't feel right. I can't—"

Evan swivelled around in her seat. Clementine was so stubborn. Anyone else would have taken the perk straight away, but not Clem.

"Look, Clem. It's just business. You'll be going around, meeting builders, architects, all sorts of people for the trust. You need a car, and my company provides. And the fact that it'll help you out with your mum, getting back and forth to seeing her, is a happy bonus."

After a short wait Clementine nodded.

"Is that a yes, m'lady, Duchess, madam?" She got a smile from Clementine at last. She loved making her smile.

"You're so silly."

Evan had the urge to reach out and touch Clementine's cheek. "You need more silly people in your life."

Clementine gazed into her eyes, then opened her mouth a few times, but said nothing. Did Clementine feel the attraction between them? Could she feel what Evan had felt since the first moment she opened the door to her gatehouse?

The moment was over almost as soon as it began, and Clementine looked back to the front window again.

"Let's take her for a spin," Evan said.

"Okay," Clementine said reluctantly. "Can I have the keys?"

"Sure, but you don't need them. They only need to be with you." Evan set them in the middle console. "Just press the ignition button. On the dash."

The engine started and the on-board systems came to life.

Clementine ran her hand over them. "This really is like something out of *Star Trek.*"

"Don't worry about that," Evan said. "It has a lot of bells and whistles, but you'll learn about them as you go. Just concentrate on the driving first."

Clementine looked down at the pedals. "This is different."

"It's just accelerator and brake—you'll soon get the hang of it."

Clementine pulled on her seat belt. "Okay, let's go."

❖

After a few stuttering starts, Clementine did get the knack of this new car. It was an amazing piece of machinery, so quiet, so smooth. She'd imagined an electric car wouldn't have much power, but it certainly was powerful enough for anything she would need.

While they were driving around the village, Evan explained the satnav and the radio and music system. Evan pointed to the screen on the dash. "So, your music apps are onscreen, and when you hook up your phone to Bluetooth, you'll have all your music available to play. Oh, and I forgot to say, as it's a leased car, if something goes wrong, the car leasing firm fixes it free of charge. No more garage bills for you."

That sounded like the biggest perk of the whole deal. Not having to worry about her car going wrong—not that it would, in a brand new car like this. It would be such a weight off her mind, to know whenever her mama needed her, she would always be able to get there.

But she still felt uncomfortable about such a big expensive gift. She had to tell Evan. "Evan, I don't think—"

Just then, Evan started to laugh. "Look, Clem. It's the Tucker twins. Slow down."

Side by side, Agatha and Ada were driving down the street. "God, I hope they're safe on those things."

"They are fine. Stop worrying." Evan put down the window.

As they got closer, Clementine spotted that Agatha had a simple headscarf on, but Ada had a World War II leather aviator's helmet, with flying goggles. "Look at Ada." Clementine giggled.

Evan chuckled. "They are adorable, aren't they?"

They stopped beside the pair and Evan said, "Good evening, beautiful ladies. You're looking fantastic on those wheels."

Agatha clasped her hands together. "Oh, it's wonderful! Ada and I haven't been out for walks like this for years."

Clementine was elated that the ladies were getting out again. It was a lovely gesture by Evan. But that was Evan, wasn't it? Kind and generous to a fault. She felt those collywobbles again and shook her head to try to get rid of them.

She leaned over, close to Evan, to talk through the window. The only problem was she was so close to Evan, she was enveloped in the smell of her gorgeous cologne. It did nothing to dispel those collywobbles.

"Are you being very careful?" Clementine said.

"Oh yes," answered Ada. "I've got my father's flying helmet from the War. Safe as houses."

"Okay, just don't go too fast. Do you need any shopping?"

"Not today, maybe tomorrow," Agatha replied.

Evan saluted the women and said, "Godspeed, ladies."

Ada giggled. "She's such a polite, well-mannered person, that Evan. Bye-bye."

As they drove on, Clementine realized that things were changing, bit by bit, and for the better, and all because of Evan. Maybe she should relax and just let things happen.

"Is there somewhere we could pull in and talk, Clem?"

"Um, yes, if we drive out of the north side of the village, there's a parking bay overlooking the cliffs."

"Sounds lovely."

❖

"This is beautiful," Evan said.

They were only about twenty feet from the edge of the cliff, with only a broken-down wire fence between them and the edge.

"I thought you would have discovered this place when you came here as a child."

"No, we mostly kept to the beach end of the village. You know what I love about the village?" Evan said.

"What?"

"It has everything. The sea, an unspoiled beach, wonderful views off the cliffs, fossil hunting at the bottom of the cliffs, fishing, farming, and countryside, with the Tynebrook River flowing past at the top of the village. There's everything someone could want."

"Why did you and your family first come here?" Clementine asked.

"When I first learned about Isadora in history class at school, I became fascinated and asked them to bring me here. Then we all fell in love with its charms."

"Isadora? Strange kind of thing for a child to become fascinated with, isn't it?" Clementine said.

Evan grinned. "I'm a strange kind of person. I had such a thirst for knowledge and facts when I was young, and my brain never wanted to switch off. If I wasn't playing with toys, or playing sport, then I was reading books, comics, anything really."

"Your poor mother and father must have been exhausted."

"Yeah, I think they were," Evan admitted.

"What is it that you wanted to talk about? Did I overstep my bounds earlier, at the meeting?"

Evan frowned. "What? No. That's what I wanted you to do, shake things up and remind us all to keep the history of this place firmly in our minds, when we plan. No, it was about the staffing report you gave me, for the house? Yeah, I was wondering if you'd do the finding candidates and interviews for me. I would ask Rupert or Violet, my PA back in London, but they don't have the experience like you do, the knowledge of what makes a person best for the job."

Evan was unsure about whether Clementine would go for this, but she wanted the help, and getting her involved with the house was getting Clem closer to her.

"That's a lot of work on top of the trust. I'm going to start meeting with the trustees to get their ideas for what needs to be done to the village. Besides, the hiring of staff is what the mistress of the house usually does."

Evan turned around in her seat. "I would like a mistress—" She could feel her cheeks getting a little hot. "I mean, not a mistress in that sense. I don't have a mistress in any sense, although—"

Clementine started to laugh softly at the muddle she was getting herself into.

"I'm making a mess of this," Evan said.

Clementine reached over and placed her hand on Evan's briefly. "Don't worry. I know what you mean. I could do it for you, but finding the time would be difficult."

"I've thought of that. You're going to be rushed off your feet with the trust work anyway, and I'm not always here to help, so what if we got you a PA?"

"A PA?" Clementine said with surprise.

"Yeah, we could get you one, then you could do the trust stuff and oversee my staff." Evan was getting excited at the thought of the future Mrs. Fox handling her affairs in the country while she split her time with the toy business.

If Clementine knew what she was thinking, she'd probably get out of the car and run. *I'm being too intense. Too excited.* Her mum was always giving her grief for that. *Calm down, Evan* was a phrase she had heard all her life.

"Wait," Clementine said with astonishment, "I'm overseeing them now?"

Evan squeezed her eyes shut and took a few breaths. "I was maybe getting a bit overexcited, but you made the excellent report on staffing, so who better than to choose at interview time, and your PA would help."

"I am an architect, remember, not an estate manager or mistress of the house," Clementine said.

"But you were born with the knowledge and experience, and you watched your mum and dad handle the estate," Evan said.

Clementine snorted. "That was mostly worrying about money and selling off land."

"Mostly, but not all. Say you'll do it?"

She watched Clementine mull over the offer, and her heart was pounding in anticipation. She wanted Clementine to be a part of her life, and this was the first small step.

"I'll say yes if I can choose my PA."

Evan smiled and her heart felt light as air. "Name them, and they're yours."

Clementine smiled. "Ashling O'Rourke."

Evan smacked herself on the head. "Of course! Ash would be perfect. A local who knows what's required. Would she do it?"

Clementine nodded. "Oh, I think so. She's a clever woman, and she's been stagnating, just looking after her father. Yes, Ash is very bright, and if things go well, she could take more responsibility with the staffing."

"Perfect, do you want me to ask her?"

"No, I think it should come from me. I'll go and visit her in the morning," Clementine said.

This was perfect, Evan thought. The little talk had gone even better than she had hoped for. "You've got it." Then Evan remembered something. "Wait a minute." Evan rummaged in the car's glovebox. "There's one more thing that goes with this car."

"What?" Clementine asked.

"This." Evan pulled out a very scaled down version of the Mr. Fox toy that she had first brought her. It had an elastic loop coming from the fox's top hat. "Mr. Fox, the car version."

Clementine laughed as Evan fitted the toy onto the car's mirror.

"Mr. Fox will bring you good luck."

Clementine smiled. "I hope so. I could do with some good luck in my life at last."

CHAPTER THIRTEEN

The next morning Evan walked down to the office with an extra spring in her step, whistling as she went. Yesterday couldn't have gone better. Clementine's first day was eventful—she put the architects on notice that they had to do better, came up with new ideas, and took Evan up on her offer of selecting staff.

As Evan lay in bed last night, she felt excited, confident, that her life was about to change, and she promised herself that she would endeavour to do everything in her power to win the Duchess of Rosebrook's heart.

But they still had so much to do, and the more she stayed here in this little idyllic village, the more ideas she got. Again, she could hear her mum's voice: *Calm down, Evan.*

The lights were already on in the office. It was a bit early for Rupert and the admin team. She opened the door and saw Archie nursing a big cup of coffee. "You're keen. Why so early?"

"The bloody rush hour. Why did you want an ecological village so far from civilization?"

"Because it's perfect. Now, we're going to need a new desk and computer. Ashling O'Rourke is joining us as Clementine's new PA."

Evan checked herself in the mirror by the door. Today she had chosen a summery light grey suit with a pink silk tie and a pink pocket square, with her customary fox tie and lapel pins.

"Don't worry," Archie said. "You haven't a hair out of place since you last checked at home."

Evan smiled at that jovial dig and walked up to the back of the hall and poured a coffee.

"So, the duchess needs a PA now too?" Archie questioned.

"Yes, and don't give me that look. It wasn't her idea—it was mine. There's a lot of work to do with the trust, and I've asked her to organize staff for the house. She's going to need help. Besides, it's great we're employing someone from the local community, the first of many, I hope, once we get our new residents flooding in."

Archie joined her to refill her coffee. "I still don't think it was a good idea to hand these people power with a trust. They have no idea of how to make this village more ecological. All they want is their village rebuilt."

"We'll make our case at the trust meetings, and with such a benefit to the world, I'm sure they'll agree. If we can't persuade them, then we are not delivering the message properly." Evan slapped Archie on the back and said, "Come on, be positive."

"What about the farmers? When are you going to talk to them about making their farms more eco-friendly? I mean, you own the lease—you could insist."

Evan shook her head. "Going forward with the new residents, I can. They are agreeing to join a community that has certain standards and maintains its duty to the earth, to making the world better, but Mr. Mason and the Murdochs need a softly-softly approach. They don't trust this vegan hippy who's suddenly turned up and wants to change everything. Let them settle in with me awhile, and then we can gently bring up the subject."

Archie nodded. "The pub being open would help. A drink shared together always makes for some social lubrication."

"Yes, we just need to find a landlord too."

"Oh, your lady friend, the duchess, dropped something off for you, first thing this morning. It's leaning against your desk."

Evan raised an eyebrow. "Really?"

She hurried back to her desk and found a large brown box. "Archie, give me a hand."

Evan slit the box open and she and Archie pulled another box out. It had a picture of a trampoline on it, similar to the one Evan had in her London office.

"A trampoline? She bought me a trampoline?" Evan said with joy in her voice.

"There's a note on your desk too." Archie handed it to her.

Evan read it out loud. "Evan, a small gift for you to enjoy. Don't subvert your personality just because you're here. Be yourself always—and please don't bounce that bloody ball."

Evan's head was swimming as that proverbial banjo smacked her in the head again. "Wow! What a woman."

❖

Clementine pulled up outside the O'Rourkes' cottage. It sat on the edge of the cove, beside the overgrown walkway at the other side of the beach. She turned off the car and gathered up her keys. She still couldn't believe she was sitting in such a good car. It still made her uneasy to accept something like this, but she'd made herself feel better by dropping off the trampoline for Evan.

She'd picked it up at a supermarket after visiting her mum last night. It wasn't much, but what do you get a multimillionaire CEO? But that was the thing—Evan didn't act like one, or what Clementine imagined a CEO would act like. Evan was overjoyed at eating an ice cream by the sea, bouncing on a trampoline while she worked, playing with her toys, and collecting rare toys. She was different to anyone Clementine had ever met.

Clementine caught herself letting out a longing sigh. *Stop it right now*. She let her head fall back against the headrest. "What am I doing?"

Every passing day she was getting deeper and deeper into Evan Fox's dreams and bright ideas, but as Kay had said, she should be on the inside. That way she could influence what was being done with her village. She was even staffing Rosebrook House for Evan now. That part secretly excited her—getting her hands, so to speak, on the house—but she had to remember it wasn't hers and never would be again.

Clementine got out of the car and opened the squeaky gate to the cottage. It looked run-down, and that was sad because James O'Rourke was a very capable man. He could have a better order, but life hadn't been kind to him and Ashling, and depression lay heavily over their lives.

But she knew Ashling was desperate to break out and make a new life, and this could be her opportunity. Clementine thought of the Tucker twins and their new wheels, and now Ashling. Evan was making a difference to their lives. Step by step.

Clementine knocked at the door. She hoped that James was out early this morning, so that Ash could talk openly. He wasn't a tyrant and Ash loved him very much, but she just felt obliged to look after him after they were so badly bereaved.

Ash opened the door and her glum expression turned into a big smile. "Good morning, Your Grace."

"*Clementine*, you know that. Good morning, I wondered if I could have a word?"

"Of course, come in." Ash showed her through to the front room.

Ash didn't seem to fit the dowdy, old fashioned decor. She was bright and beautiful with her long wavy auburn hair and her pretty yellow sundress. Clementine was more convinced than ever that Ash needed this opportunity. She needed to break out of the grief that surrounded her and live her life.

"Would you like tea or coffee?" Ash asked.

"No thanks, Ash. Is your dad in?"

"No, he's down at the boathouse. He has a fishing trip booked for this afternoon, so he's setting up for that. Did you want to talk to him? I could phone him—"

"It's you I want to talk to, Ash. Sit down with me." Clementine patted the couch.

Ash sat down. "What is it?"

"You know I'm chairing this new village trust?" Clementine asked.

"Yes, it's exciting. I can't wait to see what happens to the village. Dad is sceptical about it, of course, as he is with any change. I told him, more people will mean better business at the boathouse, but he doesn't seem to care." Ash looked down sadly at her clasped hands. "He doesn't seem to care about much these days."

"How are things now?" Clementine looked around the room at the many pictures of Ash's mother they had up.

"Um…you know. Since Mum left us, there's been a big hole in our family. Mum was everything to Dad, and now he thinks the sun will never come out again."

The family hadn't been the same since Carol died. Clementine felt guilty. She should have been paying more attention to Ash, it was her duty as duchess to help her people where she could, but she'd been so preoccupied with her own troubles with her mother that she'd let things slip. But now was her chance to make up for that.

"But would you like the sun to come out again, Ash?" Clementine asked.

Ash gulped and flicked a loose auburn lock behind her ear. She nodded. "Yes, I think that's what Mum would have wanted."

Clementine squeezed her hand. "I have an opportunity for you. Both Evan and I would like to offer you a job as my PA."

Ash's eyes went wide. "Me? Really?"

Clementine smiled. "Of course—you're local, you know all about what's needed in the village, you're bright and clever, plus I need you to help me discourage some of Evan's wilder flights of fancy. Say you'll do it?"

Ash had the biggest smile on her face. "Yes, I'd love to."

Clementine drove back up to the office. It was funny, every time she drove in through the front gates to Rosebrook, it felt like coming home, and then she remembered she wasn't, and she felt a stab of pain.

She parked her car and took the opportunity to plug it in to the charging unit outside the office. It was going to be weird getting used to not going to the petrol station any more.

Clementine heard the sound of music coming from the office. She walked in to find everyone jumping around, dancing. All except Archie, who was sitting quietly watching them. Evan was bouncing like a jack-in-the-box on her new trampoline.

"Clem!" Evan shouted. "You're back. Did she take the job?"

"What on earth is going on?" Clementine said, walking over to her desk.

"We're having a music break." With one final bounce, Evan jumped to the floor. "I love my new trampoline. Thank you so much, m'lady, Your Grace, your loveliness," she said, walking over to Clementine's desk. "Thanks for my trampoline. It means a lot to me."

"Hmm. I'm beginning to regret it. Will you turn that music down, please?"

"Sure." Evan pressed a button on her watch and the music stopped. She then turned to the admin team and said, "Everyone, back to work. The duchess would like some quiet."

"Yes, she's starting tomorrow."

"Yes," Evan said. "Everything is coming together. The advert for residents has been sent out to the national press, the architects are coming up with ideas, and we're getting new team members."

Clementine put her things on her desk and looked up at Evan's smiling happy face. She was so sweet, and handsome, looking sexy in her grey suit trousers and waistcoat. She had dispensed with her jacket.

She wanted to smile at her and so much more, but she couldn't. It would be too easy to fall under Evan's charms. *She's too young and silly for you anyway.*

"Can we get back to work please? I thought you had a toy company to run."

Evan bowed extravagantly. "Yes, Your Highness, Your Ladyship."

CHAPTER FOURTEEN

Clementine closed her front door and made her way down to the beach. It was Saturday lunchtime and the village was quiet for once with no building work going on at the weekend.

It had been a month since she'd started working for Evan, and Rosebrook village was finally starting to wake up. The pub was just about finished, the new shop was being fitted out, and the architects' plans were approved and building underway.

Clementine had ruffled a few feathers along the way. Archie thought she was interfering, but Evan backed her to the hilt as she promised. She walked down the steps to the beach and sighed. Evan.

Rosebrook wasn't the only one that was being woken up. Evan's positivity was infectious. She'd never met anyone like her before. No problem was insurmountable, no task too big, and she was always brimming with ideas to find solutions.

Clementine wasn't used to people like that. She was brought up with a glass-half-empty kind of attitude. Her father and mother were not the most positive of people. There was always a disaster lurking around every corner, and it usually materialized.

She stepped onto the sand and walked to her favourite spot to sit. She sat down, closed her eyes, and breathed in the salty air. But even when she closed her eyes, Evan's smiling face was there, just like those infernal collywobbles she got every day that she saw her.

Clementine opened her eyes and groaned in exasperation. No one else had so penetrated her consciousness, even people she'd had brief relationships with. Evan was different. She made Clementine smile every day, and she had to admit that the days Evan worked at her London office, Clementine missed her exuberant presence.

So much had changed since Evan arrived, and the villagers were starting to trust and buy in to Evan's ideas. She looked up to the other side of the beach and smiled. The old walkway at the other end of the beach had been made safe, and even James O'Rourke was impressed as it gave him and his fishing clients much better access down to his boating shop.

Clementine's stomach flipped when she saw a runner on the walkway. There was only one person in the village who ran, Evan Fox. Her instinct was to get up and leave before Evan got there, but her body wasn't cooperating. She hadn't seen Evan in two days, and her heart missed her.

Just like the last time Clementine saw her running on the beach, her body reacted to the fit, athletic figure approaching her. She had always admired sporting women's bodies. Footballers, runners, triathletes. Evan had the body and the build of a triathlete, and Clementine couldn't take her eyes off the muscles in Evan's legs and arms as she pounded along the beach.

When Evan reached her, she gave her the customary gentlemanly bow that she always did and flopped down on the sand beside her.

"Your Graceship," Evan said breathily.

Clementine was transfixed. Evan lay back on her elbows, eyes closed and breathing hard, her hair wet with sweat. Was this what Evan looked like when she was in the heat of passion?

Everything in Clementine's body was telling her to turn over and kiss Evan. Her sex was throbbing and wet at the thought of making Evan feel like that. She quickly turned her gaze back to the water, wishing she could jump in to cool off.

"Hi, Evan. Your lunchtime run?" Clementine managed to say.

"My third run of the day."

"What? Why?" Clementine asked.

"My head's too full and the house is too quiet for me," Evan replied.

Clementine felt guilty. In the month since she'd started work, Evan had asked her countless times to have dinner or lunch with her. She knew Evan was lonely up in Rosebrook House. She and Ash had set up interviews next week for domestic staff, so the house was still big and lonely.

She had made an excuse every time Evan asked because she was scared. She was getting too close and was becoming too comfortable working in and walking in and out of her family home every day.

When this village was finished, Evan would probably spend only weekends down here, if that, or worse, she would meet someone and Rosebrook would have a new mistress of the house—that thought killed her.

She decided to ignore what Evan had said about the empty house and address her other concern.

"What do you mean your head is too full?"

Evan sat up and squeezed her head with her hands. "Too many thoughts, too many plans. My head works too fast sometimes, and I pile up too many ideas. My brain goes haywire, and I've got all this energy that I don't know what to do with. It feels like I've got ants crawling under my skin."

This wasn't like Evan. It was a side she didn't show. Evan was positivity itself. "Are you feeling stressed?"

Evan rubbed her face vigorously and said sharply, "I don't let stress into my life." As soon as Evan said that she regretted it. "I'm sorry, Clem. I just find my emotions difficult to control when I feel like this."

"This really isn't like you, Evan. Do you want to talk about it?"

Evan started to draw patterns in the sand in front of her. She wanted to tell Clementine everything because she felt safe with her, but it wasn't her way. "I don't talk about negative emotions."

"I see. So you don't let stress into your life and you don't talk about negative emotions. It's no wonder you feel out of control like this."

Evan looked up quickly. "How do you know I feel out of control?"

"Because I'm the queen of negativity—well, maybe the duchess—and I know how it makes one feel, intimately."

Evan smiled for the first time today. "You're the duchess of negativity and I'm the duke of positivity. We'd make a good team."

Clementine smiled. "I think we already do. Now, tell me what's wrong. You've done so much to help me, so the least I can do is listen to you, unless you'd rather speak to Archie or—"

"No, I can't speak to Archie. I can't show—" Evan was struggling to explain that she couldn't show Archie or any of her staff this stressed side of her nature. She was the leader, the CEO, who always had the answers to all their problems.

She didn't need to answer any further. Clementine squeezed her hand and said, "It's okay. I understand. If you can tell me, it'll go no further, I promise you."

Evan had known that the first time she saw Clementine. "I can't stop thinking about everything we still have to do. We've nearly refurbished the pub but have no one to run it. The shop is being fitted out, but again, no staff. Then there's the beer factory, and the old textile factory. They are meant to be the two main employers in the village. I thought one of my old friends might take on the beer factory, but she's out of the country at the moment, and I can't reach her. I have a million ideas for the textile factory, but I can't settle on the right one. Fox Toys is releasing the sequel to our gaming app, *The Woodlanders*, next week and—"

"Wait, what app?"

"It's a game. I came up with the concept and worked with our developers to bring it to market, when I first took over from my dad. It's my baby, you could say. It's made a lot of money, and we have toy and book tie-ins to the game. It's a big deal."

Clementine nodded. "And big pressure to deliver the same with the sequel, I suppose."

Evan normally didn't admit to pressure, but she wanted to be honest with Clementine. "Yeah, and that along with everything else makes me feel like I have springs bursting out of my head. That's why Mum always tells me to calm down, because she knows I get to this point, have a bit of a meltdown, a bad few days, then pull myself up again—somehow."

"But you have me and the trust to help, and everything is going well. *You* have the grand visions, and Ash, grumpy Archie, and I try to make it happen."

Evan smiled. Archie wasn't exactly enjoying having to run plans past Clementine. Normally it was just her and Evan working on their ecology projects.

"She's not always grumpy. Archie's a good friend, but she's not really a country person."

"Or a people person," Clementine said. "She asked Ash to make everyone a cup of tea on her first morning, and they haven't gotten on well since. She told her she wasn't a bloody tea girl."

Evan laughed. "Yeah, I know. She's a bit distant."

Clementine went quiet for a few moments, then said with worry in her voice, "It's not gotten too much for you, has it? Rosebrook, I mean. You're not going to leave us?"

Clementine obviously meant leave them in a situation like Isadora did. "God, no. I promised you I'd never leave the village high and dry. This is just a temporary freak-out. Tomorrow morning I'll be positivity itself again." Evan reached out and cupped Clementine's cheek. "I would never leave you."

She felt an electricity between them as they gazed into each other's eyes, and Evan wanted nothing more than to lean over and kiss Clementine, but Clem turned away and looked out to sea. Suddenly things felt awkward between them. Evan knew she had pushed it too far too soon.

She didn't know what to say, so she asked, "Have you read my essay on Isadora yet?"

"No, but I will. I promised you I would."

She was putting it off—Evan could tell. Isadora cast such a shadow over Clementine's life that it was probably hard for her to face it.

Evan dusted the sand off her hands and said, "I better go and leave you to your solitude."

Clementine grasped her hand as she was about to stand. "Do you want to have dinner with me tonight? I mean, we could talk about the pub and the factory, and work out some ideas so your mind calms down a bit."

Evan's heart soared with joy. "I'd love that."

"I can't promise you anything exciting. I've never cooked for a vegan before," Clementine said.

"Hey, let's take the stress out of it. Why don't we get pizzas—one cheesy, one vegan?"

"Okay, sounds great. I'll walk with you back up to the house, unless you want to keep running."

Evan smiled as she stood and pulled Clementine up with her. "No, I'm feeling much calmer now. Let's walk. Do you want to drive to the nearest pizza place together later?"

"I'm going to visit mother this afternoon, so I can pick them up on my way back."

Evan had an idea. "Why don't I come with you? Keep you company. I won't come in to see your mum if you don't want me to. I'll wait outside."

"Why would you want to?" Clementine said.

Evan decided to be honest. "I like being in your company, and I'd be happy to meet the dowager duchess if you allowed me."

Clementine looked at her, silent for a time, then said, "Okay. If you'd like to. The company would be nice. But you'd better shower first."

Evan couldn't be happier. She had broken a barrier with the woman she was falling for. "Don't worry. I'll be a dapper gent again in less than half an hour."

❖

An hour later, they arrived at the nursing home. Evan brought the car to a halt.

"Are you sure you want to come in?" Clementine said.

Evan really wanted to share this with Clementine and meet her mother. It was important to her. "Yeah, I'd like to, very much. If it's okay with you?"

Clementine nodded. "Yes. When we go in if you could wait outside, just until I find out if she's having a good day or not."

"No problem," Evan said.

"Oh, and she thinks we still live at Rosebrook, so don't—"

"Don't worry, I won't say a thing."

She followed Clementine through the security door into a very smart reception area. The nurse on the front desk stood up and gave her a quick bob of a curtsy.

"Good afternoon, Your Grace."

"Good afternoon, this is my friend, Ms. Fox," Clementine said.

They exchanged hellos and Clementine led her down a corridor. What Evan noticed was how well-staffed this place was and what good facilities it had. All the staff wore extremely traditional nursing outfits and seemed hyperaware of Clementine's position as duchess—they all stopped and addressed her as they passed. It was clearly an excellent private nursing home, and probably why Clementine couldn't afford to fix her own car. It must cost her a lot of money.

That thought only made Evan feel more for Clementine. She'd sacrificed herself and her life to look after her mum.

Clementine stopped at a door and turned to her. "Give me a few minutes, okay?"

Evan nodded and walked a few paces to the other side of the corridor. There were windows right along the wall, and a glass door into a large sitting room, where elderly residents were sitting together.

Some were playing cards or board games with the staff, others were watching television, and others were sitting back in their chairs with what looked like children's toys. Evan looked more closely and saw a few ladies with baby dolls. They were rocking them and talking, and some were singing to them.

A few others had baby play mats on their knees and were busy feeling the different textures and playing with the rattles on the mats. As a nurse passed, Evan said, "Excuse me, could you tell me why some of your residents are playing with toys?"

The nurse smiled. "The residents with Alzheimer's get a great deal of comfort from the toys. Some are stuck in the past in their minds, and so the dolls calm them by helping them think they are taking care of their child. The play mats keep their minds occupied with the different textures. Most of the residents' families bring them in for them, but there are toys specifically made for patients."

"Thank you," Evan said.

Her mind started to whirl, and she brought out her phone. She made a search for articles on the subject of toys and Alzheimer's, and pages of information came up. Just as she clicked on the first link, Clementine came out.

"You can come in now, Evan."

She quickly put her phone away and followed Clementine into the dowager duchess's room. Marianne Fitzroy was sitting by the window. She was maybe ten years older than her own mother, and it was heartbreaking to think she had already been suffering with this condition for years.

Clementine had put two seats beside her mother, and she beckoned Evan over. Evan realized when she got closer that Marianne was wringing a cloth handkerchief in her hands. Clementine must have noticed her looking because she said, "It was my father's. She's holding it for him. She thinks he's out on the estate. But he never comes, of course, so she gets stressed."

What a heartbreaking illness this really was, Evan thought.

"Mama? I have someone I'd like you to meet, a friend of mine."

The dowager duchess looked up at them and Evan could see the confusion behind her eyes. What a heavy emotional burden for Clem to carry alone.

"This is my friend, Evan Fox."

"Pleased to meet you, Your Grace," Evan said.

"Are you Clem's husband?" Marianne said.

Evan looked at Clementine and smiled. Her masculine appearance had given Marianne the wrong impression.

"No, Mama," Clementine said, "Evan is my friend."

Clementine indicated for her to sit.

Then Marianne said, "I haven't seen a bow tie since Uncle Freddie died. Come closer."

Evan leaned over. She was wearing her trademark fox bow tie today, and Marianne appeared to like it.

She smiled and tugged at it. "Foxes."

"Yes, Your Grace, I like foxes."

"I hope it's not a ready-made bow tie. Dora can't abide ready-made bow ties. She'll run you off our land."

Clementine leaned over, smiling. "My grandmother was known for pulling men's bow ties at parties, to make sure they were the real thing. She thought ready-made were frightfully common."

Evan grinned and winked at Clementine. "Fear not, ladies, a dapper gentleman always wears a real bow tie, and I can assure you this is real."

"Evan is repairing Rosebrook and the village, Mama," Clementine said.

Marianne perked up at that point and said, "At last, your father will be pleased. Can we go home when it's finished?"

Clementine ignored the question and said, "She even fixed the old ramp down to the beach."

"If only we still had Thistleburn, Clem. Maybe your husband could fix that too," Marianne said.

Thistleburn. That name rang a bell with Evan—wasn't it in Clem's title? She would need to ask her later.

Marianne suddenly said, "Have you brought a chum home from school, Clemy? Go and ask Cook for something to eat."

Clementine said in a low voice, "When she's more lucid, she's aware I'm an adult, but then she slips into me being a child again. I just go with it. I don't like to stress her out." Then she turned to her mother and said, "That's okay, Mama. We're not hungry."

Marianne began to twist the handkerchief in her hand tightly. "Where is your papa? He told me he wouldn't be long."

"She's starting to get distressed," Clementine said.

Evan watched as tears of frustration began to fall down Marianne's cheeks.

"Where's your papa, where is he?"

Clementine pointed over to her mother's bedside table. "Could you get me my mother's Bible, Evan. It always calms her."

"No probs." Evan quickly grabbed the Bible and handed it to Clementine. Then a thought crossed her mind. "Clem, I've had an idea. I'm just popping out to the car for a minute."

Evan ran to her car, got what she was looking for, and after a bit of difficulty at the security door, got back in and along to the dowager duchess's room, holding the soft, plush Mr. Fox. But she was stopped in her tracks when she opened the door and found a caring, loving scene.

She closed the door behind her and stood quietly watching Clementine read from the Bible, while holding and kissing her mother's hand. Her mother mouthed the verses along with her, gaining peace with every word. If Evan hadn't been falling in love before, she surely was now.

Clementine was so caring, so gentle, so patient. Evan's heart was aching, aching to be close to her. The banjo wasn't wrong on the first day Evan met her, and Clementine was not the icy woman eager to slam the door on her face.

Evan imagined Clem and her mother on the day they were forced to leave Rosebrook, their ancestral home. The devastation must have been awful. *I'm going to get you back in that house, Clem, no matter how long it takes.*

Clementine finished the verse and looked up at Evan, giving her a strange look when she saw the toy fox in her arms.

"I thought you could give it to your mum, give her something to focus on, apart from your dad coming home. A lot of the other residents use toys this way—the nurse was telling me in the hallway. I'm not trying to be condescending or anything."

Clementine smiled. "I know they do. It's a really kind thought. Give me Mr. Fox."

Evan handed it over, and Clementine kept it on her lap until they were ready to go. "Mama, my friend gave me this toy. He's called Mr. Fox. Could you look after him for me, while we go—"

"Yes, yes, you two go out and play. I'll look after your toy," Marianne said, stroking the toy's fur already.

Evan looked out the window and said, "You say your goodbyes, and I'll pull the car up to the door. The heavens have opened out there."

"Okay."

Evan knelt down and took Marianne's hand, and gave it a gentlemanly kiss. "It was a pleasure meeting you, Your Grace."

As Evan walked out the door, she heard Marianne say, "If he's not your husband, he'd make a good one. Very gentlemanly."

Evan chuckled. Yeah, she would.

❖

Clementine gazed over her glass of cold white wine at Evan as she talked about something, she couldn't remember what, passionately, with a slice of pizza in one hand and her other making big gestures.

They left the nursing home, picked up some pizzas and a nice bottle of white wine, and were now eating at Clementine's kitchen table. While Evan gesticulated wildly, Clementine thought of the kindness and thoughtfulness shown her mother at the nursing home. When she had seen Evan offering the stuffed fox to her, she felt her well-protected icy heart crack down the middle.

"Well, what do you think?" Evan said.

Clementine shook the romantic thoughts that were making her head spin out of her head. "Sorry? What?"

"The disused factory? Making toys and sensory play equipment for special-needs children and adults, and people with Alzheimer's."

Wow. She'd missed all that.

"Sorry, could you explain that again?" Clementine said.

She could see the passion and excitement in Evan again, so unlike the stressed Evan on the beach this morning.

"Obviously I need to do a whole lot of research on it. I'll set up a research team—"

Clementine held up her hand. "Slow down, Evan."

Evan stopped, dropped her pizza on her plate, and took a breath. "Okay, I know I get excited. The thing that's been troubling me with the factory is that you cannot make toys, like Fox Toys does, in the UK and make a profit. No matter how much I want to, my shareholders won't buy it. So whatever I started making at the factory would be a labour of love. That's what I couldn't get my head around. I need jobs for the people we attract to live here, but what kind of jobs?"

"So…the toys at the nursing home gave you an idea?"

"I spoke to the nurse when I was waiting to come in to see your mother, and I realized toys didn't just need to be for the imaginations of the young. They are there to help everybody. I checked the internet, and there are online businesses that make these things, but the toys are expensive."

"It's a good idea. I would be all for helping make lower cost toys like that. I mean, my mother's nursing home is expensive and exclusive. I'm sure most local authority homes can't provide those sorts of things to residents."

Evan rubbed her hands together. "That's what I was thinking."

"But how can you make it financially viable?" Clementine asked.

Evan's enthusiastic smile made the normally negative Clementine fill with a buzz of her own excitement. Evan's joy was truly infectious.

"We don't try to make huge profits, we make the business part of the Rosebrook Trust, and after all costs are paid for, any profit goes to charity."

Evan took a breath because her mind was going too fast again, but why shouldn't it? This idea was bloody brilliant. She lifted the bottle of wine and refilled Clementine's glass.

"British made products, sold at a reasonable price, giving much needed employment to the new locals, and making the lives of some children and adults with particular needs a little bit brighter. My motto is that I want to leave the world a little bit better than I found it, and this fits that motto. What do you think?"

Clementine looked at her silently for a few seconds, and Evan was starting to get worried.

Then finally a smile started to creep up the sides of her mouth. "I think that Isadora would be so happy that you are the one to continue her legacy."

Evan was taken aback at that statement and gulped hard. For one, Clementine wasn't the biggest fan of her famous grandmother, and two, she hadn't been on board with a lot of Evan's ideas.

Evan reached over and took Clementine's hand. "Thank you. That means the world to me."

They gazed at each other for the longest time, getting lost in each other's eyes, but then Clementine seemed to shake it off and pulled back her hand.

"Now that just leaves the pub and the beer factory."

Evan rubbed her hands together. "Yeah, the pub's our hard one. It's always the heart of the community. I'm reluctant to bring in any old stranger to run it."

Clementine grinned. "I think I have the perfect solution for you."

"Oh?"

"Yes, indeed. I've been talking to Rupert and getting to know him. Did you know his partner is a manager of a pub in London? He wants to move down to Rosebrook and start a new life with Rupert. He's been trying to find a job in the next town, but it's difficult. He would be able to hit the ground running, don't you think?"

Evan smacked the table, making the cutlery rattle. "That's brilliant! How did I not know that?"

"Because your head's so full of ideas and spinning so fast you don't have enough time to see what's around you sometimes."

Evan sat back down. "I'm so glad I've got you, Your Highness-ship."

Clementine smiled and shook her head. "One problem down. Now, do you definitely want to make beer?"

The moment was obviously gone. "Who wouldn't want to make beer?" Evan joked.

"I'm sure you know that the beer factory was the start of my grandmother's downfall."

"Yes, if you read the essay I gave you, you'll see that I went into that area in great depth. She trusted someone she shouldn't have to run the plant, and he funnelled money from the business into his own bank account."

There was a flash of anger on Clementine's face. "My mother said she was warned but wouldn't listen. She went way back with this particular character. He thought Isadora and the family had so much money that they wouldn't miss it. When she did come to terms with the situation, it was too late. So it started a domino effect, starting with Thistleburn."

There was that place again. "That is part of your title, isn't it?"

Clementine nodded and took a sip of her wine. "Yes, Duchess of Rosebrook, Countess of Thistleburn, and Baroness Portford. We never owned much land in Portford, but Thistleburn in Scotland was special. There is a castle there that we inherited when Charles II granted the Fitzroys our titles and lands. It was very special. So much history, and the most beautiful little village and town surrounding it. The family used to holiday there in the summer. Isadora sold it to keep her dream afloat, but I still have duties towards it even though I don't own the land. I'm chief of one of the last private standing armies in Britain. It's ceremonial now, but in theory the men and woman of the town could be called up by me to protect Scotland and Britain."

"That's amazing! Do you get a sword and a spear?" Evan asked like a little excited seven-year-old.

"Yes, there's a very nice sword, but it's kept up in Thistleburn at the barracks there. I have to go there every year to take the salute and swear in any new members."

"That is very cool."

"Maybe," Clementine said. "Again, I have responsibilities and no land to help the people of Thistleburn. Every time I go up there, they complain about the private owner and the rents they pay. They are good people, but I'm powerless."

Interesting, thought Evan. "I won't sell anything, you know."

"Just keep your feet on the ground and learn the lessons of the past, Evan. If I can't be in Rosebrook House, then I need you in there. If you sold it on—"

"You trust me, then?" Evan asked.

"Better the devil you know, they say." Clementine smiled.

Evan gave her a mock glare. "Hey, that's not a ringing endorsement."

"Maybe…better the fox you know than the snake you don't is perhaps more fitting. Just kidding. Yes, I trust you."

"That means the world to me, Clem." Evan couldn't have been happier. What Clementine said made her nearly choke on her wine.

"Come with me up to my bedroom?" Clementine stood and held out her hand. She must have seen Evan's look of shock because she added, "Don't worry—I won't sully your reputation. I want to show you something."

"Really?" Evan took her hand and followed her up the tight staircase.

As she did, she couldn't take her eyes off Clementine's rounded bum, and her hand twitched with the urge to touch it. *Those jeans are nicely tight.* Without shifting her gaze, Evan said, "You know, I wouldn't mind if you wanted to sully my reputation, Your Highness, Ladyship, high and mighty Duchess-ship."

Clementine just laughed loudly, which was a joy in itself because apart from chuckles and smiles, this was the first time she'd heard the usually tightly controlled Clementine give an unrestrained full belly laugh.

"Come on, Foxy Loxy," Clementine said.

Good God, am I dreaming? She called me a sweet little name. Mrs. Fox is softening.

They got up to the top landing, and Clementine opened her bedroom door.

"Is it just two bedrooms you have up here?" Evan asked.

"Yes, my mother's is across there. The last member of staff to live here was the gardener."

And here she was, the duchess living where the gardener had. Evan admired Clementine. She had a position in the British aristocracy that many would envy, but not the means or the ancestral home to back it up, and rather than feel sorry for herself, she got on with leading a normal life, taking care of her mother and her own business, without relying on or using her title to curry favour with anyone. In fact, she didn't like using her title at all.

What a woman.

They entered Clementine's bedroom. It was small but tastefully decorated. There was a photo of her parents on her bedside and surprisingly a photo of Isadora and her wife on her dressing table. Clementine must have seen her looking because she said, "I did have two grandmothers, you know. Nanna Louisa may not have been related to me by blood, but she was all I knew, and I loved her very much. She was gentle, loving, kind, and a calming influence on Isadora. That's why I keep that picture there."

Evan nodded. "It's nice to hear about people you study and write about from those who loved them."

"Well, she was a good soul. Now, on to what I want to show you." Clementine opened up her wardrobe.

"What is it?" Evan asked.

Clementine went right to the back and said, "Can you help me lift these? They're heavy."

Evan saw the hangers with protective covering that Clementine was trying unsuccessfully to lift off the rail. "Here, let me."

Clementine stood back.

When Evan felt the weight of the items, she said, "Bloody hell! What have you got in here?"

"If you hang them on the wardrobe door, I'll show you. Oh, could you lift those two boxes from the shelf up there too?"

"Sure thing, Your Ladyship, ma'am." Evan pretended to tug her forelock.

Clementine laughed and gently pushed Evan. "Oh, shut up."

❖

Evan brought down the boxes and placed them on the bed. "These boxes look old."

"They are, but let's look at this first." Clementine unzipped the covering on one hanger.

"Wow. Those are your posh robes?"

"Yes, the duchess's official robes." Then Clementine unzipped the other clothing bag and revealed another set of robes. "These are the duke's."

Evan was wide-eyed and held her hand out to touch the fur collar. "Sorry, can I touch?"

"Of course." Clementine knew Evan would get a kick out of these robes. She joked, "Don't give me trouble for the fur—these robes were made generations before I came along."

"I know." Evan smiled. She touched them reverently. "This is beautiful."

"The duchess's robes are more elaborate and have a train, and once the outfit is on, you can tell my rank, my place in the aristocracy, for what it's worth."

"Will you put it on?" Evan asked excitedly.

Clementine wasn't expecting that question. Would she? She'd only worn the robes once since her father died. She hated the sight of them for what they represented, a noose around her neck, but maybe with Evan with her, she could shake off some bitterness of the past.

"If you want me to. Help me get them out, then—they are so heavy."

Evan helped lift them out, and Clementine brushed off the fur with her hand.

"They're like the Queen's robes," Evan said.

"Hmm…a bit worse for wear. They need a bit of a service. There's a place in London that takes care of all the ceremonial robes. Isadora wore these at the Queen's coronation."

"What? Our Queen? Like Queen Elizabeth?" Evan asked with surprise.

Clementine chuckled. "Of course, is there another Queen?"

Then Clementine opened the front button. "If you can hold this open for me, I'll slip it on. Kind of like an ornate dressing gown, isn't it?"

Evan helped lift the heavy robes onto her shoulders and snorted. "More like the *Queen's* dressing gown. They're big, aren't they?"

"The first duchess was a much taller woman than me, and you

have to imagine me in a big puffy white dress with gold embroidery. There's some expensive jewellery that goes with this, a gold chain with diamonds and some earrings, but they are kept in a bank in London. Isadora didn't sell them, thank the Lord." Clementine fastened the button on the robes and said, "Now open the box."

Evan did and gasped again. "You get a crown for being duchess?"

"A coronet. All the peers do, from duke all the way down to baron, but you can tell the hierarchy by subtle differences in our costumes. It's like a military uniform. All those in the know are aware of it simply by looking. Hand me the coronet and I'll tell you."

Evan picked up the coronet and carefully brought it over to Clementine. She was so honoured that Clem was sharing this with her. It was a personal thing and showed that she was trusted.

Clementine took it from her and checked inside the fur lining before putting it on her head. "There's a label inside to make sure you put it on the right way."

Evan was taken aback at how regal, how beautiful she looked. "You look stunning, Clem."

Clementine rolled her eyes. "Hardly, my hair is a mess and I've just finished a pizza. I couldn't be further from a stunning duchess."

"You are, every bit, and you won't persuade me otherwise, so tell me what everything on the gown means."

"First of all, the duchess's robe is close fitting with short sleeves, but the cape across my shoulders, the train, and my coronet explain my rank. You see these rows of spots on my cape?"

"Uh-huh," Evan said.

"That means I'm a duchess. A duke and a duchess have four rows of spots, a marquess has three and a half, an earl three, and so on down the ranks. The same with my train, the higher the rank you have, the longer the train. So I have a two-yard train and a five-inch edging. Finally, a duke's or duchess's coronet has a gold circlet and eight strawberry leaves. The lower ranks have a silver gilt circlet with fewer leaves, and some have balls instead of leaves."

"Wow," Evan said, "this is like stuff from an old period drama on TV."

"It is from an archaic world."

Evan shook her head. "It's not archaic—it's a tradition, and tradition is what this country is all about."

"It's dying, Evan. Do you know there are only twenty-four

dukedoms left in the country? The dukes are dying out," Clementine said.

"Why?"

"Because ninety-nine percent of them can only be passed down the male line. There's a much smaller pool of people to inherit under that system, and if someone has no male heirs, it gets passed from cousin to cousin, dying a little bit each time, until one day there are no male heirs left. I'm unusual in that I have one of the only dukedoms that can be passed down the female line. It's archaic and outdated. I mean, I can't share my title with whoever I marry. The rules need to be changed or done away with altogether."

Evan took a step towards Clementine and said, "If *I* married you, I'd be more of a duke."

Clementine gave her a wry smile. "Oh, really?"

Evan joked, "But I'd settle for you being Mrs. Fox."

Clementine shook her head and played along with her. "You're too young for me."

Evan folded her arms and raised a questioning eyebrow. "Am I? Eight years is nothing."

"No, it's not. I'd never keep up with you," Clementine said. "You have plenty of young things to choose from, a young, vibrant, dapper dandy like you."

Just as Evan was about to reply, Clementine changed the subject, saying, "Why don't you try on the duke's gown and coronet?"

"What? Me?"

"Yes, why not. You love elaborate clothes—it would be ultimate dress up," Clementine said.

Evan turned to the other clothing bag and unzipped it. It would be amazing and exciting to see herself as the duke, but Evan looked back at Clementine and said, "Are you sure a commoner like me is allowed to wear them?"

Clementine laughed. "Well, I won't call the police if you don't. Don't be silly, Evan. Put it on, you'll love it."

Evan was excited. "Yes, let's do this."

Clementine helped her get it out of the bag and over her shoulders, then tied the tassel at the front for her.

"You see, the duke's robes are a lot looser and more comfortable," Clementine said.

Evan eyed the box with the coronet in it.

"Let's put it on you, then." Clementine opened the box and lifted the coronet out. "The male coronet is much larger, but that will suit you."

Evan took it from Clementine and placed it carefully on her head. "This is the most awesome thing ever."

Once it was on and positioned correctly on her head, she turned to the mirror and gazed at her new outfit. Evan laughed. "I'm like a little kid at nursery school playing in the dress up box. I feel like I should have a sword."

"You would." Clementine laughed. "It suits you."

Evan took Clementine's hand and they gazed at each other in the mirrored wardrobe. "We make a nice couple."

A nervous tension crept into the air. Evan felt her heart start to beat faster, and a deep hunger built inside. She was sure Clementine could feel it too. She wanted to kiss Clementine so badly. Maybe she would scare Clementine off, but she just had to let her know how much she wanted her.

Evan turned around and took her coronet off.

"Had enough of playing at being a duke?" Clementine said.

"Nope. It would be in the way for the moment." With the coronet now back in its box, Evan took a few steps, until she was right up close to Clementine.

She could see Clementine's breathing become shallower. She was right—Clementine did feel it too, but she also had some fear in her eyes.

"What are you doing?" Clementine asked, never taking her eyes off Evan's.

Evan lifted Clem's hand and kissed her knuckles. "Showing you what a stunning woman you are."

She placed a few kisses up Clementine's arm and felt her shiver.

"Evan?" Clementine said breathily. "Don't, I—"

Evan cupped her cheek and stroked her thumb tenderly along Clementine's cheekbone. "As soon as you opened the door to me, the first time we met, I wanted to do this."

Evan leaned in and brushed Clementine's lips lightly, then as she pulled back, kissed each cheek just as lightly, lingering slightly to inhale the scent of her perfume. The scent and the sound of Clementine's heavier breathing made Evan's head swim. She had never felt like this for anyone before. This was real.

When she did finally pull back, she found Clementine with her eyes closed and her lips slightly parted. Evan wanted to kiss her fully, kiss Clementine all over her body, but she didn't want to rush things. Her dad had once said to her that when you found the right one for you, you shouldn't rush to the finish line and miss the joy of falling in love. Besides, anything more at the moment might scare Clementine off.

After a few seconds, Clementine began to slowly open her eyes.

Evan caressed her cheek and backed off. "Don't say anything. I'll help you put these things away, and I'll go. Thanks for tonight."

Later that evening, after tidying up the kitchen, Clementine made her way up to bed. Since Evan left, she could hardly think of anything else but her. Why had she been so sweet and understanding with her mother today? Why was she so much fun to talk to and brimming with positivity?

Clementine slipped under the covers and pulled them up to her chin. "And why did she have to kiss me like that?"

The kiss was tender, and it was caring, just like Evan herself. When she first met Evan, she'd assumed by the way she dressed, by her constant flattery, that she was arrogant and self-obsessed, and had a different date for every night of the week. How wrong she had been, and every moment spent with Evan was drawing them closer. She couldn't let that happen.

She worked with Evan, and people would say she was just trying to get the house back, and maybe she was getting her feelings mixed up with a desire to be close to her ancestral home. Plus Evan was too young for her. And most importantly, Clementine couldn't bear to have her heart hurt when it went wrong, and it would go wrong.

She'd had so much sadness and stress in her life that she couldn't trust this feeling of excitement and positivity that Evan was drawing out of her.

Clementine sighed and picked up her book from the bedside cabinet and opened it. She stared at the page, the words not really making sense. Then she heard the beep of her phone. She picked it up and saw it was a text from Evan.

Here I am in this big stately home, in this big bed, and not a duchess in sight. Xx

Clementine couldn't help the smile that erupted on her face, or the giddy feeling of excitement in her stomach. Collywobbles.

She typed out a quick reply. *Don't look for duchesses and you won't be disappointed. Xx*

The reply came back almost instantaneously. *You're thinking about me, aren't you?*

No, I'm trying to read my book.

The phone beeped again. *Yeah, you're thinking about me, but that's okay because I'm thinking about you too. Sweet dreams, Clem. See you at work tomorrow.*

"Bloody cheek of the woman. Thinks I'm lying here daydreaming about her?"

Clementine put off the light and shut her eyes. When she did, all she could feel were Evan's soft lips on hers. She quickly put on the light again and sat up and reached for her book again, but the essay Evan had given her caught her eye. She had faced one fear today, wearing her robes, embracing who she was, with the help of Evan. Maybe it was time to look at Isadora from her point of view too? She opened to the first page.

Chapter Fifteen

In the days since Evan kissed her, Clementine had tried to keep her distance from her and never to be alone with her. She couldn't trust herself, for one thing. She'd just stood there and let it happen, just stood there. The truth was that Clementine could hardly think of anything else since the kiss happened.

She was distracted. Clementine didn't know how many times she'd been sitting at her desk, and caught herself gazing at Evan, trying to work out why she felt like this.

Evan was so good-looking, dapper, exactly her type, but she was too young in both years and personality, and yet she felt like a giddy teenager in her company.

She tried to throw herself into her work, but building work had slowed down to a trickle since the rain had started the other day and never let up. Everyone in the office was getting a little bit testy. All except Evan, of course, who was always optimistic.

Clementine was lost in her thoughts and gazing towards Evan, when she realized Ash was talking to her.

"What was that, Ash?"

"Do you want to leave this till later?"

"No, no. Sorry, I was distracted. Where were we?"

"Why don't I make us a cup of coffee? Wake us up a bit?" Ash suggested.

"Sounds good."

Ash asked if Evan would like a coffee, and then, as she passed Archie's desk, said, "Would you like coffee, since I am your own personal tea lady, apparently?"

Archie groaned in frustration. "Look, how long are you going to keep this up? It was a mistake, okay? I didn't think."

"It was rude."

Clementine chuckled silently to herself. Ash wasn't going to let Archie forget her rudeness on Ash's first day. Their working relationship had been tense since then. Clementine turned her attention back to her computer, and then she heard her phone beep. It was a message from Evan. She looked over and found Evan had her feet up on the desk and was looking at her phone.

I think we should make Ash Archie's boss. It would make Archie's head explode!

Clementine looked over to her and smiled.

Then Evan texted again, *I caught you looking.*

Clementine felt heat flush her cheeks. She quickly texted back, *Don't be absurd.*

She tried to get back to her work, but her phone beeped again. *You're thinking about me, aren't you?*

Evan was right. She was all she could think about. She got up and marched over to Evan's desk.

Clementine whispered, "Stop texting me. I'm trying to plan the trust meeting."

Evan gave her an incredulous look. "Me? It's you who are distracting me from vital work, Your Duchess-ship. Every time I lift my head, you're gazing longingly at me."

Clementine really felt the heat in her cheeks now. "I am not. Now behave and stop with the silliness and act like the CEO you are."

When she turned around to go back to her desk, she noticed that everyone in the office had stopped what they were doing and was watching them. She felt like she was at school, passing notes and flirting. It wasn't like her at all.

She settled in her seat and Ash brought back the coffee. "Thanks, Ash."

Ash must have noticed where she was looking because she said, "Gorgeous, isn't she?"

"What?"

"Evan, she's gorgeous," Ash said.

Clementine sighed. "Yes, she is, and she doesn't even know it, which makes her even more fanciable."

"Unlike Archie," Ash said. "She thinks very highly of herself."

Clementine turned to Ash. "You like women, Ash?"

"Yeah, but don't tell Dad. I haven't told him yet," Ash said.

"Of course I won't. But probably best not to keep him in the dark too long. Secrets have a habit of coming out."

Ash started tapping her nails nervously on the desk. "He's had so much to deal with—I just didn't want to add to his stress or disappointment. I had a girlfriend in the next village, but he never knew."

"Do you still see each other?"

Ash gave a rueful laugh. "No, she didn't understand why I stayed at home. She went to university and wanted to live her life, and that was it."

Clementine squeezed Ash's hand. "I'm sorry."

"It was never going to be a great love. I believe I'll know when that one person comes along. Do you think?"

Clementine looked up at Evan, who was now bouncing on her trampoline. "Yes, I think I would."

Evan tried to look busy at her computer. Everyone had gone except Archie and Clementine. Normally she wouldn't stay this late, but she wanted to talk to Clementine. The tension between them today was palpable, and she couldn't wait to get her on her own.

Clementine was still working at her computer, busy with her own work. It was wonderful to see how engaged Clementine had become with the Rosebrook project. The change in her since Evan first met her was night and day. She had a purpose now, a purpose that she was born to fulfil.

Archie walked over to her desk. "I'm heading back to London now. Have you spoken to her about the wind turbines yet?"

Evan placed her fingers to her lips. "Shh, not yet, but I'm building up to it."

Archie shook her head. "You do realize this is your land now, not hers?"

Evan got up and walked Archie to the door. "I want everyone on board, especially Clem. She…this is her home, and I want her to be comfortable with what we do."

"She hated the solar panels on your house, and then there's the new cattle feed we want the farmers to use."

"Just give me some more time, okay?" She patted Archie on the back.

"The equipment starts to arrive next week, so don't take too long. The rain holding us back is bad enough, without walking on eggshells around Her Ladyship."

Evan sighed. She had to make Archie understand. "Archie, I'm falling in love with her."

"Oh, Jesus Christ." Archie slapped her forehead. "I knew it. Just be careful. This is your dream—don't compromise for her, okay? She has different priorities."

Evan leaned against the wall. "There's one other thing I'd like you to do."

"To do with this project?" Archie said.

"Yes…in a way. There's a little village in Scotland called Thistleburn. It has a castle, a village, and some other historical monuments. Do a report for me like you did for Rosebrook. Who owns what, that kind of thing."

"Of course I will. But please bring up the wind turbines."

"I will. Pinkie promise," Evan joked.

Archie shook her head. "You are the biggest kid at Fox Toys."

"May it always be so."

When Archie left, Evan turned around and saw Clementine packing up her things. She sidled over to her and said, "So, you all done for the day?"

Clementine winked and said, "Yes, boss."

"That's a laugh. I think we both know who's the boss around here," Evan said.

Clementine put her hand on her hip. "Are you saying I'm bossy, controlling?"

Evan tapped her chin as if thinking deeply. "Hmm, not in a bad way."

"Is there a good way?"

"Sure there is. There's positives to everything."

Clementine walked around the desk and pulled on Evan's polka-dot tie. The tension was ramped up by a hundred percent.

"Oh, you like a woman to be in control?"

Evan gulped and her mouth dried up. "More along the lines of I love strong women. I mean, I love and respect all women, but I do like strong-willed women. They help me run my life. There's my mum, who if given the power could change the world, then there's Violet my PA in London—"

"Is she twenty-two and more interested in which colour lipstick she wears than your schedule?"

Evan laughed. "Eh, no. She's sixty-one and more concerned that I get to meetings on time and that I remember to eat. My mum always says that I fly in the clouds, dreaming of new ideas, and she and Violet keep me from flying away. I think I can add you to that list."

"We'll see," Clementine said enigmatically.

Clementine went back around to pick up her bag. It was a lot of fun to flirt with Evan. It was something she hadn't done in years. Flirting and relationships took the back seat when her mother got ill, but this was fun, and it was safe because she trusted Evan. She wasn't deceitful, conceited, or playing any game. She was lovely, sweet, and thoughtful. Oh God, she was falling for her, wasn't she?

"So? Where do you want dinner, yours or mine?"

Clementine said, "Who decided we were having dinner together? You shouldn't be making assumptions."

"Well, stop gazing at me like you want to lick me all over, all day."

"Excuse me?" Clementine squeaked.

Evan walked up to her slowly and took her hand. "We've got this sexual tension going on, and I think we should just cut out the middleman and admit we're hot for each other."

She threaded her fingers through Clementine's, and she, in turn, caressed Evan's face.

"I have to check on my mother," Clementine said.

"I'll drive you or come with you. Just spend time with me. I've been thinking about you all day, and you're only a few feet away."

Clementine was getting lost in Evan's eyes and fighting the urge to kiss her. *Don't fight it*, her subconscious said to her. *Just enjoy the feeling. It's not as if it's serious.*

Evan made her decision for her and closed in on her lips. The kiss was soft just like the first time Evan kissed her. Clementine's heart sped up, and her whole body was yearning for more. She deepened the kiss and teased Evan by slipping the tip of her tongue inside her mouth.

Evan moaned and slid her hands down Clementine's sides, grasping her bottom and pulling their pelvises together. Clementine responded by running her hands through Evan's hair, grasping the longer locks on top.

Their kiss became more frantic, breathy, and desperate. Clementine had years' worth of sexual frustration and days of longing since Evan's first kiss, bursting to come out.

Evan manoeuvred her to the edge of the desk and lifted her up onto it. Clementine immediately opened her legs and pulled Evan close, wrapping her legs around Evan's calves.

Clementine was so turned on that she wanted to rip Evan's clothes off. It was so unlike her—she'd never truly let go with any of her few lovers over the years, but just a few kisses with Evan, and she wanted to offer her everything.

She grasped and loosened Evan's tie, then popped open the top button of her shirt, then slipped her hands inside and around her neck. Evan groaned when Clementine dug her nails into her neck.

Evan ran her hand under Clementine's skirt and grasped her thigh. Clementine was losing herself. All that mattered was that Evan would touch her. She held on to Evan's neck with one hand while fumbling and trying to undo Evan's belt with the other.

She succeeded, and Evan started to push her back onto the desk—then Clementine's phone started to ring.

Clementine recognized the ringtone straight away. It was the Tucker twins, and it felt like she'd been doused with cold water.

She pushed Evan back. "Stop, stop, I need to answer this."

"Ignore it," Evan pleaded.

"I can't. It's the Tuckers. I need to make sure they're okay."

Evan sighed and stood back. "You're right."

Clementine hurried to get the phone out of her bag and answered. "Hello?"

"Clementine, it's Agatha, Ada's fallen and I can't get her up. She's in pain."

"Don't worry—I'll be right there." Clementine hung up and grabbed her bag.

"What's wrong?" Evan asked while tucking her shirt back in.

"Ada's fallen. I need to get there."

Clementine was taken aback for a second as she saw all she had done in the heat of passion, as Evan tried to make herself presentable again.

What am I doing?

She felt awkward all of a sudden.

"Give me your keys," Evan said. "I'll drive."

"Okay, I'll phone Kay on our way. We might need some help."

Evan fastened her belt but didn't have time to fix her now messy hair and do up her shirt button as they ran out of the office.

❖

Evan hated this silence. Since they were interrupted at the office, Clementine had pulled away from her and only said anything when it was to do with Ada.

Kay had met them at the Tuckers' and gotten Ada off the floor. Ada was in a lot of pain, and her sister Agatha was upset.

The ambulance was going to take too long, so Evan had suggested that she and Clementine drive her to hospital, and Kay would stay with Agatha. Now she and Clementine were in the waiting room with the awkward silence hanging in the air.

Evan got up and walked over to the window. Waiting was not her strong suit, especially as the woman she couldn't stop thinking about had clammed up. How could they have come to this after nearly ripping each other's clothes off in the office?

To make matters more gloomy, the rain was battering against the window. Evan just had to fill the silence.

"The rain is terrible."

"Yes," Clementine said flatly.

She turned around to sit on the edge of the windowsill. Evan crossed her arms and sighed. "The rain's been awful this summer. We get a few days where the sun is beating down on us like Spain, then a few days of torrential rain. Another symptom of global warming."

"Seems like it," Clementine replied.

Evan was sick of this. She wanted to provoke a response in Clementine one way or another.

"Speaking of global warming, there is something that I haven't run by the trust yet, something I plan on going ahead with."

"Oh? What?"

"You know the wind turbine in Rosebrook grounds?"

Clementine rolled her eyes. "How could I forget. It's a worse eyesore than those solar panels."

"It harnesses the power of nature and gives us free energy, with no cost to the environment. How could anyone object to that?"

Clementine looked at her silently. "I suppose not."

Evan clapped her hands together. "Excellent. Well, they're going to be installed in the village next week, and with the trust's approval, with each cottage we renovate."

"No, you're bloody not." Clementine's anger was instantaneous. "You are not going to turn this village into an eyesore. It's a place of natural beauty."

"I want to make Rosebrook as self-sufficient as it can be," Evan said, "an example to the world. We're on the coast and it would be insane not to use the power on our doorstep."

Clementine stood up angrily and was just about to give what looked like a furious reply when a nurse opened the waiting room door.

"Ms. Fitzroy? Ms. Tucker is all ready for you. Her ankle's been put in plaster, and we'd like to see her back here in a week."

Ever the well-mannered duchess, Clementine instantly calmed down. "Thank you. She'll be well taken care of."

❖

"That's it, in you come." Kay held the door open while Evan bumped the wheelchair into the Tuckers' cottage.

"I'm sorry to have caused so much fuss," Ada said.

"Don't be silly, Ada," Evan said. "We're just happy you're all right."

Agatha was over to her sister as soon as they were in the living room. She hugged her. "I was so worried about you, you old goat."

Clementine was behind the chair and squeezed Agatha's hand. "She's going to be fine. We'll all make sure of it."

"We certainly will," Kay said. "Now, we're all ready for you. Casper brought our double folding bed over, and we've set it up in the dining room. That way you can sleep down here and not have to worry about the stairs."

"We're so lucky to have you all," Ada said.

"Let's get you into your armchair and get you a cup of tea," Kay said.

Between them they got Ada into her chair and her plastered leg up onto a footstool.

"Is there anything else I can do?" Evan said. "Get some shopping? Anything?"

Clementine sighed. "No. Kay and I will be fine from here. You can head off now."

"No, I'll wait on you," Evan said firmly.

Clementine shot her a look. "I don't need you to wait."

Evan narrowed her eyes. "Well, I am. I'll go and put on the kettle."

When Evan left, Kay nudged her. "What's that all about?"

"What's what about?"

"The tension." Clementine went over to the window to shut the blinds and Kay followed. "Well?"

"She wants to put wind turbines all over Rosebrook. I mean, have you seen those ugly things?" Clementine said.

Kay folded her arms. "That's not what this is about. Wind turbines don't make you look like you're either going to kiss or kill each other."

Clementine started to tell Kay, when Evan popped her head around the door.

"I can't find the teabags."

❖

Clementine drove Evan up to the door of Rosebrook House in silence, apart from the heavy patter of rain on the window.

"Do you want to come in for a drink?" Evan asked.

"No, I'd like to go home. It's been a long day."

Evan sighed. Why was Clementine pulling away from her like this? "I'm going to London tomorrow, not just for the weekend, but the whole week. We're launching *The Woodlanders*. I'd like to talk about what happened before I go."

"There's nothing to talk about."

"Of course there is. We were trying to rip each other's clothes off earlier, and now you won't even talk to me. Why?" Evan asked.

Clementine gripped the steering wheel more tightly. "It was a mistake. Nothing like that can happen between us. I'm not interested in any kind of relationship, especially with someone who has their head in the clouds and my former estate."

Instead of becoming annoyed, Evan felt a grin creep up on her face, because if she could make Clementine this annoyed or flustered, then she did care about her.

"You fancy me, don't you?" Evan grinned like a Cheshire cat.

Clementine clearly wasn't expecting that response and so couldn't hide her natural reaction of a sweet smile forming on her face.

"I do not."

Evan took her hand and chuckled. "Why are you smiling, then?"

Clementine was trying to do her best at hiding her smile, but clearly failing. "I am not smiling."

Evan kissed her hand. "I care about you, Clem, and there's no reason why we can't explore what we feel."

"I can't."

Evan cupped her cheek. "You can. You're just frightened. I'm not Isadora."

Before Clementine could respond, Evan leaned in and kissed Clementine deeply. Clementine didn't resist and in fact moaned as Evan traced the inside of her lips with her tongue.

When she eventually pulled away, she rested her forehead against Clementine's. "While I'm away, think about us, and what we could be together. An unstoppable force. There's nothing that we couldn't face, and nothing that's keeping us apart."

With that she got out of the car and quickly ran inside before she was drenched with the rain.

Chapter Sixteen

The next day Kay called for Clementine and they decided to walk to the old church, now The Meeting Place, for the trust meeting. The meeting where she would have to sell the idea of the bloody wind turbines. Archie had emailed her the details—the costs, and the green power it would generate for the village—and she couldn't really argue with them, but convincing the other villagers was another thing entirely.

"So? What got Evan Fox all ruffled up yesterday, as if I didn't know?" Kay said.

Clementine sighed and Kay looped her arm through hers. "Come on. You can talk to me."

"I'm not myself, Kay. I mean, I'm not behaving like myself," Clementine said.

"How so? I know there's some super-duper electricity between you."

"That's just it. I did that to her. At the office after everyone had gone, we kissed and ended up on my desk about to…Then Agatha called."

Kay squeezed her. "That's wonderful. You deserve some excitement in your life."

"That's the thing. What's between us is so electric, so desperate, and I've never been like that with anyone before. My lovers, not that I've had many, have always been nice, pleasant, but this feeling that Evan stirs up in me is frightening."

"Why not just go with it? Listen to your heart and your body?"

"What about my head? I need to be sensible. I've got my mother to look after, I can't fill my life with distractions, but every time I look at her, I want to rip her clothes off. I'm too old for this, for her, not to mention the fact that everyone would say I'm with her to get my hands back on Rosebrook."

"Who cares what people think. You know that's not the case, and Evan knows that. Don't listen to anyone else, and don't let your head get in the way of finding happiness."

"I care what people think. I do have some pride left in me, despite all the setbacks I've had to take on the chin," Clementine said. "Besides, it would be like having a relationship with a jumping bean. She has so much energy, and she's eight years younger than me."

Kay waggled her eyebrows. "I see that as a good thing. Just think about it, okay? She's a good person."

As they got nearer to The Meeting Place, they saw Mr. Fergus and waved to him.

"Well met, ladies," Fergus said.

"Hi, Fergus," Clementine said, "at least the rains stopped for us for tonight."

They'd had nearly nonstop rain for the last few weeks, torrential rain, a lot of the time.

"Yes, thank goodness. The river at the top of the village is quite high. We'll need to keep an eye on it. Now, shall I escort you good ladies in?"

❖

"Not bloody likely," Mr. O'Rourke said.

"Dad, language," Ash reprimanded him.

"I should say so, James," Fergus said. "Remember, there are ladies present."

"Sorry, Your Grace. But I've seen these things on the news, and they're an eyesore."

His reaction wasn't dissimilar to the one she'd had, but in the cold light of day, turbines made sense.

Mr. Murdoch joined in, saying, "So much for the trust, so much for giving us control of our village."

Clementine looked to Kay for support. "But if we don't change our ways and use greener energy, villages like this on the south coast will be underwater when the polar region warms up."

"Why do we have to be the vanguard, making all these changes?"

Mr. Mason said. "Murdoch is right. Fox said we would have control of how our village changed."

Clementine had to find a way of getting through to them. "It's not a matter of control. This trust is a partnership with Fox Toys. We have to compromise—after all, we are going to reap the benefit of all the money Ms. Fox is putting into the village, and in turn we have to be flexible on the things that are important to her."

Mr. Murdoch slammed his hand down on the table. "This is not her village, and I will not have one of those windmill things in my garden for anything."

Time to bring out the big guns. "I'm sorry to hear that, because it would more than halve your power bill every month."

"What?" Mr. Murdoch was quite caught off guard with that statement.

"Yes, but since that's not important to you…"

"Hang on, hang on. Will it?"

"Oh yes. Easily," Clementine said.

Mr. Murdoch grinned. "Now you're appealing to my finer nature. Tell us more."

Clementine looked at Kay and Fergus, who were grinning back at her. *Not a bad negotiator*, she told herself.

As Evan drove into Rosebrook, she sighed with relief. It had been a long and busy week launching *The Woodlanders 2*, but more than anything she'd missed Clementine. In fact being apart made her more convinced that Clementine was her love story.

They had texted back and forth, and although stiff at the start because of the way they'd parted, Clementine's warmth soon came back. Evan's parents were in the car behind, and she couldn't wait for them to meet Clem, and hopefully they would get on.

Evan slowed as the first cottages came into view at the start of the village, with scaffolding all around them. These were the uninhabited cottages that needed the most work. She pulled the car onto the side of the road. She looked in the mirror and confirmed her dad had pulled over as well.

"I feel nervous. I wish Clem was here." She was nervous because her parents' good opinion meant so much. She got out of the car.

Thankfully it had stopped raining—for a time, it had been thundering down on the journey from London. The forecasters had even warned that this might be the wettest summer on record. That was all they needed. Construction would be held up even more.

Her parents got out of the car. Her dad stretched out his arms and said, "This is amazing, kiddo."

Like her, her dad could find positivity in any situation. Her mother, on the other hand, was more down to earth. Lucky someone in the family had their feet on the ground.

Her mother got out and put on her sunglasses. "Show us around, Evan. There's still a lot to do, I see."

"Yeah, the rains really held us up." Her parents joined her at the side of the first cottage.

"Who would have thought," her dad said, "that our little Evan would own Rosebrook one day, eh, Cass?"

"Hmm, we spent some wonderful day trips here." Her mother reached out and touched the wall of the cottage.

"We're working on revised plans now." Evan pointed to various places around the house—the windowsills, the door frame—all were trimmed with seashells embedded in the cement. "This was Clem's idea, making every cottage a little different, rather than having them all uniform, because they were originally built at different times and they are all a bit different stylistically."

"What's the power source?" her mother asked.

"A battery powered by wind turbine. Clem wasn't too happy about it at first, but I convinced her of the benefits. She's been breaking it to the residents this week, while I'm away."

"Fantastic," her dad said. "Isn't it wonderful?"

"I've heard you talking about this duchess nonstop. Do you think it wise to allow the former family owner to act as chair of your trust?" her mother said.

"I knew I needed her onside to get things done. She may not have the land, but she's still the duchess to these people, their leader, and it turned out she really is the perfect person for the job. It's in her blood."

"Are you attracted to her, munchkin?" her mother said softly. "Because that could make things tricky on this project."

Evan couldn't conceal the truth from her parents. She nodded. "When I looked in her eyes the first time I saw her, fate smacked me about the head with a banjo. She's my love story—I'm sure of it."

Her father pulled her into a hug. "Didn't I tell you? Fate always finds the right one for you."

"Donny, we haven't even met her yet. She could be a gold-digger or just after getting her ancestral home back."

"She's not like that, Mum. I had to strong-arm her into working for the trust. She didn't want anything to do with the project at first. Clem blames her grandmother Isadora for blowing the family fortune and losing their home. When I first met her, she had an old broken-down car and worked as a freelance architect. Her mother is in a nursing home, and all her money goes to that. The last thing Clem wanted was to get on board with another dreamer like her grandmother."

"Hmm. I'll meet her before I pass judgement. Is she coming to dinner tonight?"

"I think so. She said she would the last time we talked on the phone," Evan said.

Her dad put his arm around her. "Don't listen to your mum. If I had listened to her, I would have never gotten a first date at the fiftieth time of asking."

Evan laughed. She loved the story of her mum and dad getting together.

Her mother rolled her eyes. "I'll withhold my judgement till tonight."

Evan took her mum's hand and kissed it. "I know you'll like her. She's not the typical duchess. She doesn't think she wants to be one, but her presence in this village is the only glue that kept them together. I want tonight to be special. The new housekeeper started work while I was away, so I've asked her to make us a fancy dinner. I know we're not fancy people, but I want Clem to experience a night like her parents and grandparents used to have. Black tie, champagne, eating in the dining room with lots of different wines, laughter, and genteel conversation. The full *Downton Abbey* type thing."

Her dad snapped his fingers. "That's why you wanted me to bring my dinner suit?"

"Yeah, but you didn't need much persuasion, Dad," Evan said.

"You two are like peas in a pod. I think your father would wear a tie on the beach if he could," her mother said. "You're making a lot of effort to woo this woman. What age is she?"

"She's eight years older, Mum."

"Ooh, toy boy," her dad said immediately.

"Come on, toy boy," her mother said. "Show me more. Onward."

❖

Clementine was both nervous and excited. Evan was calling for her any minute to take her to meet her parents and have dinner. She had hoped that her week away from Evan would cool her attraction and feelings, but the opposite had been the case.

She had missed Evan's positivity, her fervour for life, and Clementine's usual glass-half-empty attitude started to creep back in. The office had felt empty without Evan, and she was checking her phone constantly to see if there were any texts from her, something she had never done with anyone.

Clementine heard the door knocker and her heart jumped. She was going to see Evan again. She checked her hair, which was pulled up into a chignon, one last time and smoothed down her green cocktail dress.

She walked downstairs, opened the door, and her breath caught. Evan looked gorgeous, sexy, all of the above. She was wearing a modern dinner suit complete with bow tie and impeccably styled hair.

Evan bowed then kissed her hand. "You look stunning, Your Grace."

She got her title right for once. "You look very handsome, yourself."

Evan looked down at her suit with a satisfied grin and brushed off her lapel. "Dad and I thought we'd go the whole hog and make it special. I wanted tonight to be like the dinner parties Rosebrook used to have."

Clementine closed her door and took Evan's offered arm. "I remember nights like that when I was a little girl. I used to sit on the stairs and watch them all coming in the front door."

"Well, this will be fabulous. So, did you miss me? What am I saying? Of course you did."

Clementine couldn't help but laugh. From anyone else it would seem like arrogance, but Clementine knew Evan didn't take herself too seriously. It was all banter—and wooing, she was sure.

"How did your app launch go? I downloaded it, by the way, but I'm not really sure how to play it. I'm not a game sort of person."

"I'll show you later. It was amazing. We are number one in the app store, and a percentage of each game goes to forestry conservation in the country it's downloaded. A great business model, if I do say so myself."

"And you usually do. Your family has found a great way of working in the corporate world, making money, but with a conscience."

"We like to think so. My great-great-granddad, who started Fox Toys, was a religious man. A philanthropist a bit like Isadora. Our company was built with the attitude of helping make the world a better place, and then my mum came on board and really ramped it up. She's an amazing woman. How's your mother?"

"All right. The same as usual, although she's been losing weight. She doesn't like eating any more. The nurses give her build-up drinks to try to make up for it, but she won't always take them."

"I'm sorry. Is there anything I can do?" Evan asked.

Clementine sighed. "No, there's nothing anyone can do. It's part of the condition towards the end."

Evan stopped in the middle of the driveway and took Clementine into her arms. "I find a hug always helps when other things can't."

"Your hugs can." Clementine stepped back from the hug and said, "She's still holding on to Mr. Fox. It's given her a lot of comfort."

"I'm glad."

They reached the doorway and two torches were lit on either side of the entranceway. "The torches. Just like the old days," Clementine said happily.

"I told you I made an effort, my lady."

"The torches used to light the way for the carriages arriving."

The front doors magically opened to reveal a man in butler's uniform. "Where did he come from?"

"You got me the housekeeper, but I did some organizing myself. I asked the agency where you got the housekeeper, Sarah, from to send some extra staff for the night. Thank you, Winston."

"You are adorable sometimes, you know that?" Clementine admitted.

Evan grinned. "It has been said. Come on, let's meet Mum and Dad."

❖

Evan watched on with pride as Clementine chatted to her mother. It was nice to see this elaborate dining room being used as it was meant to.

Her father clapped her on the back and said, "What a smashing girl—sorry, woman, your mum will give me trouble. Smashing *woman* your Clem is."

The waitstaff came into the room and cleared away the delicious vegan meal they had just enjoyed.

"She's not mine yet, Dad. Clem's intelligent and careful and has a lot to deal with in her life. She's not about to jump into a relationship quickly." Evan took a drink of her wine.

"Kiddo, if she's the one, then make it happen. Don't just sit here on the sidelines hoping it'll all turn out right. Remember what your mother called me when I first asked her out?"

Evan chuckled softly. "A capitalist bastard."

"Exactly! But did I let that deter me?" he said. "No, I persisted, and here I am today with the most wonderful woman in the world."

"Clementine threw me out of her house the first time I met her."

"You see, she's a passionate woman. Go for it."

Her mother and Clementine looked right at them, and her mum said, "What are you two talking about in such hushed tones?"

Her father replied quickly, "How wonderful women are."

"I'm sure," her mother said. "Why don't we go through to the drawing room for coffee."

Her father jumped up quickly and said to Clementine, "Let me escort you, Your Grace."

Clementine giggled and took Donny's arm. Evan then offered her mother her arm and followed them through.

She heard her dad ask Clementine, "Have you tried the trampoline room? It's simply marvellous."

"What do you think, Mum?"

"She's a lovely woman. A little serious, but she has a lot to be serious about, I suppose, but she seems genuinely dedicated to your cause, this village, and making the world a better place."

"You approve, then?" Evan asked.

"If she's the one you want, then yes," her mother said.

"She's worried that people will think she just wants the house back."

"Then make her understand it doesn't matter to you. People, including your grandmother, thought I was after your dad's money. I won them over."

"I'll try. She's my dream girl, Mum."

"Woman, Evan," her mum corrected her.

"Woman—sorry, Mum."

Chapter Seventeen

Clementine was starting to relax and enjoy herself. She had been nervous at dinner, talking to Cassia. She was such a powerful personality, and such a beautiful older woman. Her short ash-blond hair suited her perfectly. It also felt so strange to be a guest here. The last time she and her parents had dinner in the dining room was her last birthday before her dad died.

Clementine could see why Evan liked powerful women. It was obvious who was in charge in the Fox family. She was sitting with Cassia on the couch in the drawing room while Evan got the village plans so they could show her parents.

"Are you enjoying working with Evan?" Cassia asked.

"Yes, it's a lot of fun. She's so exuberant in all that she does. It really lifts the whole office."

Cassia pointed over to Donny, who was trying to get to grips with Fox Toys' new app. "I think you can tell who she gets that from. I try my best to keep their feet on the ground. I'm sure you do that with Evan."

Clementine laughed. "There have been times when she needed some grounding. One day she got quite down because she had too many ideas—her brain was working too fast."

"Yes." Cassia sighed. "That happens, but I'm glad she had you to help her."

"Evan's been kind to me and everyone in this village. She's kind, considerate, a gentlewoman."

Cassia put her coffee cup down on the table. "My daughter is very keen on you, Clem."

Clementine didn't know what to say. There was a part of her

that thought Evan's attention was just a lot of flirtation, but she had obviously talked to her mother about her.

"I like Evan very much too," Clementine replied.

"It's more than *like* for her, so if you don't feel the same way, be careful with her heart. She's never had a long-term girlfriend or anything serious. She always bought in to the love story that her dad told her about us. She's waited, and you seem to be the one she wants, so if you don't feel the same, then don't play along if you don't mean it."

Clementine was quite taken aback. Evan had never had a long-term girlfriend. So this was serious to her. These feelings they had for each other were serious.

"I won't, I care about her too, I just—" Clementine was interrupted by Evan bounding into the room.

"I've got them." Evan held up the folded-up plans.

"Did you get the photos from my suitcase?" Cassia asked.

"Right here, Mum." Evan handed them to her mother.

"I brought some pictures of our family days out here in Rosebrook when Evan was a child. I thought it would be nice to look at them."

"That would be lovely. I imagine Evan was the cutest little girl."

Evan laid the plans down on the coffee table. "Hey, baby pictures after the plans. You don't need to embarrass me yet, Mum."

Donny and Cassia sat side by side to see the plans, and Evan knelt down by the coffee table.

"Okay, so the main things are housing, obviously. The refurb plans have been altered to Clem's suggestion of making them reflect the cottages' history and position in the village."

Evan pointed to each section of the housing units. "We have the Seascape Houses, the Woodlanders Cottages—"

"Great name," Donny interrupted.

"Thanks, Dad." Evan grinned. "And the Countryside Cottages. We are getting applications for our new community online—"

Clementine added, "We've had a lot of interest already, Evan. We'll need to start going through them soon."

"Absolutely. So, we have likeminded people who want to live here, who want to build a better community, a safe, inclusive community. Each house will have a wind turbine and a battery power cell, to cut consumption of electricity from the grid. How did the trust members take the news about the turbines, Clem?" Evan had figured maybe the turbine news would go over better coming from Clem.

"Like I did at the beginning. Then I appealed to their finer nature and told them that their bill would halve. They seemed more inclined after that."

Evan nodded happily and went back to the plans. "Of course we need employment, and we'll have the shop, and the pub, but the main sources of employment will be the beer factory and the toy factory. Dad, I told you about my plans to make toys and sensory equipment here in the village."

"Yes, fantastic idea. Making toys right here in Britain. Back to your great-great-grandfather's days."

"And what about conservation of the plants and wildlife of Rosebrook?" her mother asked.

Evan knew that would be upmost in her mother's mind. "This big area of land here is going to be a bee garden."

"Wonderful," her mother said. "Bees are vital to our food supplies."

"Yup, we have it all in hand, Mum. Don't worry. Once we have the community set up and residents moved in, we'll have teams of people looking after the hedgerows, litter picking, animal welfare volunteers…"

Clementine leaned forward and pointed to a big space on the map. "We wanted to turn this area into allotments so the villagers can grow their own organic produce, and we're keeping the army barracks as a piece of social history, but we're not quite sure what to do with them yet."

"What do you think, Mum, Dad?" Evan asked.

"It's fantastic," her father said. "In fifty years' time there will be Fox eco villages the world over."

"Let them finish one first, Donny. I think it's brave, it's bold, and I'm very proud of you, munchkin. You too, Clementine. It couldn't have been easy to see your village taken over like this."

Clem smiled at Evan, and Evan could feel her heart pounding hard.

"Maybe not at first, but the more I got to know Evan, the more I knew this was something special."

"Evan's always been a special kid," her mother said. "Let me show you her holiday pictures." She lifted the pictures, and Evan's heart sank. Now she was going to be embarrassed.

❖

Evan felt her cheeks flush with heat and held her hands over her eyes, as her mum and Clementine laughed and *aww*ed at Evan's childhood pictures.

"Oh, she's so cute!" Clementine said.

"I know," her mother said. "That was taken outside the ruined cottages at the beginning of the village, I think, and that T-shirt with the dog on it was her favourite. I couldn't get her out of the thing. It had a squeaker in it, you see. She was constantly pressing her chest. Squeak, squeak, squeak, it went day and night."

"Oh God." Evan looked to her dad for support. "Dad? Mum's ruining my cool dapper image."

"Well, you were cute. The cutest child in all the world." Her dad grinned with pride.

Her mother went on, "Of course, that was the only T-shirt she wanted to keep on. The rest of the time she wanted to run around with no top on, like a boy."

"Right, that's it." Evan got up and made her way over to the couch. "No more, Mum. It's embarrassing."

Clementine took her hand and pulled her down beside her. "Oh, stop it. I'm enjoying seeing these. You're such a cutie."

"It's the beach photos next," her mother said as she passed them one by one to Clementine.

"Look, Evan. Here's one of you playing in the World War II gun placements. What's that you've got in your hand?"

Evan sighed. She would just have to go with it. "A large stick I'm using as a rifle. Mum didn't allow me toy guns when I was little, so I improvised."

"I don't know why I bothered banning toys of violence, because anything she picked up, she turned into a weapon," her mother said.

Evan squirmed for a few more photos, her mum and Clementine loving every embarrassing image, until one made Clementine go quiet.

"What's wrong, Clem?"

"I don't believe it. Can I see the other ones of the beach, Cassia?" Clementine asked.

Clementine looked at the next five photos, and they were all the same. A young Evan was building sandcastles, playing with a beach ball, and paddling in the water, and all the time a younger version of herself was sitting feet away, in her favourite spot.

She gave the first picture to Evan and pointed. "It's me. I'm in your beach photos."

"You're kidding," Evan said with shock.

"I'm not, and look at this one. I caught your beach ball and was throwing it back for you."

"That is astonishing," Cassia said.

"It's fate, kids." Donny's comment was what Clementine was hearing in her heart.

Just then there was a loud crack of thunder. The evening had become surreal.

❖

Evan walked back into the drawing room after escorting the waitstaff and her housekeeper out to their cars. She had dispensed with her dinner jacket and undone the buttons on her waistcoat.

Clementine was sitting alone on the couch. Her parents had discreetly withdrawn to their bedroom for the night.

"Well, that's them off. It's bucketing down out there, and the thunder is still going strong," Evan said.

"Fergus said the river was high. We'll need to be careful."

"I'll get some of the builders to put some sandbags along the river just in case." Evan clapped her hands together. "Now for a drink. What can I get you?"

"A small brandy, I think. I need it. I'm still in shock," Clementine said.

Evan poured out the drinks and brought them over to the couch. "It just goes to show we were meant to meet."

She gave Clementine her drink and sat down, slipping her arm along the back of the couch, like a teenage kid at the cinema.

"Do you believe in fate?" Clementine asked.

Evan nodded. "I think so. I mean, everything about my life has been leading up to this. I've always been connected to Rosebrook. Life has always been pushing me here. Maybe Isadora wanted me here to finish her work and meet you."

"I've never really believed in fate, but those pictures, you coming here—it's, I don't know, there feels like there is a reason." Clementine looked over to the rug in front of the fire. "You know, I used to lie there on the rug colouring and drawing. It was a nice safe place."

Evan wanted to get closer to Clementine to pick up where they'd left off before she went back to London. She had to be brave.

Before she could say anything, Clementine said, "I finished your essay."

"Really, what did you think?" Evan asked.

"It was very good. I saw a different side to Isadora, the young idealist side to her. I think I would like to have known her then, before she got lost in pursuing her dream at all costs. She reminds me of Captain Ahab in *Moby-Dick* with her relentlessness to make this place work."

Evan put down her drink and moved closer. "Do you think you have a little more sympathy towards her?"

"Maybe. She made mistakes and was unlucky. Her cause might have been noble—to bring affordable housing to the masses—but somewhere along the way she forgot about us, her family."

Evan stroked her fingertips down Clementine's cheek, making her shiver. "I would never forget about you, Clem."

Clementine bit her lip, and Evan's heart thundered like the storm outside. She'd been dreaming of those lips and couldn't hold herself back any longer. She leaned in to Clementine's lips and whispered, "I think you're my destiny."

Clementine closed the space between them and kissed her, pulling at her bow tie and undoing her shirt collar, and it was Evan's turn to shiver as Clementine gently scratched the skin around her collarbone.

Their kiss became fervent, and as their passion mounted, lightning lit up the room, and a huge crack of thunder crashed. The lights went out in an instant and Clementine pulled away.

"What happened?"

"I don't know," Evan replied, "but every time I try to kiss you, something interrupts us. Let me go and check the fuse box."

"I'll come with you. I don't like the dark."

Evan held her hand out. "Come on, m'lady. I'll keep you safe."

She used the torch on her iPhone to check the fuse box down in the kitchen. "Everything seems fine. It must be the stormy weather has brought down the electrical lines or something. We can call someone in the morning to get it fixed. You see, this won't happen when we get the wind turbines and the Powerwalls in each house. We'll always have backup power then."

"Okay, okay. You've made your point. I should text the Tucker twins to make sure they're okay. They were probably already in bed by the time the electricity went out, but I'd just worry if I don't find out."

Clementine quickly typed out a message. She didn't want to call and disturb them if they were already sleeping.

As she sent the text, Evan said, "The power from the wind turbine should have kicked in. It must have gotten hit too. Listen, I don't like the idea of you alone in the gatehouse without power. Why don't you stay here—in your mother's room. It is the duchess's room, after all."

Clementine knew Evan made her bedroom in the duke's room, and there was an interconnecting set of doors between the two. She would feel safe, and she would also be close to Evan.

She got a message back from Agatha Tucker that they were safe and well, and in bed. "The Tuckers are fine, so yes, I'd like that."

Evan's face lit up with excitement and happiness. "Really? Excellent, I'll give you something of mine to wear. Let's go."

❖

Clementine hung her dress up in the wardrobe and closed the door. Evan had given her a large T-shirt to wear, and it was comfortable.

There was a knock on the connecting door. "Come in."

Evan walked in and hung back by the door. "Are you okay?"

Clementine saw what Evan was wearing and walked right up to her. "You look adorable, Foxy Loxy."

Evan wore a navy-blue pair of sleep shorts with foxes printed on them, and a matching blue T-shirt on top.

"Thank you," Evan said. "I always try to look jaunty for every occasion."

Clementine took her hand, needing the comfort of her touch.

"How does it feel to be back here?" Evan said.

"Strange isn't the word to describe standing here again. The last time I was here was when I tried to buy the house back from one of the previous developers. I tried to put together a fund among all the remaining distant family members. I thought I had enough, but then my cousin, the one I told you about, pulled out at the last minute."

"Bastard. Why would he do that?" Evan asked.

"It turned out he had been stringing me along. He's a bitter man, and when my father died, he was extremely disappointed that

I inherited, being that he was the only male left. When he called me, he laughed, he actually laughed. I stood in the middle of the floor and cried. My last hope had gone."

As she spoke, the tears returned, and Evan pulled her into her arms. "Hey, hey, don't cry. That excuse for a guy is a complete and utter prick."

Clementine grasped Evan's T-shirt and rubbed her face on her chest. She was so comforting. When Evan was this close to her, Clementine felt safe, and comforted.

"I think I lost my last bit of hope that day."

"But what you didn't know was that old Foxy Loxy was on her way into your life, to make your village and your home a better place."

Clementine chuckled and wiped away her tears. "That's right. You've made me feel hope again, Evan."

After they stood there for a while enjoying holding each other, Evan decided to take a chance, just like her dad had told her to.

"Clem? Would you like to sleep beside me tonight? No funny business, I promise."

"How can I resist the lure of those fox sleep shorts?" Clementine joked.

"No one could," Evan joked back. "Come on, then."

"Where are your parents sleeping? They won't mind, will they?" Clementine asked.

"If they had been there when the lights went out, they would have suggested it themselves."

Evan pulled Clem by the hand into her bedroom, or the duke's bedroom, as Clementine would have known it.

"It's so much cosier than I remember it," Clementine said.

"Yeah, now the heating is revamped, it's nice and toasty," Evan said.

"It was always cold when we lived here."

"You jump in, I'm just going to finish up in the bathroom." Evan brushed her teeth and sprayed on some cologne. She couldn't wait to get back to Clementine.

But she was suddenly nervous when she went back into the bedroom. Her palms were sweaty and her mouth drying up. All those nights alone here, she had been imagining what it would be like to have Clem here, and that moment had finally arrived.

"Um…shall I put on the TV, or—" Evan smacked her forehead. "I'm forgetting the electricity is out."

"That's okay. I think I'd rather just listen to the rain and thunder, and enjoy your company anyway."

Evan slipped into bed and listened to the rain battering the windows. Her nervousness didn't ease.

Then out of the darkness Clementine said, "This is nice."

"Yeah it is. It's the first time I've gone to bed without the TV on since I left home."

Clementine raised herself up on her elbow, her blond hair cascading down her neck. "Why is that?"

Evan hesitated. Should she tell the truth? It would make her look weak, but she couldn't look in Clementine's eyes and lie to her.

"I hate to be alone."

Clementine cupped her cheek, "Oh, my darling." Then Clem gave her the kind of kiss that made her toes curl.

Clementine never wanted the kiss to end. Evan's honest confession made the love and caring she was trying to keep under control flood out. Her hair cascaded onto Evan's face and Evan grasped it gently and moaned.

One of the things she loved about Evan was that she was true to herself. If she experienced an emotion, she embraced it and didn't hold back like she did.

She pulled away from the kiss and gazed down at Evan. "Don't ever change, Foxy."

Evan stroked the hair away from her eyes and said, "The only thing I want to change is how close I am to you. You're the most beautiful woman I've ever seen and the most graceful. You take every problem life throws at you and don't complain, but get on with it. You are my dream woman."

All Clementine wanted to do was feel Evan's skin against hers, but it was so long since she had done anything like this. In fact there was no other experience she'd had that made her feel like this.

Evan reached down for the hem of Clem's T-shirt and pulled it off in one go, leaving her naked apart from her lacy knickers.

She gasped and said, "You're beautiful, Clem." She reached out towards her breasts, but hesitated. "May I touch you?"

"Please," Clementine said.

Evan cupped her breast and squeezed softly. Clementine moaned and put her head back. She hadn't experienced this intense need to be touched before, the need for Evan to touch her, and so she just paused for a time and let her body feel.

Evan let go of one of her breasts and trailed her fingers down the centre of Clementine's chest, then her stomach, and teased the waistband of her knickers.

Clementine's sex was pulsating, anticipating what Evan's touch would be like. Evan rolled her over and began to kiss her more fervently.

In between her kisses Evan said, "I want to touch you everywhere, make you feel what I feel in my heart."

Evan was overwhelmed with what she was feeling. Her heart was bursting, and she could only hope Clementine felt a fraction of what she did, but she would show her. Evan would love her body until Clementine understood what her heart felt.

When she took Clementine's nipple into her mouth, Clementine grasped her hair painfully. She pulled back and blew on the nipple.

"You like that?"

"Um, uh-huh. Yes."

Evan used her tongue to lick and flick her nipple while still squeezing her other breast. Clementine rocked her hips against Evan's, clearly needing some relief.

The fact that this beautiful lady, this gentlelady, wanted her, blew her mind, but she wanted to feel, to taste just how much Clementine wanted this.

She let go of her nipple and kissed her way down to Clementine's sex.

"Yes, Evan. I need you."

Evan could see the wetness through Clementine's tiny underwear. She couldn't resist her first impulse to lick her sex and taste her. Her inclination to go slow and enjoy every second was forgotten after that first taste, when Clementine's hands rested on the back of her head, encouraging her not to take it slow.

She didn't even stop to take Clementine's underwear off. She just pushed it to the side and licked as she had before. Clementine's legs tensed and her hips raised off the bed.

"Oh God, Evan."

Encouraged that she was doing exactly what her lover wanted, she opened her up and placed short teasing, rhythmic strokes on her clit. It had just been instinct, but she'd obviously hit on something her lover liked.

Clementine's hips started to undulate in time with her strokes. "God, where did you learn that, Foxy?"

Evan stopped and smiled to herself, then drew long slow circles around the outside of her clit. Clementine moaned at the loss of the strokes directly on her clit, so Evan began again. Then each time her lover's breathing got more erratic, her hips matched, and her moans more desperate, Evan stopped abruptly and circled around the outside again.

After the third time of doing this, Clementine's groans almost became cries. "Please, please, make me come."

Evan teased Clementine's entrance with her tongue a few times and then got back to her clit. Clementine closed her legs tightly around Evan's head as if trying to control her from stopping, but Evan had no intention of stopping this time.

She went faster and could hear her lover was going to come soon. Then Clementine went still and almost crushed her head with her thighs. As quickly as she tensed up, all the tension was let go just as quickly. Clementine was left audibly trying to get her breath back.

Evan moved back up and stroked Clementine's hair from her face. "Are you all right, Clem?"

"Yes. That was—"

Instead of answering she pulled Evan down into a kiss. Evan got caught up in the moment and the feeling of being close to Clementine again. Her mind was mush, and all she could think was how much she wanted, how much she needed Clementine

Evan's hips betrayed what her body wanted and started to thrust between Clementine's thighs. She kissed, licked, and gently bit at Clementine's neck, making her shiver.

Clementine moved her hand down between them and slipped her fingers into Evan's sex, splitting her fingers around her clit.

"Oh yes," Evan said.

"This is what you want, isn't it?" Clementine whispered in her ear.

Clementine's breath made her shiver. "Yeah."

It was perfect. She got to be on top, the way she liked, and thrust herself onto Clementine's fingers. Controlling the pace, but giving herself over to Clementine completely, being vulnerable, and enjoying the deep kisses she was giving her.

She so wanted to take it slow, but her body was demanding she thrust her hips faster, so she could assuage this deep need inside her. Evan could feel herself ready to lose control. She pulled away from Clementine's lips and buried her face in her neck. She moaned and said, "Oh yeah."

Her thrusts took her to the precipice, and she fell off into the deepest, almost painful orgasm.

She collapsed on Clementine, and she wrapped her arms around her, soothing her as she regained control.

"Evan?" Clementine kissed her head.

That was so mind-blowing. Evan knew Clementine was the right one for her. Fate sent her here, and now all she had to do was convince Clementine that she would love her forever.

Evan started to wake and her memory of last night filtered slowly back through her mind. She smiled and opened her eyes, expecting to find Clementine next to her, but she wasn't in bed.

She sat up and was relieved to find Clementine was still in the room, sitting on the wide windowsill, her knees pulled up to her chest. She was staring out the window, looking lost, deep in thought.

Evan was almost frightened to let Clem know she was awake. What if she said this was a mistake? She dreaded that. Clementine could see into all her darkest places, the places where she was fearful, anxious, not the happy-go-lucky Evan Fox that she showed the world. It was such a relief for someone to see the real her, and still care, still kiss, still touch her.

Clementine was the strong woman Evan needed in her life, and she prayed that she wouldn't run from her.

"Clem?" Evan said while she sat up on the bed.

Clementine looked back and gave her an anxious smile, which made Evan nervous.

"Morning."

"Are you okay, Clem?"

She nodded. "I used to sit here when I was a little girl. It was my favourite spot to survey the estate."

"And here you are again," Evan said.

Clementine just nodded in response. Something wasn't right. Evan got up and slipped on her sleep shorts but didn't worry about a T-shirt. She walked over and kissed Clementine on the cheek.

"Are you sure you're all right? After last night and everything?" Evan sat on the large sill with Clementine.

"Last night was wonderful. I can't remember ever feeling like I did last night."

Evan reached over and took her hand. "Then why do you look worried, or whatever?"

"It's not you. It could never be you. I woke up and walked over here just to see if everything was all right after the storm. Then I remembered the day we left here, and I sat here for what I thought was the last time."

"Yeah? And what?" Evan couldn't quite work out what the problem was.

"I began to think, here I am again, in my family home, and all because I slept with the new owner."

Evan was hurt at that remark. "You really think that?"

"No, Evan. That's what other people will think. The poverty-stricken duchess gets herself a cushy job with the estate, and then sleeps her way back into the house."

"Who cares what people think, Clem? All that matters are our opinions, our truth," Evan said firmly.

"What is our truth, Foxy?"

"That we have something amazing between us. My dad has told me ever since I can remember that when he first saw my mum, he felt like he had been hit over the head with a banjo. I've carried that story with me as a benchmark for the people I've dated, but those dates were always just one or two with each person because I didn't feel it. Then I come here ready to start a new chapter in my life. The first time I met you…remember?"

Clementine laughed. "I was beastly to you. I was having a hard time, and the house was gone for good with you buying it—but I'm sorry."

Evan took her hand. "I don't need any sorrys. When you opened the door to me, that banjo I'd been waiting for smacked me so hard around the head, I should have had concussion."

"Really? You liked me since then?"

"Yeah, but you weren't ready to accept me. Now I think you know I am committed to the village, and a half decent person."

"Of course you're a half decent person, you're a wonderful person. It's just too soon," Clementine said. "Too soon for people to know. I was brought up with these people, and I don't want them to think I'm jumping in bed with you, to work my way in here. I have my pride."

"Okay, as long as you'll give us a chance. It's nobody's business but ours," Evan agreed.

"There's Archie and the office staff too."

"What about Archie?"

"I've heard her warning you about me."

Evan sighed and stood up. "It's only because she cares about me. Plus, she has a very jaded view of commitment and relationships. She's relationship phobic, but she'll come around. I don't want you to care about gossip or whispering behind your back. Do you not think I get looks and whispers for the way I present myself? How awkward it is when I walk into a public lavatory? I can hear it, I can feel the stares, but I choose positivity. I live by it."

Clementine stood up and put her arms around Evan's waist. "And I choose to think the worst because then no one ever disappoints me."

Evan cupped her cheeks. "I'm going to show you that there's a different way to look at things. Positivity rules, and no one can change how we feel about each other by gossip or tittle-tattle."

Clementine couldn't help but want to try Evan's way. "Your enthusiasm is so infectious. You know that?"

"That's my job, m'lady, Your Highness. Don't worry about anything else—just concentrate on enjoying each day." Evan swept her off her feet, making Clementine laugh, and said, "I'm going to show you how fun life is, but why don't we have this further discussion in bed."

"Are discussions not best held sitting or standing?" Clementine asked.

Evan scrunched her eyebrows and pursed her lips. "Oh no. I always think more clearly when I'm lying down."

Chapter Eighteen

Evan was right. She did make life more fun for Clementine. The next couple of weeks were as happy as Clementine could remember. After a day's work at the office, she and Evan would eat dinner together, walk on the beach, spend time watching TV together, or as Evan called it, "Netflix and chill." Nobody knew they were seeing each other except Kay. Clementine couldn't keep it from her closest friend, and Kay encouraged her to explore the relationship.

The weather had cleared up, although the river was still high, letting the builders get caught up on lost time. The residents' cottages had been mended—from leaky roofs to stonework needing to be redone, kitchens and bathrooms refitted. Even the most critical villagers, the Murdochs and Mr. Mason, were delighted with the improvements and the cut in their electricity bills from the new wind turbines.

This evening was an important one for the village. The pub was reopening under the landlordship of Rupert's husband, Jonah. To celebrate, Evan was hosting a party in the beer garden with a barbecue.

Evan, of course, took charge of the barbecue and was having the time of her life. Clementine and Kay sat at a picnic table with the Tucker twins and Ash. Everyone else stood around chatting, and Kay's boys sat in the corner playing Evan's new app on their iPad.

The Murdochs, Ash's dad James, and Mr. Mason had been initially quiet when they met Rupert and Jonah. They had never met a gay male couple, Clementine supposed, but within twenty minutes Jonah, a big bear of a man, had the other men onside, telling naughty jokes and discussing the finer points of real beer.

"Look at her," Kay said, gesturing towards Evan. "She's having the time of her life."

Clementine chuckled and shook her head as she watched Evan in full chef whites and a chef's hat, dancing away as she cooked the food.

"She likes to play dress up. I don't think she's progressed from nursery level sometimes," Clementine said.

Agatha, who was holding a near empty glass of sherry, said, "We think she's a breath of fresh air to this village. Don't we, Ada?"

Ada was chirpy despite still being in plaster and a wheelchair. "Oh yes, indeed. This is a lovely afternoon. It's quite a treat for us."

Clementine's heart sighed in the most nauseatingly romantic way. She'd never been a romantic, had always held a disdain for romantic movies and books, and here she was, her heart sighing at the sight of her lover in a silly chef's hat.

Jonah interrupted them with some more drinks. "Ladies, some more sherry?"

"Oh yes, Jonah. Fill them up," Ada said, handing him her glass.

After he refilled the drinks he left to take more drinks around.

"Isn't he just a lovely big man," Agatha said.

"Yes," Ada agreed, "like Thor, one of those big strong Greek gods."

"*Norse* gods." Ash laughed.

"I think our elder ladies have taken a shine to Jonah," Kay whispered.

Fergus and Archie, who had been talking, walked over to their table.

Archie said, "Food will be ready in a few minutes."

Clementine stood up. "Why don't I go and make a plate up for you and Ada and Agatha, before there's a rush."

"Good idea," Kay said with a wink, clearly spotting her ulterior motive of wanting to talk to Evan.

As she approached Evan from behind, she heard her singing along to the music playing in the background.

"Enjoying yourself, Foxy?"

Evan jumped. "God, I was lost in my own world there. What can I do for you, m'lady?"

"I'm here to get the Tucker twins food, but secretly I wanted to see you."

"Lucky me," Evan said.

Evan couldn't believe how lucky she was. The past few weeks had been amazing. Clementine was opening up to her more every day, and they were just loving every moment they were spending together. The only thing that irked Evan was that, apart from Kay and Archie, no one knew they were together. She didn't see the need for the secrecy any more, but Clementine was insistent that she wasn't ready to go public.

"So how's the food going, grill master?" Clementine asked.

"Perfectly." Evan tended two barbecues side by side. She pointed to the one on her right. "This one is for all the meat products, and the one next to it has all the vegan and vegetable choices."

"You don't feel uncomfortable cooking the meat? You want me to do it?"

"No, I'm fine. It's obviously not ideal, but I'm seeing this as a teaching moment. Everyone who's having a meat burger has agreed to try the vegan plant-based burgers." She pointed to the vegan burgers. "These bad boys come from a plant-based butcher's in London, and they are as near meat as you could get. I think they'll surprise a lot of people."

"A plant-based butcher? Seriously? How does that work?" Clementine asked.

"They're popping up in all major cities now. They use plant-based ingredients to make meat-style products. They make it look like a butcher's shop. Very cool."

Clementine chuckled. "You are positive about everything, aren't you? Even serving vegan burgers to farmers. That takes guts."

"Nah, I just believe in compromise and bringing people over to your side of things, through understanding and tolerance."

"I bet your mum wouldn't."

"You're right. She's a firebrand, but I got the mellowness from my dad." Evan took Clementine's hand discreetly and leaned over and whispered, "Do you fancy meeting inside the pub after I've fed these people for a bit of a kiss in the basement?"

Clementine laughed. "You say the most romantic things."

"Is the food ready yet?" Fergus asked as he walked up behind them.

To Evan's annoyance, Clementine snatched her hand away.

"Any minute, Fergus," Clementine answered.

Evan was getting frustrated with this. This had happened too often, and the feeling of rejection Evan felt was bubbling away underneath and was going to explode eventually.

They were going to London for a few days at the end of the week. The interviews for prospective residents of Rosebrook cottages were taking place at Fox Toys. Evan was looking forward to showing

Clementine her other world, and she was determined that they were going to talk about this.

Evan wanted to shout about her new relationship from the mountaintop, not hide away like they were doing something wrong.

❖

Clementine held her mum's hand. "Mama, I'm going away for a few days. I want you to promise you'll listen the to nurses and eat when they ask you to."

"Are you going to school, Clemy?"

"I'll just be a few days, okay?" It filled Clementine with worry to leave her mother. She'd never been away from her for more than a day before, but she had to go. She and Evan were holding interviews at Fox Toys for the first phase of cottages, and Evan was excited to show her London offices to Clementine.

She gave her mum a kiss and a hug. "I'll be back soon, Mum."

On her way out she saw the sister in charge. "I can be reached at any time and I'll come straight back."

"Don't worry, Your Grace. We'll look after her. Enjoy your few days away," said Sister.

Clementine walked to the front door and put up her umbrella before descending the steps from the nursing home.

The rain was back with a vengeance, and if this summer didn't show the effects of global warming, she didn't know what did. They had been going from some of the hottest days on record to torrential rain and storms, from one day to the next. Meeting Evan and Cassia Fox had educated her to the problems, and their activism was certainly rubbing off on her.

Evan and her green Beetle were waiting at the bottom of the steps. Evan jumped out and hurried around to open the door for Clementine.

"You didn't have to get out in this rain," Clementine said.

"Good manners cost nothing, m'lady. Now get in and we'll be off, Your Grace."

When Evan started the engine, Clementine said, "No romantic audiobook this time?"

"No need. I'm living my romance story right now."

That comment left Clementine dumbfounded. *She's serious.*

They were soon off on the road to London. Clementine couldn't wait to see where Evan lived. When they pulled into the gated driveway of what looked like an old building, she couldn't have been more surprised. The building called Garden Mews was sectioned off into modest flats, by the look of it. At the side of the building was a line of garages, and Evan pulled her car into one.

"This is not what I was expecting, Foxy," Clementine said.

"What were you expecting?"

"I don't know, a dockside penthouse or something?"

"Nah. That's not me. I like life simple. This building used to be a baker's. It's been here for over a hundred years, but it's been made into flats."

Evan was the most down-to-earth businesswoman she had ever come across and, despite her flash, enthusiastic nature, was extremely humble.

"Which one's yours?" Clementine asked.

"Bottom floor. Here." Evan reached into her pocket and handed a set of keys to Clementine. "You take these. The fob will get you into the lobby. I'll bring in the bags, save you from getting wet."

"A true gent."

Evan smiled and saluted her. "I always aim to please, m'lady."

Clementine ran for the lobby area and waited for Evan. She came in drenched from the rain.

"You're soaking wet," Clementine said.

"It's okay. I'm not made of sugar. Let's get inside."

Evan opened the door and led Clementine into a large airy flat. From the front door you walked into an open-plan living area. The kitchen was on the other side of the large open space, with a breakfast table beside it. A pool table, a vintage arcade machine, and a pinball table sat in the living area. Above them was a balcony which you got to by a spiral staircase.

"This is so sweet."

"Head up, and I'll bring the bags."

Clementine walked upstairs and saw it was actually quite a big space, as the large bed must have been super king size.

Evan plonked the bags down and said, "What do you think?"

"It's so cosy. No wonder you like it here. So different from Rosebrook."

"Yeah, it's been great having you with me at Rosebrook." Evan clapped her hands together. "So what do you fancy tonight? Dinner out at the best restaurant London has, and then drinks at a swanky lesbian wine bar I know, or—"

Clementine wrapped her arms around Evan's neck. "Or?"

"Or we have takeaway dinner and cosy down here for the night."

Clementine smiled, then kissed Evan lightly on the lips. "I think takeaway and cosiness sound perfect."

"I was hoping you'd say that."

❖

Later they lay in bed with some soft romantic music playing in the background. Evan was in heaven, with Clementine lying with her head on Evan's chest.

Evan stroked Clementine's hair and let out a contented sigh.

"What was that for?" Clementine asked.

"It was contentment and happiness. We eat a quick dinner, forgo the movie, and you drag me to bed. What could make me happier?"

"You didn't take much convincing." Clementine kissed her chest. "Besides I've got a lot of time to make up for. Before you came along, I hadn't had sex in six years."

"Six years? Well, I'm glad I'm young and fit to be able to service your needs, m'lady."

Clementine leaned up on her elbow. "Ooh, you make it sound like you're the gardener who's attending to the lonely lady of the manor. Sexy."

Evan reached up and stroked Clementine's cheek. "You know I do have toys for adults if you're interested in making up for lost time."

"Okay, I'm game to try anything with my toy boy."

Clementine laughed as Evan jumped up like a shot and hurried over to the wardrobe, then the bathroom. She came back with a distinctive bulge in her underwear, and Clementine groaned internally while a heavy beat started inside.

Evan jumped under the covers quickly, suddenly looking a little unsure of herself. "Uh, this is new, by the way. I haven't—"

Clementine touched Evan's chest and drew her fingernails down her sensitized skin. "What's wrong? Are you uncomfortable or something?"

"No, I bought this last year. I always wanted to use one, but there was never the opportunity. I mean, I only went on first or second dates at the most, and it's not really something you bring up on a second date and—"

Evan was babbling because she was nervous. Clementine could

see their difference in age now. Evan liked strong women, so she would be that for her.

She pushed Evan onto her back and straddled her.

"Clem, I'm not—"

Clementine leaned over and kissed Evan sweetly. "I know you like to be on top, Foxy, but I think you need the older lady of the manor to teach you how to make love with this."

Evan groaned. Oh God. Clementine had read her mind. Since Evan had begun staying at Rosebrook, she'd had a few fantasies of Clementine in her role as duchess.

"You read my mind, Your Grace. I've had a few fantasies."

"Oh? What about?"

"Just like you said. You as duchess calling your gardener or workman to her room to service her." Evan grinned.

Clementine's eyes lit up. "Oh, really?" Clementine traced her nail along her lips. "I've called you to my room, and…what?"

"You say 'get undressed and lie on the bed' and use me for your own wicked purposes." Evan couldn't help but smile.

"Oh, naughty." Clementine kissed her deeply, sliding her tongue into Evan's mouth.

Evan felt Clementine lift her hips and ease the tip of the strap-on inside her. Evan kept her hips still for the moment and allowed Clementine to set her own pace.

Clementine lowered her hips inch by inch, until she let out a long groan. "Oh, you're quite big, aren't you?"

"Yes, ma'am." Evan tried to sound as deferential as she could.

Evan couldn't be more turned on. She was inside Clementine, and she was beginning to move her hips. Evan let herself do the same until their rhythms matched.

"God, this feels amazing," Evan said.

"Yes." Clementine put her hands on either side of Evan's head and closed her eyes. "You feel good inside me."

Clementine's words were enough for Evan's orgasm to build fast, and she knew what she was doing. Clementine sat up again and ground her hips down on Evan, making the base of the strap-on tightly rub against her clit.

Evan arched her back, thrusting against Clementine even more. "Jesus, you can use my cock anytime, m'lady."

Clementine moaned when she said that and started to thrust up and down faster. "I hope that's a promise, gardener."

"Promise." Evan put her hands on Clementine's hips, holding her tightly as they thrust faster towards orgasm.

Orgasm came up on Evan suddenly, and she lost control. "Fuck, I'm coming. Sorry."

Evan's hips moved erratically as her orgasm washed over her. She tried to pull Clementine's hips and push as deeply as she could inside her. She tried to catch her breath, but her sex was still on fire.

Evan looked up and saw Clementine, her eyes screwed shut and pleasure etched on her face. Just when Evan thought Clem was going to come, she said, "Need more."

Evan wasn't quite sure what she meant.

Clementine slowed her thrusts and opened her eyes. "I need something else from you."

"Anything," Evan said.

Clementine eased the strap-on out and moved onto all fours. Evan's mouth dried up. "I need your cock deeper."

"Jesus, yes." Evan supposed this was the plus side of going out with a slightly older woman. She knew exactly what she wanted. Evan jumped up and grasped Clementine's hips. "God, you're fulfilling all of my fantasies in one day."

Clementine looked back at her and said, "Make me come."

Evan didn't waste any time. She wanted to be inside her again. She held the strap-on, and this time it slipped in easily as Clementine was so wet.

Evan groaned as Clementine took her all the way in. "You're so wet."

She started softly, getting used to the feel of it. Clementine's hips were moving quicker. Evan loved the sight of taking her from behind. She sped up to match Clementine.

"I need you to be deep, Foxy."

Evan could feel herself building up to an orgasm again. "Yes."

She was losing herself in Clementine, going faster and harder as Clementine demanded.

Soon Clementine was groaning loudly, until she threw her head back and cried out. Evan followed with an even more intense orgasm than her first. They both fell to the bed, breathing hard.

"That was so fucking good," Evan said.

"Language, Foxy." Clementine smiled and stroked Evan's face. "No one has ever touched me like you do."

Evan's heart sped up. She knew this was her moment to say what was in her heart. "I love you."

Clementine looked unsure, but Evan kissed her lips. "It's all right. You don't need to say anything."

"I do. I'm sorry I pull away from you every time we're around the villagers. I'm just scared."

"I'll chase that fear away. The glass doesn't have to be half empty any more. When I'm around you, it's half full."

"I love you, Evan," Clementine said.

Evan felt like her chest might burst. "Thank you for being brave. I love you."

CHAPTER NINETEEN

This is beautiful, Evan."

Clementine was overawed by the grand foyer of Fox Toys. They had enjoyed breakfast at a local coffee shop and then taken the Tube to Evan's company headquarters. There were no flash chauffeur-driven cars for Evan Fox. It wasn't her style, and Clementine admired that.

"It's a bit special, isn't it? Archie helped make the place over once my dad retired. I wanted to bring the outside indoors."

"It's like Kew Gardens or something."

Evan took her hand and said, "Before we go upstairs, there's someone I'd like you to meet."

She followed Evan to a secured doorway just off the foyer. Once they were inside it was clear this was for children. There were murals on the wall, many featuring the character of Mr. Fox.

Evan rang a buzzer on the inner door and the door was unlocked. The noise of children's chatter and laughter came out loud and clear.

"This is our staff nursery. I wanted you to meet the manager, Jess. She's a university friend of mine. When we opened this place, I asked her if she would come and manage it for us."

Clementine walked into the nursery. It was big, with different coloured areas for different kinds of play, she guessed. "This place looks wonderful. Does it cost a lot for the parents?"

"Not a penny. It's a perk of working for Fox Toys," Evan told her.

"Really? Because childcare costs a fortune."

"I know. Mum and I wanted to create an environment for women where childcare wasn't an issue and didn't hold women back in our workforce. It works. We have far fewer absences from the parents, knowing that they can bring their kids here."

Something caught Clementine's eye. She saw two dogs walking about with the children as they played.

"You have dogs?" Clementine asked.

"Those are our service dogs. Remember I told you we have a service dog trust?"

Clementine nodded.

"We have a few children with special needs or autism. Our dogs come here every day to help the children get through their day."

"That's a wonderful thing."

A good-looking brown haired woman in a Fox nursery T-shirt came walking up to them. "Fox, you've come back from the country."

"Yes, I'd like to introduce you to my friend, Clementine, Duchess of Rosebrook."

"Pleased to meet you, Your Grace. I'm Jess."

"Call me Clementine, please. Nice to meet you, Jess. You have a wonderful facility here."

Jess looked around and smiled. "We're very proud of it. Come and I'll show you around. We were just about to start story time."

"Yes! I love story time," Evan said.

Clementine smiled and shook her head. Evan was a big kid in dapper clothing.

After enjoying a story with the children. Evan escorted Clementine upstairs to her office. She had felt so proud showing Clementine the building and the nursery. Clem really seemed to understand what they were trying to do here. The lift doors opened and they walked out onto her office floor.

Violet immediately stood up and had a big smile on her face. She knew Violet was excited to be meeting a duchess.

"Clem, come and meet the other strong woman who tries to keep my feet on the ground—Violet, my PA."

They shook hands and Violet said, "It's an honour to meet you, Your Grace."

"It's wonderful to meet you. Evan has told me all about you and that you try to keep her on the straight and narrow."

"I don't always succeed, but I try, Your Grace."

"Is the conference room prepared for the interviews?" Evan asked.

"All ready. Shall I organize for tea in your office for the duchess?" Violet said.

"Please. Come and see my office, Your Graceship." She led Clementine into her office and said, "Before you say anything, let me do one thing."

Evan raced over to the desk, pressed a button, and her train started to move around the track on the walls.

Clementine started laughing. "You see, this is what I thought you'd turn the Rosebrook office into."

"I do have some decorum," Evan joked.

Clementine pointed to her trampoline and said, "You've even got your precious trampoline."

"You're not seeing it to its best advantage. Give me a sec." Evan grabbed her mini basketball off the floor and bounced onto her trampoline. "This is what makes it so good. Look." Evan pointed to the basketball hoop on the wall and, as she bounced, threw the ball into it.

"You, Foxy, are the biggest child I know." Clementine laughed.

"I take that as a compliment. Fancy a bounce?"

❖

Three hours later they had seen nineteen of the twenty applicants and were up to the last couple. Clementine looked down at her notepad to refresh her memory about their application.

Most of the individuals and families they had seen were interested because of the environmental aspect of the village they were trying to create, but the couple that they were interviewing now had different reasons.

Blake Campbell and Eliska Novak were quite different from each other. Blake did all the talking while Eliska sat there like a little mouse. There was great pain in Eliska's eyes.

Evan led the questioning. "Blake, you are a doctor with the Red Cross?"

"Yes, that's how I met Eliska. We were working in Ustana, trying to help those caught up in the civil war. I managed to get Eliska and her daughter out of there and granted asylum here in Britain."

Clementine jumped in, "You have a daughter, Eliska?"

Eliska looked to Blake, who smiled and nodded to her. She wrung her hands nervously and said in her accented English, "Yes, she is eleven."

Blake took her hand again. Clementine was impressed with Blake's care of her partner. She was so protective and gentle.

"Why do you want to be part of our community?" Clementine asked.

Blake answered, "Eliska and her daughter have been through a long asylum process and now have been given leave to stay. They, sorry, *we* need to heal, and when I saw your advert about building a community that's safe for LGBTQ people, I thought it was ideal. Where Eliska came from was the polar opposite to that. I want them to feel safe, and we have a lot to contribute. Eliska is a nurse, and I'm a doctor."

The tension and nervousness the two were exhibiting showed how much this meant to them. Clementine didn't want to give their standard reply, that they'd hear the committee's decision by letter in a week. Blake and Eliska needed security and hope now.

"Would you give us a moment?" Clementine got up and signalled to Evan to follow her.

"What is it, Clem," Evan asked.

"I want this couple to get the first available cottage. They need it, and I want to tell them now, not have them nervously waiting. They need hope now."

"Fine by me. Let's do it."

They walked backed to the table and Clementine said, "We'd like to offer you a place in our village."

"Thank you," Blake said before hugging Eliska.

Evan continued, "The cottages aren't finished yet, but we'll put you down for the first one. You'll be in well before Christmas."

Eliska looked straight at Clementine for the first time and said, "Thank you."

"You're welcome. I hope you'll feel safe and be happy in Rosebrook."

"I'll show you out," Evan said.

When Evan came back in, she said, "You're a kind woman, Clementine Fitzroy."

"Well, they needed that hope. These are exactly the type of people we need to build up our village."

"Our village?" Evan said as she sat down.

"Your village."

Evan leaned in and kissed Clementine. "No, you were right the first time. Now we just have to decide on the rest of the applicants."

"There's some good people there," Clementine said. "And we need a mix of single people and families."

"Talking of families, I had an idea," Evan said.

"What?"

Evan took her hand. "Why don't you bring your mother to stay at Rosebrook next weekend?"

"Really? You think that's a good idea?" Clementine asked.

"You're always saying how distressed she is that she's not at Rosebrook. I think it would make her calmer."

"It will be a lot of work to look after her. You're sure?"

"Yes, I love you and she's your family," Evan said.

Chapter Twenty

The next Friday Evan got back from London early. She was taking Clementine to pick up her mum and bring her back to Rosebrook. Luckily it was a dry day. The nurses and Clementine helped the dowager duchess into her wheelchair, and Evan wheeled it out to the car. They'd brought Clementine's car since it had more room.

"Where are we going, Clemy?"

"I'm taking you to Rosebrook."

"We're going home? We're going home?" Marianne started to cry, which in turn set Clementine off.

"Let's get her into the car, Clem. I'll drive, so you can sit in the back with your mum."

On the car journey home Marianne seemed to come alive with new energy. She started to recognize familiar landmarks as they drove.

Evan looked in the rear-view mirror and saw Marianne grasp Clementine's hand tightly and smile and point out the window. Clementine was smiling too. It was wonderful that she was getting these quality moments with her mum.

"Clem? Let's not just go back to the house. Let's take her around all the places she remembers."

And so they did. They drove to the cliff lookout point, then walked, with Marianne in her wheelchair, through the village, which overwhelmed her with joy, especially when she saw the cottages being rebuilt. Marianne put that down to her husband finally finding the money to upgrade the village.

Then the house. The look of joy on Marianne's face, and on Clem's to see her mother so happy, was worth every penny of putting this place right.

❖

After dinner in the dining room, Clementine saw her mother flagging. It had been such a busy day for her, so she decided to get her upstairs for an early night.

Clementine settled her mum in bed and said, "I'll be back in a few minutes, Mama."

She walked out of the bedroom, and Evan was waiting for her. "How is she?"

"Happy. This was such a great idea."

Evan put her arms around Clementine. "I'd do anything to help you and make you happy."

Clementine buried her face in Evan's chest. "I've been alone for so long, trying to cope with Mama and struggling to look after her properly—now I don't feel alone. You've taught me to dream there can be a better future."

"You never have to feel alone again, Clem. I love you."

Clementine caressed Evan's cheek. "I love you."

She saw tears coming to Evan's eyes. Evan deserved everything. She deserved the certainty of a committed relationship that everyone knew about.

"No more secrecy and pulling away from you in public. That's going to change from now on."

"It is?" Evan asked cautiously.

Clementine kissed each of her cheeks, then her nose and lips. "Well, if we're going to be partners in business and life, people have to know."

Evan swept her up and kissed her. "Thank you, you don't know what that means to me. We can have your mum to stay anytime you like, and if you move in with me one day, then she could live with us, and we'd get her a full-time nurse."

"Really? You'd want me to live with you, and bring my mum to live with us? That wouldn't bother you? Starting a new life with my mother alongside us?"

Evan gave here the biggest smile. "Don't be silly. You *do* for family, whatever it takes. My grandma stayed with us. She died at ninety-eight years old, at home, in her own bed, with her family. That's how I was brought up."

Clementine rested her forehead against Evan's. "I'm going to miss you so much tonight. I could never have imagined such a good, kind person."

"You forgot exceptionally good-looking," Evan joked then put her arms around Clementine and squeezed her in the biggest hug.

"I'll miss you too, Clem, but it's important to spend time with your mum. I'll find a cosy old movie to put on TV, and I'll soon fall asleep."

"Okay, goodnight, Foxy." Clementine kissed her goodnight and walked back into the bedroom.

"Clemy? Is that you?" Marianne said.

"Yes, Mama. It's me."

She slipped under the covers and took her mother's hand. She hadn't been able to do this for such a long time.

"Do you want your fox back, Clemy?"

Clementine turned around and kissed her mum on the cheek. "You keep him, Mama. Let's go to sleep."

As they lay there in the dark, all that could be heard was the tick-tock of the clock.

Then out of the darkness Marianne said, "Thank you for bringing me home, Clemy. I always knew you would."

"It's nice to be home with you, Mama."

"Dora said you would."

Clementine sat up slightly. "What do you mean?"

"Dora said you would get Rosebrook back."

Clementine was a little bit freaked by that remark. "When did she say that, Mama?"

"I can't remember, but she's waiting with Louisa and Papa."

"Where?"

"The end of the lane. Down there. Night night, little Clemy."

Logically Clementine knew that this was probably a product of her mother's confused mind, but here alone in the blackness, it did make her slightly uneasy. Regardless of that, it appeared to give her mother comfort, and that was a good thing.

"You're safe at Rosebrook, Mama. Have a peaceful sleep. Night night."

❖

Evan jumped when she heard her text message tone. The twenty-four-hour news was playing on the TV and the bedroom lights were still on. She must have fallen asleep without putting them off.

She grabbed her phone. Six a.m., and there was a message from Clem.

I need you.

Evan jumped up and pulled on a T-shirt. She hurried through to the duchess's room and found Clementine sitting on the floor by the bed, tears streaking her face.

"Clem? What's wrong?"

Clementine looked up and said, "She's gone."

Evan walked over to the bed and saw Marianne deathly still, but peaceful looking.

"She's gone."

Evan went immediately down on her knees and pulled Clementine into her arms. "I'm so sorry, Clem."

"She's gone," Clementine repeated.

Evan could feel her trembling. She had to get her warmed up. "Come through to my room. You're cold."

Clementine allowed herself to be helped to her feet, and then Evan lifted her up in her arms and carried her through to the other bedroom. Evan put her on her bed and grabbed a blanket from the armchair in the corner to wrap around her shoulders.

"Hold on to this blanket. It'll warm you up."

Clementine just stared off into the distance.

"Clem, I'll call for an ambulance and make you a cup of tea, okay?"

She got no reply. Evan didn't want to leave her, but she was going to have to.

❖

After the ambulance, police, and undertakers had come to take Marianne's body away, Kay arrived with some fresh clothes for Clementine to change into. Then as word spread, one by one, people started to arrive to pay their respects. If the villagers didn't know about Evan and Clementine being a couple before, they did now. Clementine hadn't let go of her since they came down to the drawing room. Fergus had been the first to arrive, then Barbara and William Murdoch, closely followed by Albert Mason.

Evan was thankful that Kay was here taking charge and helping her housekeeper Jane with food and drinks for everyone. It was nice to see everyone showing their support for Clementine.

Once everyone left, Evan returned to the drawing room, but Clementine wasn't there. She hurried into the reception hall, and Jane was just coming up the stairs from the kitchen.

"Evan, would you like me to stay on later and make you dinner?"

"No, you go off. I'll make us something later. Thanks for all your help today," Evan said.

"You're welcome. I hope the duchess is okay."

"Thanks, see you tomorrow."

She was sure Clementine would be in the duchess's bedroom or hers, but she wasn't there. Evan started to panic. Clem had been so quiet that she didn't know where her mind was at. Then an idea came into her head. Would she go out to the family burial ground? Evan ran downstairs out of the garden room and ran across the gardens at the back of the house.

The gate to the burial ground was open. Evan's hunch was correct. She found Clementine standing by her father's and Isadora's graves, hugging herself and shaking.

"Hey, what are you doing out here?"

"Visiting Papa," Clementine said with little emotion.

"Come inside. How about we have an early night? Cuddle up, and starting tomorrow we can plan what needs to be done?"

"Mum thanked me last night for bringing her back."

"Did she?"

Clementine nodded.

"Well, as I said earlier, at least she passed away in the home she loved," Evan said.

Clementine turned her attention to Isadora's grave beside her. "Mum would have spent her declining years in her own home if it wasn't for Dora, and my father might not have died so early. Mama always said he died because of the stress, trying to keep the house afloat."

"You don't know that, Clem." When she got no response, Evan said, "Come on inside. You're cold."

"Would you mind if I buried Mama here? With Papa?"

Evan put her arm around Clementine's shoulders. "Of course not. You don't need to ask."

"I do," Clementine said flatly. "It's not my house any more."

Clementine slipped away from Evan and said, "I think I'll go home now."

"You want to stay at the gatehouse tonight?"

Clementine nodded.

Evan supposed it might be hard to stay close to where her mum passed. "Okay, just give me twenty minutes to pack a bag for myself, and I'll be right with you."

"No, I meant *I'll* go home now. I'd like some time to myself."

Evan tried to hide the little bit of hurt she felt. She had tried to be Clementine's rock all day and felt it was her job to take care of her girlfriend, and maybe it was childish, but she was kind of hurt at the rejection. Not to mention worried about Clementine being on her own.

"If you're sure that's what you really want."

"It is," Clementine said and began to walk back to the house.

It seemed a lifetime ago when Clementine told Evan she loved her. She didn't know why, but Evan had a bad feeling that their burgeoning relationship wasn't going to run smoothly.

Clementine felt numb. She sat on her bed and stared blankly ahead, unsure of what she was meant to be feeling. The only emotion she was sure about was one of loss, a gaping expanse of blackness, and it frightened her.

She'd had one purpose since her father died when she was a teenager—to look after her mother and make sure she was as comfortable as she could be. With her mother's mental instability after her papa passed, she'd had to become an adult before her time, then even more so when her mother had started to show the signs of dementia.

Now she was gone, and Clementine's purpose for getting up every day and working as hard as she possibly could was gone as well. What was left was a great big frightening hole. She slipped under the covers and curled up on her side.

She heard her mobile beep. Then after she ignored it, it beeped again. Clementine opened the text. It was from Evan asking if she was all right.

Clementine typed back quickly, *I'm fine. I'm going to sleep, goodnight.*

Seconds later Evan replied, *Don't hesitate to call me if you need me. Any time during the night, I'll be right there. I love you.*

The words *I love you* jarred inside her. She didn't want to feel or think about love just now. That big gaping hole of loss was swallowing up any positive or comforting emotions, so she replied simply.

Goodnight.

CHAPTER TWENTY-ONE

The next morning Evan got dressed quickly and walked down to the office. She wanted to leave some instructions for Archie, then go to the gatehouse. As she neared the office, she saw Archie's car pull up and Rupert and Ash walking up the driveway, ready to start their day.

Archie got out of her car and said, "Fox? How is Clementine?"

"Not great. She insisted on being alone last night. That's why I was coming in early to see you. Can you take Ash and meet with the shop outfitters and the new manager—they are hoping to sign off on their work. Clementine was due to meet with them—"

"Absolutely, anything I can do to help, just let me know," Archie said. "Are you all right?"

"Yeah, I need to spend the day with Clem."

Ash and Rupert came alongside them, and Archie said, "Good news, Ash. You're working with me today."

Ash rolled her eyes. "Oh, hang out the flags. Don't worry, I've been practising my tea-making skills."

"What a good start to the day," Archie said sarcastically. "Go ahead, I'll be there in a minute."

Rupert went to unlock the door, but it was already open. He turned to Evan and said, "Someone's beaten us to it."

"What?" Evan walked with them inside and saw Clementine working away at her desk.

"Could you give us a minute, everyone?" Evan asked.

Archie nodded and said, "Ash? Let's have some of that nice tea you promised and take it into the conference room."

When they walked away, Evan went over to Clementine's desk. "Clem? What are you doing here?"

Clementine looked up briefly, then returned her attention to her laptop. "Working. Isn't that what normally happens on Monday mornings?"

"Not after your mum's just passed away. Come on, I planned to take the day off to be with you. Pack up and we can go back to yours, or Rosebrook if you want."

"No, I'm working. I have a very busy day. I'm meeting the shopfitters in the afternoon, and I have to chase up the contractors down at the Seascape Cottages. They're still a week behind."

This was going to be difficult, Evan thought.

She walked around Clementine's desk and knelt down beside her chair. "Clem, you shouldn't be here, or working. You've just lost your mum."

Clementine gave her a hard look. "What am I supposed to be doing? Getting my nails done?"

Evan sighed. "No, but there's arrangements to be made with the undertaker, plans for the wake. I was going to take the day off to help you do that."

"The arrangements have already been done. I emailed the funeral directors first thing this morning with my wishes. It's all done, and as long as your offer to hold the burial and wake at Rosebrook stands, then it's all under control."

Evan was worried. Clementine wasn't being harsh or bad-tempered, but she was cold and emotionless, which was a whole lot worse than anger.

"Of course you can still have it at Rosebrook. I'll do anything you need me to do," Evan said.

"Then don't fuss. I'm fine."

"You don't seem fine."

"Look, just let me be and do my work. It's all I have, now that Mama is gone."

Evan shouldn't feel hurt. It must be the grief talking. Still, the rebuff hurt all the same.

❖

Clementine felt her brain and the day were going a million miles an hour, and her head hurt from it.

She popped a couple of painkillers before leaving the office and hoped her raging headache would calm. Ash tried to keep up with her as she walked quickly through the village to the shop. They could have driven, but Clementine wanted to walk.

"Are you sure you're okay, Clementine?" Ash asked.

"I'm fine," came her stock response. She had to keep busy. If she slowed down, she would lose herself in the black hole that had opened inside her.

They passed the pub and saw Jonah sweeping up outside. "Morning, Your Grace, Ash."

"Morning, Jonah," Clementine tried to say as cheerily as possible. "What have you got on the agenda today?"

Jonah looked surprised at the normal tone of her enquiry. Clementine hated the way everyone was walking on eggshells around her. She just wanted everything to be normal.

"The kitchen people are coming back to finish off the kitchen refurb, and I've got interviews for the cook's position. Some good quality pub food will lift this place to another level."

"Good, good. All systems go, then. Carry on."

Clementine was soon at the shop, and the site manager for the shopfitters was waiting outside. When another car pulled up, Ash said, "I think Ms. Badger has arrived."

"We can get down to business, then."

"Mr. Jones, Ms. Badger, thanks for coming."

❖

Evan couldn't think about work this afternoon. Before Clementine had left to go to the shop, she had snapped at Evan for hovering and fussing, as Clementine put it. She was confused and unsure what to do. She thought of going for a run, but instead of being full of energy as usual, she felt lethargic and down.

Instead she decided to go and visit the Tucker twins, to see if they needed anything and check on Ada's ankle. When she arrived, she was happy to see Kay's car in the driveway.

Kay opened the door. "Hi, Evan, I thought you'd be with Clem."

"So did I. I thought we'd both not be working today, but apparently I was wrong."

Kay furrowed her eyebrows. "Oh? Come in and tell me all about it."

Evan walked into the living room and was met with two smiling faces in Agatha and Ada.

"Afternoon, ladies."

"Evan!" they both said at once.

At least someone was pleased to see her. She kissed both ladies' hands. "Looking radiant today, ladies."

That compliment made them laugh.

"Oh, stop it," Agatha said.

"So gentlemanly," Ada added.

"And how is the ankle, Ada?" Evan asked.

Ada was sitting with her leg on a footstool.

"Not so bad. It'll be just the ticket in no time."

"Excellent."

Kay walked over to the kitchen door and said, "Let's have a nice cup of tea."

Evan sat down in the armchair by the fire. She wondered how Clementine was. She felt so cut off from her, physically and emotionally, and it was killing her.

She realized Agatha had asked her something. "Sorry?"

"I was saying at least the rain's off for an hour or two. Mr. Fergus says the river is very high."

"Yes, but we're keeping a watchful eye on it, and my builders have laid sandbags along the banks."

"Good," Agatha said, "because we've seen it flood a few times, haven't we, Ada?"

"Oh yes, quite a few times over the years."

As Kay brought the tea tray through, Evan said, "I meant to say, don't worry about the inside of your cottage being redone. I know the other village houses are finished, but yours is just delayed. We can't cause so much disruption when you're not on your feet. The roof and the outside are all completed, Ash tells me."

"We're just thankful you're here to look after the village and the duchess," Agatha said.

Kay put down the tea tray and started to pour out three cups. "How is Clem?"

Evan clasped her hands together. "Working hard."

Kay looked at her with surprise. "Working? At the office?"

"Yes, she insisted on staying at the gatehouse herself last night. I was going to take the next few days off and help organize the funeral.

Turns out she's the first one in the office this morning and has already sent out all her instructions for the funeral. Just now she and Ash are at the new village shop meeting the manager we appointed, and with the shopfitter, to sign off on the building. I don't understand it. She wants to do as much work as possible, and I can't even think about work."

"Oh, dear," Ada said, taking a sip of tea.

"Hmm. She can be a bit of a control freak at times. She's probably finding comfort in controlling her job and everything around it."

"Sounds about right. I'm just worried that she's not dealing with these emotions about her mother, and she'll end up blowing her top."

"Evan," Agatha said, "we remember when her father died. She was only a girl and couldn't grieve properly because she was propping up her mother. Isn't that right, Ada?"

"Yes, indeed. The dowager duchess suffered with anxiety and depression most of her life, but the duke was her strength. He was her voice when she thought she didn't have one herself."

Agatha nodded. "Exactly and when the duke passed on, Clementine had to become the adult too soon, and thereafter they had to leave their family home. Since then her life has been consumed with working and taking care of Marianne. You see what I'm saying?"

"I think I do," Kay said. "She's always been the responsible one. Work and caring for the dowager duchess are what kept her going, and now there's a big hole in her life and she's in flux."

Evan knew what they were saying. "She's trying to fill that hole in her life with work so she can feel in control. So what do I do?"

Kay squeezed her shoulder. "Be close by and offer your support. She'll reach out for you when she can't cope any more."

"I love her."

"Then that's all she'll need," Agatha said.

CHAPTER TWENTY-TWO

The week had been a long blur for Clementine. Between her job with the trust and her mother's funeral on the next Saturday, she didn't have a minute, but that was the way she wanted it. She wanted to be so busy she couldn't think.

The worst times were those in bed on her own late at night, when her mind had no other distractions. She thought about her grief, her guilt at not being able to look after her mother full-time and not being able to give her Rosebrook. Then there was Evan.

Clementine looked up from her computer and gazed over at her. She knew she had pushed Evan away. Even as she did it, she'd slapped herself mentally, but she couldn't help it. Clementine didn't want comfort, didn't want to feel better or loved, when her life was so in flux.

She had infected Evan's normally happy-go-lucky positive attitude with doom and depression. Evan hadn't bounced on her trampoline once, and Clementine knew what a big part of her workday that was.

But still, Evan hadn't given up on her.

Every morning Evan texted her good morning when she woke, and at bedtime texted that she loved her and would be there whenever she was ready. It would be so easy to take comfort in Evan's love, but if she did, Clementine feared falling apart. To get through this week, she had to stay in control. Today was Friday, the day before the funeral, and it was starting to become all too real. A lot of extended family and friends were due to arrive at their hotel today and had been texting and phoning as they arrived.

The service was to take place in the church in the next village, High Walton, then back to Rosebrook for the burial and wake. High Walton had grown from a village to a small market town, so the guests had booked rooms there at the medium-sized Walton hotel.

They usually finished work early on a Friday, and Rupert, Archie, and Ash were starting to pack up, she noticed. Her chest started to constrict, and a sense of foreboding and panic started to sweep her body. If the workweek was over, then the funeral was upon her, and there was no place else to hide emotionally.

She had been so distracted by her sense of panic that she didn't hear Ash talking till the last minute.

"Sorry, Ash?"

"Do you need me to do anything before I leave?"

"No, no. Off you go," Clementine said.

"And you don't want me to do anything tomorrow?"

"No, thanks. There's a catering company coming in, so they'll take care of everything."

Ash got up and gave her a kiss on the cheek. "I'll be thinking of you."

Rupert was not long behind her. "Jonah will be up early tomorrow to set up the drinks."

Clementine experienced a tingling sensation from her neck and down her upper arms. Oh God. It was happening. This was it. She tried breathing to regain control but was interrupted by Archie.

They hadn't had the closest of working relationships since Clementine joined the Fox team. In fact Archie appeared annoyed that she was stepping on her toes initially, but she looked open and sympathetic as she said, "I know how hard tonight and tomorrow will be for you, Clementine. I just wanted to say I'll be thinking of you. I lost my brother five years ago, and—well, I know how this feels. I'll be thinking of you."

She didn't know what to say. It somehow made her feel more emotional that the normally stoic Archie was showing such an understanding side to her nature.

"Thank you," Clementine managed to say.

Archie left and the tingling spread down her lower arms, and suddenly it felt like she couldn't get enough air in her lungs. She got up and, on wobbly legs, bolted for the office door, her vision narrowing as she went.

When Clementine got outside she gasped and braced herself against the wall, her stomach threatening to rebel against her, and her knees about to give out. Then two strong arms wrapped around her and stopped her from falling.

Evan tried to pull her into a hug, and her last bit of control resisted. "No, don't, don't, I can't—" She pushed and pushed against Evan's chest, but Evan wouldn't be deterred.

"Shh, shh, it's all right. I'm not letting you go, Clem. I've got you," Evan said.

Evan held Clementine, not giving up on her. She had kept her distance from Clementine all day, just as Clem seemed to want it, but she saw a change in her demeanour when everyone had said their words of support before they left. She saw panic.

Now was not the time to sit on the sidelines and let Clementine deal with her grief in her own way. Evan had to look after her.

Clementine's struggles and demanding words started to ease and were replaced with tears and a total breakdown in emotion.

"I've got you. It's okay."

Clementine grasped her lapels and cried into her chest. Evan was just strong and held her, rocking back and forth until Clementine's gasping sobs slowed down.

"I'm sorry, I'm sorry," Clementine said.

"You don't need to be sorry for anything. All I care about is being there for you."

Clementine held her more tightly, as if she would be set adrift without Evan as an anchor.

"Don't leave me." Those were the words Evan had been longing to hear all week. She wanted to be useful and take care of Clementine, but on the advice of Kay, she'd let Clem deal with it in her own way.

"I won't ever leave you. Let's get some things packed for you so you can stay at Rosebrook."

"No, I mean—" Clementine pulled back a bit from Evan. "I mean, would you stay with me at the gatehouse? I really don't think I can cope with my memories there. Not tonight, anyway."

"Absolutely, I'll be anywhere you need me to be."

❖

They ate a very light supper and went to bed early. Evan stroked Clementine's hair, as she lay with her head on Evan's chest.

"How's your head, Clem?"

After crying and all the stress of the day, Clementine had a raging headache.

"Better, but I feel like I want to sleep for days. I'm so tired all of a sudden," Clementine said.

"It's the stress. You've held yourself together all week, and now you're letting go. Your body is exhausted."

Clementine sighed. "I'm sorry I pushed you away."

"You have got nothing to apologize for. You just needed to do what you had to do. I was always going to be waiting for you."

"Let me explain why—I mean, I think I have to explain why."

Evan kissed her head. "If that's what you need, then go ahead."

"That evening, when all the guests were leaving, you were seeing them off. Well, I looked at the time and thought, I'm late for visiting time with Mama at the nursing home. Visiting Mama is—*was* such a big part of my life, of my every day, that in that split second, I forgot that she was gone."

"I understand. Is that when you ran out to the family graveyard?" Evan asked.

"Yes, I panicked. When I remembered that she had gone, I realized there was this gaping hole in my life. Before you came along with your dreams and passions for this village, life was pretty grim, and the only thing that drove me from day to day was taking care of Mama and trying to make enough money for her nursing home. Without that I was, I *am* lost. I knew if I let you close, I would break down. I had to submerge myself in work."

"And it got too much today?" Evan asked.

Clementine nodded. "Everyone was being so kind. I had a panic attack, I think."

"Yeah, that's what it looked like. But even though it seemed as if you were on your own, I was always there waiting, ready to be there when you needed me. I'll always be there if you want me."

Clementine sat up slightly and stroked Evan's hair. "You know what Mum said to me the night she died?"

"What?"

"We were lying there in the dark and she thanked me for bringing her back to Rosebrook. I told you that bit, but what I didn't say was that she said Dora told her I would."

"Really, when?"

"I think it was just in her muddled mind, but there in the dark it felt eerie. Then she said Dora, her wife Louisa, and my papa were waiting for her down the lane."

"Which lane?"

"I don't know, but if it made her calmer at the end, I don't care where the thought came from."

As much as Clementine was trying to rationalize it away, her mother's words clearly had an impact on her. Evan chose to believe Dora, and that she had guided her to Clementine.

"Our whole lives have had too many coincidences. The pictures of the beach, my interest in Dora and of building a community…"

"Our lives have intertwined since we were children, that's true," Clementine said.

Evan took Clementine's hand and put it on her heart. "You see, you don't have this gaping hole in your life. I mean, you'll always feel the loss of your mum in your life, but you do have a life to look forward to—if you want it."

Clementine smiled as much as her sadness would allow. "You mean you, Foxy?"

"Well, who else loves you and worships at your feet, Your Grace?"

Clementine's heart felt so much lighter being with Evan. Her positive outlook on life was infecting her again. "I think you're yang to my yin."

Evan rubbed her thumb along Clementine's cheekbone. "Why do you think that?"

"Because my glass is half empty and you keep filling it up."

Evan kissed her softly, sweetly, reminding her that she would never be alone.

"Tomorrow will be difficult," Evan said, "but no matter how hard it is, we'll get through it together."

Evan held up her hand to encourage Clementine to take it. She slid her fingers through Evan's and repeated, "Together."

Clementine looked at herself in the freestanding mirror and brushed her hands down her black skirt. She had brought her funeral outfit up to Rosebrook to get changed there before the car arrived. She heard the connecting door open and Evan walk in. Clementine never turned around but felt Evan's arms slip around her waist and watched in the mirror as Evan rested her head on her shoulder.

"Are you doing all right?" Evan asked.

Clementine leaned her head back against Evan's. "Yes, surprisingly. I don't know how I'll be at the church, but I know that I will get through it with you by my side."

She turned around and into Evan's arms. She gently took hold of Evan's black tie. "You look smart in your black suit."

"I'm used to more colour but I think I still rock this."

Clementine smiled. "I was just thinking before you came in the number of times I watched my mother get ready in this room. I sat on the bed or on the window ledge. It seems appropriate that I get ready here."

"Did your mum and dad not sleep together in my room?" Evan asked.

"Yes, but Mother used this room for her wardrobe and dressing room. I'm glad that if she had to pass, she passed here in what she thought was still her home."

Evan nodded in understanding.

Clementine wanted to say something else. "I was wondering…?"

"Yeah?"

"Can I stay here tonight? I don't want to be on my own, and I'd feel closer to Mama up here."

Evan cupped her cheek. "You never have to ask."

"I do—it's your house, Evan," Clementine said.

"It doesn't have to be. I love you, Clem. I want to share my life, my house, this village. I mean, it's yours anyway, whether legally or not. You are the cornerstone of this community. You've helped me make my dreams come true. Move in with me?"

Clementine was surprised, to say the least. "Isn't that a bit sudden? A bit too quick?"

"I know what I want. The banjo smacked me over the head, remember? I'm not meant for living on my own, and I think about you every second of every day, so why shouldn't we live together? I mean, I would rather marry you and make you Mrs. Fox, but you're not in the right frame of mind for that kind of question, so think about it, okay? You don't need to answer right away."

"I'll think about it, for the future." Clementine heard the sound of tyres on gravel. "It must be the cars."

Evan took her hand. "I'm with you every step of the way, okay?"

Clementine nodded. "As long as I have you, I can face anything."

Chapter Twenty-three

Clementine did so well at the service. Evan was proud of her and proud of her staff, Archie and Rupert, for coming to the funeral, along with all the villagers, to lend their support. It had been a good turnout between distant family and the dowager duchess's friends, and they had all returned to Rosebrook for the wake.

The drawing room and reception hall were full of people circulating and talking. Waitstaff circulated with trays of nibbles and wine. Evan had left Clementine talking with some people and went to get them some drinks from the bar Jonah had set up.

Jonah smiled as she approached. "Evan, what can I get you?"

"A St. Clement's for the duchess and just a Coke for me. I want to keep on my toes."

"Coming right up," Jonah said.

"You know, you didn't have to do this, Jonah. I could have gotten one of the waitstaff to do it."

"I'm happy to. It gives me more of a chance to get to know the locals. Rupert and I are still foreigners to them."

"I wouldn't worry about it," Evan said. "Clementine tells me it takes about ten years to be considered a local around here."

"I'm sure." Jonah chuckled. "Here's your drinks."

"Thanks."

Evan wandered back into the room to find Clementine. She had moved from the group she had been talking to, to speak to her goddaughter, her cousin Lucille. Clementine had pointed her and her father Peter out at the service, but they hadn't been introduced. Lucille appeared to be a smiley, open girl, but Peter seemed to have a permanent scowl on his face.

They were an odd mix. Lucille was only fifteen but her dad was in his sixties. Clementine had explained that he had Lucille late in life, in the hope of the title staying in his line after his death. It wasn't likely that he would get the title, given his age, but he made sure that he at least would have a child who would.

"Evan? Come and meet Lucy. Lucy, this is my—" Clementine hesitated a moment, then said, "My girlfriend, Evan."

Lucy smiled brightly. "Hi, Evan. It's really nice to meet you."

Evan handed over Clementine's drink. "You too, Lucy. Can I get you anything?"

"No, I'm fine, thanks." Lucy had a sweet blush to her cheeks at meeting someone new.

Clementine noticed Lucy's shyness around Evan and said, "You know, Evan, Lucy was telling me about her favourite toy."

"Uh, yes," Lucy said, "Mr. Fox. I got him when I was born, and he's been my favourite toy ever since."

"That's wonderful. I gave Clementine a Mr. Fox when we met. He's a dapper little guy."

Clementine smiled, remembering throwing Mr. Fox along with Evan out of her house. "I was just saying, Lucy should come and stay sometime. So I can get to know my lovely goddaughter. We haven't spent enough time together."

"Sounds like a great idea," Evan said.

"I'd love that. It would be nice to get a break from Father," Lucy said.

"Is he still as bad?" Clementine asked.

Lucy hugged herself and nodded. "At least I'm at school most of the time."

Clementine put her arm around Lucy and said, "Let's go and say hello to your father, then, before he accuses me of ignoring him."

Clementine couldn't stand Peter. Since she was a child he'd been unpleasant to her at family events and whenever their paths crossed. He resented the fact that she inherited the title and that they had lost the house and fortune.

"Peter, thank you for coming and bringing Lucy. It's so nice to see her again."

Peter downed the glass of whisky in his hand. "I was surprised, to say the least, that the wake was to be held at Rosebrook. I heard that you may have found a way to get Rosebrook back."

"Papa, don't," Lucy said.

Peter sounded as if his tongue had been loosened by strong drink. "Excuse me? What do you mean?"

❖

"No, in all honesty I have to admit that my cattle are doing well on it," Mr. Mason said.

"Didn't I tell you?" Evan said.

She, Mr. Mason, Mr. Murdoch, and Mr. O'Rourke were standing together enjoying a drink.

Evan continued, "You see, you get a top-quality food for your animals, and you help save the planet. Got to be good."

Mr. O'Rourke joined in, "It's the sea we need to do something about. When I take my fishing parties out, they're more likely to catch plastic and rubbish than fish."

Evan nodded. "Yeah, that's something. What we need is—"

"Excuse me, Evan?" Lucy interrupted.

"Hi, Lucy. Everything okay?"

Lucy appeared to be a mixture of embarrassed and panicked. "No, my papa said something rude and mean to Clem, and she ran. I don't know where she went. I'm so sorry."

Evan could feel the fury rise up in her in a millisecond. "Bloody idiot. On her mother's funeral day. I'll kill him."

Mr. O'Rourke place a hand on her shoulder. "Just go and find the duchess. We'll deal with him."

What a show of support this was to Clementine, but she had no time to dwell on it. She ran out to the reception hall, spotted Kay talking to Fergus, and said, "Kay? Fergus? Have you seen Clementine?"

"Oh yes," Kay said, "I saw her hurrying out the front door."

"Is everything all right, youngster?" Fergus asked.

"I really hope so."

❖

Evan looked everywhere, but her final port of call was the beach, and as she hurried down the steps, she saw Clementine, sitting in the sand, halfway up the beach. Whatever Peter had said must have been really upsetting, and that was all Clementine needed today.

She ran up the beach until she reached her. "Clem, what's wrong? Lucy told me you were upset. What did Peter say?"

"Only what everybody will be saying." Clementine wiped her eyes, but fresh tears kept coming.

Evan dropped to her knees beside her. "Hey, don't cry. Tell me what he said."

She heard a rumble in the distance and looked up at the ominous dark clouds heading into shore.

"He said that I had managed to get back into Rosebrook the same way the very first duchess had gotten the titles and land—on her back. He supposed that kind of behaviour ran in the female line of the family."

"Fucking prick. He says that to you the day you say goodbye to your mother? If I ever see him again, I'll knock him onto his bony arse."

Clementine shrugged. "That's what everyone will be thinking."

"Why do you care about gossip? We know the truth—our friends know the truth."

"I was brought up to care about gossip. Gossip is an enemy in small villages like this. I've had people talking behind my back my whole life, and I hate it. You know, before my father died, we had debt collectors at the door all the time, them swanning into the house, sitting in the drawing room, and refusing to leave until they'd been paid."

"I'm sorry, Clem. I didn't realize how bad things had been for you," Evan said.

"At boarding school, I was picked on and laughed at by the other girls. All their parents knew of the money problems we had, and the penniless duke, and then when the school wouldn't wait any longer for their fees, I was sent to an ordinary primary school. I was already an oddity, because my father was a duke, but then the gossip reached them and everything got so much worse."

"But you're an adult now. You don't need to care about what people say about you. Let's walk back to the house. It looks like a storm is closing in," Evan said.

"I can't. People heard Peter, they won't—"

Evan was frustrated. Clementine didn't seem to understand what high regard the villagers held her in.

"Are you kidding? When I left, James O'Rourke, Mr. Mason, and Mr. Murdoch were about to throw him bodily out of the house." The rain started to fall, but Clementine didn't say anything or start to move. "Let's go before the rain gets any worse."

Clementine did get up and Evan took her hand. The dark clouds in the sky and claps of thunder mirrored Clementine's mind. Her grief and hurt were clouding her mind.

As they walked Evan said, "We'll get back home and settle in for the night."

The word *home* jarred Clementine. Evan kept pushing this idea that Rosebrook was hers too, and it wasn't. Evan was moving way too quick, and it was making her panic and question herself. Was she conflating her feelings for Evan with getting her family home back?

Clementine was worried and feeling overwhelmed. She needed time alone.

The rain was falling heavily now, and when they got to the gatehouse, Clementine stopped.

"Come on, we need to get out of this rain," Evan said.

"I'm going to stay here tonight."

"But you asked earlier if you could stay at the house. I want to look after you."

"I know I did, but now I think I'd like to be alone, to think," Clementine said.

"What do you need to think about?"

"Us, this. It's all moving too fast. This afternoon you were talking about getting married. It's too much, okay? You're jumping into this like every dream you have—without thinking."

Clementine saw anger etched on Evan's face for the first time, her look made worse by the rain dripping down her face. That voice inside her head was screaming, *Why are you pushing her away again?*

"You want to be alone. I'll give you exactly that. I don't jump in without thinking. I just know who and what I want, but if you don't or are too scared to take it—I'll leave you alone. No problem."

Evan marched away up the driveway to Rosebrook.

❖

It was twenty-four hours since Clementine had asked her for space, and she had given it to her. Evan's anger had dissipated overnight, and all she wanted to do was text Clementine. Make things right between them. It was so hard not to contact her—when there was a problem, Evan wanted to solve it. Evan was sometimes impulsive, yes, but only because she was clear about what she wanted.

Evan sat on the edge of the trampoline and stared at her phone.

She wished Clementine would text or call. To Evan it was so simple—she loved Clementine, so why wait? She jumped off the trampoline and walked over to the window. Her mum would probably say, *Calm down, Evan. Give her a chance.*

The summer evening was dark and ominous as the dark clouds covered the sky and the rain battered off the windows. She gazed at the gatehouse longing for Clementine.

"Fuck it. I'm texting her."

But before she could, Evan's phone sprang to life. But it wasn't Clementine. It was Casper.

"Hello?"

"Evan? We need your help."

Clementine pulled on her clothes quickly while talking to Kay on the phone. "I'm coming, I'm coming."

"Don't come yourself, Clem. It's too dangerous. Casper is going over to meet Mr. Murdoch at the Tucker twins'."

"Did anyone phone Evan?" Clementine asked.

"Yes, Casper did."

"You need to get yourself and the boys down to Rosebrook. The water won't get up there."

The wild storm last night and today had finally pushed the Tynebrook to its limits and burst its banks. Water was cascading through the village, seeping through front doors and into homes.

"We called the emergency services, but they can't tell us when they can get here. The roads are flooded everywhere, all over the south coast. Cars stuck, people stranded. They say the build-up of rain and storms over the summer is unprecedented. We just need to do what we can ourselves."

"Make Rosebrook the meeting point. You'll be safe there."

"I'm going to meet Mrs. Murdoch and Fergus. We'll be safer together."

"Okay, keep in touch."

Clementine hurried downstairs. As she stepped off the last step, she splashed into water.

"Bugger."

Clementine's first floor was starting to flood too. She grabbed her wellies by the front door and pulled them on, followed by her jacket. When she opened the front door, more water flooded into the house.

She could worry about that later. Now she had to get to the Tuckers'. The rain was battering down a lot harder than it looked inside. Clementine saw a torchlight at the gates to Rosebrook.

"Clem? Is that you?" Evan shouted.

"Yes."

Evan being Evan was dressed in green tweed trousers, a green waxed jacket, wellington boots, and a flat cap. Typical country gentleman, bad weather attire. She couldn't help but smile to herself. Even in unprecedented weather, she was still the dapper gent.

"Is the gatehouse flooding?" Evan asked.

Clementine tried to pull her hood further over her face. "Yes. Kay says there's flooding all over the area. Emergency services can't get through, and the Tuckers' cottage is right on the river, so we need to get them out quickly. They're sleeping downstairs, remember, so we need to get to them. I've told Kay to make Rosebrook our base and to head there. Did you leave it open?"

"Yes." Evan had to shout over the din of the storm. You could even hear the noise of the waves down on the beach crashing onto the shore. "You go up to the house and wait on Kay and the others."

"Not likely. These are my people. I'm going too," Clementine said.

Evan was silent for a few moments, then said, "Then take my hand so you don't fall."

Clementine took Evan's hand and entwined her fingers through hers.

Evan wasn't crazy about Clementine coming with her, but it was so good to touch her again, even if it was in the middle of such chaos.

"Has anything like this ever happened before?" Evan asked loudly against the noise of the wind and rain.

"Flooding, yes, but not like this. It feels like we're in the middle of a typhoon."

Evan couldn't go any longer without expressing her feelings. "I've missed you."

Clementine stopped and turned around to face Evan. "I've missed you too."

That look and those words were enough to give Evan hope. "Let's make sure everyone is safe, and then maybe we can talk?"

"Yes."

They made their way slowly through the floodwater, down into the village. The Seaside Cottages, the ones that were nearest completion, were all flooded, by the looks of things.

Clementine pointed to them. "Evan, look. All that hard work, they'll be ruined. I think this village has a curse on it or something. Every time someone tries to make it better and rebuild, something goes wrong."

There was a flash of lightning in the sky, and Evan pulled Clementine closer. "There's no curse, no bad luck. We make our own luck. Anything that gets destroyed or damaged tonight is only material, it can be fixed. I promise you—I will not let this village die. Tomorrow we can assess the damage, but tonight we make sure everyone is safe."

"You're right. I love you, Foxy."

Evan was surprised and filled with joy at that admission. She leaned in and kissed Clementine quickly on the lips. "I love you too. Let's keep going."

Their slow progress led them past the pub. Jonah was there putting sandbags in front of the door.

"Jonah? How's the pub?" Evan asked.

"It's filling up. I'm trying to keep the worst out. Where are you headed?"

Clementine led Evan over to the pub doorway, so they could be heard more easily.

"The Tucker twins are trapped in their house, next to the river," Clementine said.

Jonah threw down a bag of sand at the door. "You head on, and I'll catch you both up."

Evan held Clementine's hand tightly and they waded on through the village. The thunder and lightning continued, and then there was a loud crack of thunder directly above them.

Clementine jumped with fright and slipped into the floodwater. Evan grabbed her and pulled her up.

"Thanks," Clementine said.

"We're a team."

They heard shouts from further up the road and tried to hurry to see who it was.

Kay was with her two sons and Mrs. Murdoch, and Mr. Fergus, who had fallen in the water.

"Is everything all right?"

The water was gushing harder down the street, and the noise was making it almost impossible to be heard.

"Fergus slipped in the road," Kay said.

They helped Fergus up. "Can you walk on it?" Evan asked.

"Not very well. I'm a bloody fool."

The two boys were quiet and looked scared.

"What do we do?" Clementine asked.

"We split up. You stay with Kay and Fergus and the boys. We'll call Jonah and ask him to help you back to Rosebrook."

Clementine nodded. "I think you're right. You will be careful, won't you?"

"Of course I will. I've got you to come back to."

Rosebrook House was filled with the low murmurings of sombre chatter and the occasional squeals from Kay's two boys as they ran around. Clementine, Kay, and Ash were running up and down to the kitchen fetching tea, food, and hot water bottles to warm everyone up.

Clementine gave hot water bottles to Agatha and Ada and made sure they had enough blankets.

"Thank you, dear," Agatha said. "That was quite an experience."

The Tucker twins had been troupers and very brave. The water had gotten high in the downstairs of their cottage, but Jonah and Evan carried them both out, and James O'Rourke had brought one of his inflatable dinghies, since they couldn't walk. The sight of the twins being pulled through the flooded village in a boat was quite something to see.

Clementine then went over to Fergus, who had sprained his ankle and had it resting on a footstool.

"How are you doing, Fergus?"

"I feel like a bloody fool. I should have been helping you ladies get here safely, and instead I bugger up my ankle. What a bloody nuisance."

Clementine gave him a kiss on the cheek. "You're a gentleman, Fergus."

"One does one's best," Fergus replied.

Evan brought him over a glass of brandy. "Here you are, Fergus."

Clementine looked quizzically at Evan. "Should he be drinking that? We gave him painkillers."

Fergus took the glass. "Stuff and nonsense. Don't worry about it. I was downing a bottle of champagne when I was ten. A brandy is nothing. It'll just warm up the old cockles."

Clementine followed Evan back to the drinks table.

Evan said, "Mrs. Murdoch is crying. They're all really down. All the downstairs refurb of their homes is destroyed."

"What do you want me to do?" Clementine asked.

"Talk to them. Make them believe that we will get through this. You're their leader. You know that you always have been. When I met you, you said that you would give up your title if you could, but if a title is worth anything in this modern world, then it's as a focal point. Someone to look to in time of difficulty, someone who will express how they feel *in* their time of difficulty. Like the Queen does in a national emergency or tragedy. Take your place, Duchess of Rosebrook."

Evan's words made sense, and her title made sense for the first time in her life. She nodded and took a step away from the fireplace, then stopped and looked back at Evan.

"I'll be moving back in on Monday. That all right with you?" Clementine said.

"You mean here? Live with me?" Evan stuttered over her words.

"Yes, well, it is the duchess's house."

Evan grinned. She had her. Clementine was going to commit. "You're quite right."

"Oh, and I thought I better ask, because it's not the done thing to ask a duchess yourself—will you marry me?"

Evan's mouth hung open in shock. "Um…yes, I'd love to, Your Graceship, Mrs. Fox."

"Mrs. Fox? Has a nice ring to it, doesn't it?" Clementine said, then she walked to the centre of the room.

She heard Evan say, "What a woman."

"Excuse me, everyone?"

The chatter died down. "Thank you. I just wanted to say a few words. This summer's weather has been unprecedented. The severity of the rain and storms is not normal—they're a consequence of the damage we are doing to this world, to our ocean and the land, exactly as Evan has been telling us from the start."

Everyone was shocked when James O'Rourke interrupted, "We have to find a new way of living. I'm sick of plastic and pollution in the water. I see every day the damage it's doing."

Then Mr. Mason piped in, "And my crops will be ruined. We need to change before it's too late."

"Exactly, we need to buy in to Evan's ideas to make this world a better place. I know it's frustrating sometimes, but as Evan said when she first came here, we have a chance to make Rosebrook a shining example to the country, of how to live."

Mrs. Murdoch put up her hand. "What about our homes, and the new cottages that are nearly finished? The floodwater will have ruined them."

"We rebuild. The trust has the money, and as someone reminded me recently, material things can be fixed or rebuilt, but people cannot. We have to come together as a community and make it somewhere to be proud of, the vibrant, thriving village it used to be." Clementine put her hand on her chest. "I am here for you all, and I'll make sure everything is done properly. I'm going to be working on this with my team, full-time. There will be no more part-time duchess."

Evan walked beside her and slipped an arm around her waist. "The Duchess of Rosebrook is moving back into her ancestral home, and she has agreed to marry me."

Kay was first to jump to her feet and congratulate them. "Oh, Clem, I'm so happy for you."

Then Ash followed suit along with all those that weren't injured. Fergus waved Evan over, and Clementine heard him say, "Congratulations, youngster. Bagging a duchess isn't half bad."

"And a countess and a baroness, don't forget," Evan joked. "I think I've done pretty well for myself."

Once everyone had been settled in the many bedrooms Rosebrook had to offer, Clementine and Evan retired to the duke's bedroom. Evan took a shower first and was waiting in bed for Clementine to come back from hers.

She came out of the shower room dressed in one of Evan's T-shirts. She looked so sexy with her wet hair hanging down her back. Evan was overjoyed by Clementine's proposal. She couldn't wait to hold her.

"I'm too tired to dry my hair," Clementine said. "It'll just have to wait until the morning."

Evan patted the bed. "Come in here."

Clementine slipped under the covers and let out a breath. "I'm so exhausted. Tomorrow will be even more tiring. We'll probably have company staying with us for a week or so, until the water in the cottages can be pumped out."

Evan leaned up on her elbow and smiled down at her. "Don't worry about that now. The more the merrier, as far as I'm concerned." Evan stroked Clementine's wet hair from her face. "You are going to be my wife. I can't believe it."

"Neither can I. I just think it's the right time."

"The way you took charge down there, you really turned me on," Evan said.

Clementine chuckled. "You like strong women. You told me."

"I did."

Evan was overwhelmed with the need to touch Clementine. She trailed her finger down Clementine's chest and lightly stroked her hand across Clementine's breast. Clementine's breathing caught and her nipple became hard.

"I know you're exhausted, but do you think I could touch you?"

Clementine nodded.

Evan sneaked her hand up Clementine's T-shirt and cupped her breast lightly. Clem groaned and Evan placed soft kisses on her lips.

"I'm going to love your body so gently, just relax and feel."

Evan moved her hand down to Clementine's sex. She cupped it and squeezed in the gentlest of fashions. She wanted to rock her tenderly and gently to her orgasm, and then to sleep.

Clementine moaned and grasped the back of her neck.

"Slowly and softly, m'lady."

Evan pushed past Clem's underwear and felt that Clementine was already wet. She slipped her finger into her wet folds and split her fingers around Clem's clit, so that she would be barely touching it.

She began a gentle, rubbing motion and felt Clementine's clit become hard. Clementine rocked her hips at the same pace.

Clementine had her eyes closed and was just concentrating on the feeling of being rocked to her orgasm in utter love and devotion. It built so slowly that it was almost overwhelming when the wave of orgasm washed over her. It felt like pure love, and Evan had given her the love that she never dared to dream of.

❖

Evan woke from sleep and found the bed empty. She scrubbed her hands through her short hair and sat up. Just like the first time they slept together, Clementine was sitting on the window ledge, but unlike last time, Clementine had a large sketch pad on her knees and was scribbling away.

Evan got up and wandered over to her. "Morning, m'lady."

Clementine looked up and gave her a bright smile. "Good morning."

Evan leant in and kissed her. "What are you up to here?"

"Planning."

She looked down at her sketch pad and saw drawings, notes, and lists filling the page. "What kind of planning?"

"Things we need to do with the village, staff we'll need for the estate, new buildings and cottages we've still to build, and of course there'll be lots more work to do once we assess the damage from the storm," Clementine said.

Evan had never heard Clementine so animated. She spoke with such speed and excitement in her voice that it sounded like her ideas were running away with her, and all of it was said with the biggest smile.

"Oh, and I had an idea for the military buildings. Why don't we refurb them as lodgings for students? We could set up a scheme where students could come and spend time with us, learning and helping us with our ecological work here. Like an internship. Young people often have the best ideas. What do you think?"

Evan shook her head. "Wow, you're just blowing me away. I think there's a lot of Isadora in you. You're daring to dream."

Clementine put her sketch pad down and stood up. "I didn't know I was capable of dreaming."

Despite waking up to the aftermath of one of the worst storms Rosebrook had ever known, Clementine had never felt more positive. Evan had taught her it was safe to dream again, and she was loving it. Her creative spark was bursting out of her brain when she woke, and now Clementine couldn't wait for the future.

Clementine placed her hand on Evan's chest and said, "I'll never be as optimistic and positive as you, I don't think anyone is, and I'll always have to rein in your wilder flights of fancy, but yes, I can't wait to see what dreams we'll come up with together." She pushed on Evan's chest and grinned. "Let's go back to bed. I have a lot of energy this morning."

"But what about our guests? Your villagers will be surfacing and will be needing tea and breakfast."

"*Our* villagers," Clementine corrected Evan. "You can be quick, can't you, Foxy?"

Unusually Clementine had Evan mentally and physically off balance. When they got to the bed, Clementine pushed her back onto the mattress. She pulled off her nightie and saw the look of hunger on Evan's face.

"I think I like it when you're positive and demanding," Evan said.

Clementine climbed on top of Evan and leaned over to within a few inches of Evan's lips.

"I'm learning so many new things about myself. Like, dreaming and planning make me all hot and bothered."

Clementine kissed Evan so deeply and passionately that Evan moaned. Evan grasped her bottom with her hands, squeezing and making Clementine rock her hips on Evan's stomach. But this wasn't about her. She wanted to make Evan feel good, loved, and appreciated for the wonderful person she was.

She broke away from the kiss and felt Evan try to turn her onto her back. She wagged her finger. "Uh-uh. This morning you're mine, Foxy."

"Oh God," Evan replied.

Clementine moved down Evan's torso, kissing and teasing as she went. Evan gave the biggest moans when Clementine's breasts brushed against her thighs.

She teased Evan with her tongue, lightly licking around her clit.

Evan sat up propped on her elbows and begged Clementine, "Jesus, Clem, don't tease. Suck me."

Clementine stopped and met Evan's gaze. "Well, I did tell you to be quick."

She winked at Evan and returned to her clit. Clementine sucked it in, and Evan groaned. "Oh yeah, yeah, just like that."

As Clementine picked up the pace, Evan's hips thrust right along with her, and as she got closer to her orgasm, Clementine felt Evan's hand in her hair, grasping it tightly. She sucked and licked faster, matching the thrust of Evan's hips and her moans until she went rigid and still.

"Fuck!" Evan cried out.

After she had squeezed every ounce of pleasure out of Evan's orgasm, she climbed up to Evan, who was trying to get her breath back. Clementine stroked her face tenderly.

Evan pulled her into a deep kiss, then said, "Can you be positive every morning?"

Clementine laughed. "I can try." Before she could stop her, Evan had flipped her onto her back. "We don't have time, Foxy. Our guests will be waiting for us."

Evan trailed her fingers down Clementine's body, and without any teasing or preamble slipped her fingers into Clementine's wet sex.

Clementine moaned, and then Evan lowered her lips down to Clementine's, and as she had done, Evan whispered, "You can be quick, can't you?"

EPILOGUE

Five months later

It was a crisp, frosty winter morning in mid-December. Clementine was in the family burial ground out at the back of Rosebrook House. She told herself that she wanted to visit her mother, but deep down it was the grave beside it she wanted to talk to. Isadora Fitzroy, who was buried with her wife, Louisa.

Clementine sighed. "I've spent most of my life trying to hate you, Grandmother. Life wasn't good after you lost our money, and I didn't want to acknowledge that you were trying to do good, that your social conscience was something to be admired. I've never been a dreamer, never understood anything but order and precision. I never understood it's the dreamers that make the progress that advances us as humans. Some will fail, some will succeed—"

She heard the telltale crunch of gravel that meant someone had walked through the gate.

"Those who succeed need people like you to keep their feet nearish the ground." Evan stood beside her with her hands behind her back.

"Nearish is right. Is it time?" Clementine asked.

"Just about. Mr. Fox wants to give you something." Evan took her hand from behind her back to reveal a hand puppet of Mr. Fox, holding some papers tied with a red bow.

"What's this?"

"A wedding present," Evan said.

"It's not our wedding for another two months."

"It's early—open it."

Clementine took the present and then started to untie the bow. Some very old and extremely tattered papers were amongst the pile.

"Read the top one."

Evan looked so excited, and that worried Clementine. Every time Evan was excited, it usually meant more dreams and ideas to try to make come true.

Clementine opened the first document, which had an old wax seal on it.

"My gift to you, the future Mrs. Fox."

She scanned it quickly and her heart started to pound. *These are the deeds to Thistleburn Castle and its land. Owned by Clementine Fitzroy, Duchess of Rosebrook, Countess of Thistleburn, and Baroness Portford.*

"You bloody didn't?"

"I bloody did. I had Archie do the research and the business. The local council didn't know what to do with it. It was too expensive to refurbish, and they were thinking of knocking it down. I bought it lock, stock, and barrel."

"Why?"

Evan cupped Clementine's cheek. "Because I want you to have your family lands back, and when we have this village up and running, Thistleburn can be a second site for us to develop." Evan gesticulated wildly. "Think of it. We can show the world how we can make communities work and make them green, not just as a one-off village but two, and maybe three or four—"

Clementine saw that Evan was starting to get too excited and lost in the clouds, as her mother had put it.

"We could have a village in every corner of the kingdom, then maybe towns, then cities—"

She grasped Evan's hand. "Evan? Calm down. How about we make one village work first, and then see about the second, and so on."

The summer storm had wreaked havoc on the village and the building work already done, but in a way it had been a positive thing. It brought the community closer together and proved to the more reluctant members of the tiny community that they had to try and make changes to the way they worked, farmed, and lived, so that natural disasters didn't become the norm.

"I'm getting overexcited, aren't I," Evan said.

Clementine kissed her cheek. "Just a bit, but this"—she held up the deeds—"it's too much. I mean, what do I bring to this marriage?"

"Are you kidding me?" Evan picked her up and twirled her around. Evan straightened her best fox tie and said with smugness, "I get a duchess. The third highest ranked dukedom in the country. Even Archie couldn't get a duchess. In fact, I think I shall get a lapel badge and a bumper sticker for my Beetle: *I'm married to a duchess.*"

Clementine laughed. "Be serious, Evan."

"I am. Besides, isn't this the way things used to work in Jane Austen–type times? One partner brought the money, one brought the title." Evan imitated her future wife's posh voice and said, "A very prudent match, wouldn't one say, what? What?"

"That is not how I speak."

Evan kissed her. "Near enough, come on, we better get going."

"I love you, Foxy."

"I love you, m'lady, Your Graceship."

"Come on, you." Before they left the burial ground, Clementine reached out and touched Isadora's grave. "Look after Mama, Dora, and if it was you who brought us together, thank you. We'll try to make Rosebrook everything you dreamed of."

❖

"Why are you not up there? It's your baby, Fox," Archie asked Evan.

They both stood at the back of a crowd, in front of the newly completed Seaside Cottages. Clementine was in front of a ceremonial red ribbon drawn around the beginning of the row of cottages, with Ash beside her. Twenty new residents stood intermingled with all the locals, including Blake Campbell, Eliska Novak, and their daughter, Ola. Those carefully chosen first twenty people included single people as well as families of all sizes and kinds, all enthusiastic about the opportunity for a new life.

They had promised Blake and Eliska that they would have their new home, their safe haven, by Christmas, and they did. Blake had said it was the best Christmas present they could have. Evan looked forward to getting to know the couple.

She folded her arms and smiled. "Nah. It maybe started out as that, but that strong woman there is the leader of this village. When I first met her, Clem was weighed down by the world and her problems. She felt a responsibility to these people, to their living conditions, but couldn't do anything about it. Look at her now." Clementine was laughing and taking an oversized pair of scissors from Ash. "She has her purpose back. Look how much everyone else has changed. Clementine told me that Ash hardly ever went out, but now she's learning the business and happily mixing with people."

Archie leaned over and whispered, "Just don't ask her to make you a nice cup of tea. She has a long memory."

"Well you deserved it."

"True. Oh, Griffin got back to me. She's really interested in your offer."

Evan had finally gotten hold of her old friend Griffin, who was an expert in craft brewing. Evan thought she would be perfect to make the beer factory a success, but that was for another day.

"Excellent. It's all coming together," Evan said.

"I bet Isadora is smiling down on you both."

"I think she'd be happy that a Fitzroy is mistress of Rosebrook House again. It seems like my whole life has been leading me here, to her."

As Evan gazed at her soon-to-be wife, she filled with so much love. She had gotten her love story at last, and it had been so worth waiting for.

"Ladies, gentlemen, and children," Clementine said, "I'm delighted to open the first of what will be many new housing areas in Rosebrook. We haven't had an easy time while trying to bring this dream to fruition, but we never gave up, we kept going forward, because we want to make the world a better place. As my partner Evan says so often, we want to leave the world a little bit better than how we found it, and these affordable, ecologically friendly houses are just the start."

Clementine looked right at Evan and said, "I didn't always believe in dreams, but without the dreamers of this world we would be nothing. I declare the Seaside Cottages open!"

About the Author

Jenny Frame is from the small town of Motherwell in Scotland, where she lives with her partner, Lou, and their well-loved and very spoiled dog.

She has a diverse range of qualifications, including a BA in public management and a diploma in acting and performance. Nowadays, she likes to put her creative energies into writing rather than treading the boards.

When not writing or reading, Jenny loves cheering on her local football team, cooking, and spending time with her family.

Jenny can be contacted at www.jennyframe.com.

Books Available From Bold Strokes Books

Forging a Desire Line by Mary P. Burns. When Charley's ex-wife, Tricia, is diagnosed with inoperable cancer, the private duty nurse Tricia hires turns out to be the handsome and aloof Joanna, who ignites something inside Charley she isn't ready to face. (978-1-63555-665-0)

Journey to Cash by Ashley Bartlett. Cash Braddock thought everything was great, but it looks like her history is about to become her right now. Which is a real bummer. (978-1-63555-464-9)

Love on the Night Shift by Radclyffe. Between ruling the night shift in the ER at the Rivers and raising her teenage daughter, Blaise Richilieu has all the drama she needs in her life, until a dashing young attending appears on the scene and relentlessly pursues her. (978-1-63555-668-1)

Olivia's Awakening by Ronica Black. When the daring and dangerously gorgeous Eve Monroe is hired to get Olivia Savage into shape, a fierce passion ignites, causing both to question everything they've ever known about love. (978-1-63555-613-1)

The Duchess and the Dreamer by Jenny Frame. Clementine Fitzroy has lost her faith and love of life. Can dreamer Evan Fox make her believe in life and dream again? (978-1-63555-601-8)

The Road Home by Erin Zak. Hollywood actress Gwendolyn Carter is about to discover that losing someone you love sometimes means gaining someone to fall for. (978-1-63555-633-9)

Waiting for You by Elle Spencer. When passionate past-life lovers meet again in the present day, one remembers it vividly and the other isn't so sure. (978-1-63555-635-3)

While My Heart Beats by Erin McKenzie. Can a love born amidst the horrors of the Great War survive? (978-1-63555-589-9)

Face the Music by Ali Vali. Sweet music is the last thing that happens when Nashville music producer Mason Liner and daughter of country royalty Victoria Roddy are thrown together in an effort to save country star Sophie Roddy's career. (978-1-63555-532-5)

Flavor of the Month by Georgia Beers. What happens when baker Charlie and chef Emma realize their differing paths have led them right back to each other? (978-1-63555-616-2)

Mending Fences by Angie Williams. Rancher Bobbie Del Rey and veterinarian Grace Hammond are about to discover if heartbreaks of the past can ever truly be mended. (978-1-63555-708-4)

Silk and Leather: Lesbian Erotica with an Edge, edited by Victoria Villaseñor. This collection of stories by award-winning authors offers fantasies as soft as silk and tough as leather. The only question is: How far will you go to make your deepest desires come true? (978-1-63555-587-5)

The Last Place You Look by Aurora Rey. Dumped by her wife and looking for anything but love, Julia Pierce retreats to her hometown only to rediscover high school friend Taylor Winslow, who's secretly crushed on her for years. (978-1-63555-574-5)

The Mortician's Daughter by Nan Higgins. A singer on the verge of stardom discovers she must give up her dreams to live a life in service to ghosts. (978-1-63555-594-3)

The Real Thing by Laney Webber. When passion flares between actress Virginia Green and masseuse Allison McDonald, can they be sure it's the real thing? (978-1-63555-478-6)

What the Heart Remembers Most by M. Ullrich. For college sweethearts Jax Levine and Gretchen Mills, could an accident be the second chance neither knew they wanted? (978-1-63555-401-4)

White Horse Point by Andrews & Austin. Mystery writer Taylor James finds herself falling for the mysterious woman on White Horse Point who lives alone, protecting a secret she can't share about a murderer who walks among them. (978-1-63555-695-7)

Femme Tales by Anne Shade. Six women find themselves in their own real-life fairy tales when true love finds them in the most unexpected ways. (978-1-63555-657-5)

Jellicle Girl by Stevie Mikayne. One dark summer night, Beth and Jackie go out to the canoe dock. Two years later, Beth is still carrying the weight of what happened to Jackie. (978-1-63555-691-9)

My Date with a Wendigo by Genevieve McCluer. Elizabeth Rosseau finds her long-lost love and the secret community of fiends she's now a part of. (978-1-63555-679-7)

On the Run by Charlotte Greene. Even when they're cute blondes, it's stupid to pick up hitchhikers, especially when they've just broken out of prison, but doing so is about to change Gwen's life forever. (978-1-63555-682-7)

Perfect Timing by Dena Blake. The choice between love and family has never been so difficult, and Lynn's and Maggie's different visions of the future may end their romance before it's begun. (978-1-63555-466-3)

The Mail Order Bride by R. Kent. When a mail order bride is thrust on Austin, he must choose between the bride he never wanted or the dream he lives for. (978-1-63555-678-0)

Through Love's Eyes by C.A. Popovich. When fate reunites Brittany Yardin and Amy Jansons, can they move beyond the pain of their past to find love? (978-1-63555-629-2)

To the Moon and Back by Melissa Brayden. Film actress Carly Daniel thinks that stage work is boring and unexciting, but when she accepts a lead role in a new play, stage manager Lauren Prescott tests both her heart and her ability to share the limelight. (978-1-63555-618-6)

Tokyo Love by Diana Jean. When Kathleen Schmitt is given the opportunity to be on the cutting edge of AI technology, she never thought a failed robotic love companion would bring her closer to her neighbor, Yuriko Velucci, and finding love in unexpected places. (978-1-63555-681-0)